Bone Yard

Book 2 of the Aspect Wars

Jesse Sprague

Chapter 1

Flynt stretched out her bone fingers. Clothed in nothing but a long, black satin glove over her skeletal left arm, she perched on the edge of her berth. The flesh fingers of her right hand clenched. She longed to rip the covering off. That glove was a lie—it hid the essential truth of Flynt's existence.

While in space aboard the *Seer's Sword*, Flynt could usually go without her glove—the soldiers on Captain Lem's voyagecraft all knew what she was already. But docked on-planet, as they currently were, or on the piddling missions that had filled her life for the past six months, she needed to worry about discovery.

The native Uvian woman behind her, sprawled across Flynt's shipboard mattress, made the glove necessary.

Removing the glove over her bone arm wasn't expressly forbidden, but Queen Milisade had cautioned against revealing Flynt's true self in a broad sense.

The queen's instructions to Flynt had been clear. Don't reveal her Necro-equitem abilities or admit to them while away from the Coil space station that was the center of Milisade's power. And Flynt had been charged with learning how to use her command over Death-aspect and her unique connection the Goddess of Death, so when her true calling came out, Flynt would be ready to defend herself and the Milisade's Coil from backlash from the other Coils and their queens.

Flynt suspected that the citizens of this backwater planet wouldn't know what her bone arm meant. Nevertheless, revealing her skeletal arm was a risk. There were already rumors circulating about Flynt being a Necro-equitem—a powerful type of Aspect manipulator that had been thought extinct for nine hundred years since the Federation of Coils had hunted them all down and killed them. Though the rest of Flynt was clothed in flesh, pale and womanly, that arm was the kiss from her Aspect—the kiss of Ayal, Lady Death. Even lightyears from the Coil space station, Milisade would expect Flynt to hide that connection to her Necro-equitem abilities.

The voyagecraft's flooring retained a leeching cold that slid up through the carpet and soles of Flynt's feet and permeated the square cabin. Nothing adorned the space except a few button panels on the metal walls used to call up various amenities, a berth on either side of the door, and the soldiers' uniform that Flynt had worn on-planet the night before, crumpled on the paper-thin carpet.

The woman behind Flynt made a series of sighing sounds. She was waking up. Her short hair stuck up in uneven spikes, partially a style and partially from sleep. Her wide mouth and equally wide nose gave her a soft but strong appearance.

What was her name? Flynt winced when she realized she couldn't recall. No amount of alcohol excused forgetting the name of a bed companion—even a partner with a one-night shelf-life.

Flynt stood, letting her black hair fall over her pale, pink shoulders. She glanced up at the room's security camera mounted in the center of the ceiling.

The black lens gave nothing away.

As she often did, Flynt wondered if Captain Lem was watching. She pointedly never turned on the privacy screen. He *could* watch. But if he ever did, he gave no sign.

After six months on his ship, she'd practically given up on tempting him to her. He hadn't even spoken to her—except to bark orders in public places—since their first night aboard the Seer's Sword.

"You are just gorgeous in the morning," said the woman in

a burred, alto voice.

Flynt tensed. How could she really respond? Saying, *"You kind of resemble the man I really want in my bed... less so in the morning"* wasn't really an option. As much as she saw herself as honest, some statements were simply cruel. She turned to the woman. "You're not bad yourself. However, my roommate will be back from her shift soon..."

"Maybe next time you're in port." The woman sat up and retrieved her dock uniform—a dark green jumpsuit and white vest—from the foot of the bed amid a tangle of blankets. Her broad shoulders and muscular arms were just as sexy in the morning as they had been the night before.

But it was time to be clear that this was a one-time thing. "I hope you find something better by then," Flynt said.

There was no doubt that the *Seer's Sword* would return to this planet. Uvus was Captain Lem's homeworld, where his estranged wife and both children lived. That was also why this glorious dockworker looked so much like Lem. As Flynt had learned on her first visit here, Lem's human sub-species had evolved on Uvus. Due to the high gravity and hot temperatures, they all shared a certain look, short and strong with equally blunt features. Other than the compact and powerful builds, they looked human.

Flynt had never asked him where else his sub-species broke from the base-line humans.

Her own species, the Leshmen, differed mainly in gender and breeding habits.

The woman sat there, waiting for more.

"One-night stands don't make great long-term plans," Flynt added.

The woman chuckled.

Good. Flynt disliked it when bedmates got annoyed. She owed them nothing.

"Point taken. No repeats."

"Sorry, I'm sort of hoping I'll have a relationship by then —but he likes *monogamy*." Flynt said the word with derision she couldn't control. "I'm not entirely sure what that means, but…"

Her erstwhile bedmate shot Flynt a smile—so like Lem's smile. "Got it." The woman tugged her jumpsuit up over her hips. Was that humor part of the planetary culture, too? And the thick skin. She slid into her uniform and secured her dock boots. "What's with the glove?"

Flynt pulled her left arm to her chest. "Nothing."

"That's the only thing you never took off, that's all."

Flynt lifted her bone hand, staring at the black satin and emeralds decorating the wrist. This woman looked like Lem. Perhaps Flynt could find the same acceptance that she'd once believed she'd found in Lem. The desire to connect with another person without a lie between them overwhelmed Flynt. She reached over and loosened the top button near her shoulder. "My arm tends to scare people."

"I know lots of people with deformities and scars. No need to be ashamed." To belie her casual statement, the woman leaned eagerly forward.

Flynt itched to take the glove off, but her fingers paused. Showing her affected limb revealed not only bone, but the other truth that scared people. What the glove really kept hidden was her true calling, her connection to the Aspect of Death, Ayal, as a Necro-equitem. Sure, she could explain away the bone to most people's satisfaction by claiming to have the lesser calling of Death-magister… but that too tended to scare people off, even though being a Death-magister wasn't against Coil law. The night before, she'd worn a soldier's uniform, but she wasn't a soldier. Her Death-magister robes hung in the cabin's closet, hidden behind a metal panel. Those black-and-acid-green robes were closer to the real her.

"What have you got to lose?" The woman's dimples showed when she smiled. "Especially if we're never going to see each other again."

But Flynt had a lot to lose: her life, her father's life, and that of the myriad of siblings she'd never met, along with their children. Anyone related to her was at risk if it came out that

Flynt was a Necro-equitem rather than a garden-variety Death-magister. And yet... if this woman looked without fear, maybe Flynt could hope that others might as well.

Still, Flynt's hand dropped. "I can't."

The woman rolled her eyes. "*Srikes*," she swore, a term Flynt had never heard before coming to Uvus—probably this Uvian's name for one of the Aspects of Creation.

Flynt's chest ached. Maybe a partial truth, anything just to be reassured that there was a place for her in the universe that didn't rely on hiding the best pieces of herself. "I'm a Death-magister. I hide the evidence of my trade under the glove."

That wasn't entirely a lie. She was hiding the evidence, just not the withered flesh of a Death-magister. But admitting she was a Necro-equitem was explicitly forbidden.

"Ayal's void!" the woman swore, a look of disgust on her face.

At least she was swearing by the right Aspect's name now. Even if the Aspect of Death seemed to offend her. Flynt's stomach sank. She clearly wasn't going to find her acceptance here.

"You should warn people..." The woman crept along the wall toward the door.

Flynt's eyes snapped up, and she felt the Aspect rising inside her. She knew her normally green eyes would be showing the same acid hue as the hidden Death-magister robes, and that if she let the Aspect take over, they'd turn red. "What are you afraid of?" Purple billowed from her breath.

Balance. She needed balance. Without thinking, her flesh hand jerked up, and the fingers spread. Her obsidian finger-cuffs parted, and the chain between them tightened, making a bridge between her middle and ring fingers. This cord allowed her to maintain her balance on the correct side of the veil and not slip over into the very Death-aspect that she controlled.

"*Freak*," the woman hissed as she fled toward the metal door, which slid open at her approach. She exited the room, pushing past another person, who seemed to have been quietly waiting in the hall.

After a breathless moment, the Death-aspect retreated. The pressure of unspent Aspect inside Flynt was getting worse— the longer she hid, the more the truth sought to burst from her. The Death rioting inside her wanted to kill.

She feared she would let it.

The person in the hall was Flynt's roommate, Nightshade. She entered, her Life-magister robes impossibly neat around her. The white and yellow colors suited Nightshade's purple- and green-streaked "skin." The truth was, Nightshade only resembled a human in shape. And though Flynt thought of Nightshade as a woman, they really had no gender. They, or *she* as Nightshade had confirmed either was acceptable when Flynt asked, was a Diethyrian tree-person. She had been painstakingly grown in the shape of a humanoid, slender and shapely, neither male nor female in appearance. Her skin consisted of a multitude of intertwining vines. Her eyes were carved from white stone, each painted with a pupil and iris.

She was the only Diethyrian to ever live among humanoids or communicate directly with them. But she'd been grown to look humanoid enough that few outside of a trusted circle ever guessed she wasn't just another human derivation.

The two shared a room because everyone else on the warship was terrified of them both. No one off the ship might know what Flynt really was, but it wasn't possible to hide her powers from the soldiers and Magi who traveled with her. And Nightshade was just as "other" in her own way as Flynt was.

Flynt ripped off her glove and threw it on the bed. She glanced at her bare bones, emerging from the stump of her bicep, gleaming like pearls. No messy tendons, blood, flesh, or skin interfered with the flow of Death-aspect that circled her left hand. Her shoulders relaxed. The sight was beautiful.

"Get dressed," Nightshade commanded. She never *asked*. As far as Flynt could tell, Nightshade didn't see the point in being polite or conciliatory.

Flynt sighed and went to the closet. No way was that

damned glove going back on. The people on the ship had all seen her gloveless anyhow. She pressed a button on the wall and a closet rack slid out. Flynt pulled out the green-and-black Death-magister robe. Having been through a series of fittings, the cloth fit both her body and her clothing preferences perfectly—namely, she wanted to be on display.

As Captain Lem had commented, back before he had started avoiding her, magic was almost a sexual act for her. And she needed to feel beautiful and powerful to perform her duties as the ship's "Necro." Along with being one of the Magisters on board who supervised and helped train the lower-tier Magi, Flynt used Death-aspect to help navigate. She'd expected missions to unclaimed worlds and battles where she raised undead critters to protect them, but thus far, Milisade had sent her on no such missions. Even so, she'd used a few critters as part of transport missions to scout ahead—undead rats could travel most places unseen.

The robe's cool fabric draped over her skin, the left sleeve cut back at the shoulder in order to display her glove or her bone arm. More cutaways in the fabric peeked out along her waist and revealed a fun portion of leg. The black silk was shot through with the vivid green of all Death robes.

"I don't understand why you do that," Nightshade said, turning her head and her blind-stone eyes toward the door through which the local woman had fled.

"Scare people?" Flynt adjusted her robes to be sure they displayed a proper amount of cleavage. Then she shifted her obsidian finger-cuffs to her bone fingers.

"No." Nightshade's voice lowered with disapproval. "The one-night stands. Your fluid exchanges with strangers seem counterproductive to your goals."

Flynt wondered if Nightshade was referring to her desire to be accepted and belong. But surely, sex helped a person belong! So this conversation must have been pointing to Flynt's desire for Lem. "I'm proving I'm capable of monogamy."

Nightshade moved just inside the cabin, keeping the

sliding, metal door open. She settled her attention on Flynt. "I fail to see how committing the sex act with a multitude of people proves that."

"I'm not emotionally involved," Flynt said, annoyed. Why did everyone always question her? She was entirely capable of being true to one romantic partner. She'd done it the entire time she'd been married. Both she and her late husband, Cyniel, had gone through multiple lovers, but their only commitment had been toward each other. As far as she understood, that was true monogamy—sharing your heart and your soul with one other partner.

"I don't believe that you understand what 'monogamy' means." Nightshade motioned for Flynt to follow her, and they walked out into the passageway. The space was sufficient for both of them to walk abreast and for others to pass them. The walls were a matted metal with a cool blue tint that married well with the gray-and-black patterned slats of the floor.

"'Monogamy' means having only one romantic partner," Flynt said. Though currently she had no romantic partner, which was annoying.

"Sexual."

"What?"

"Monogamy means having only one *sexual* partner," Nightshade said. Her bare feet slipped out from the hem of her robe and made soft padding noises. She had no toes, just the vague shape of them.

And what would the Diethyrian know about monogamous sex? Flynt thought, but she realized the thought was unfair and didn't voice it. Nightshade knew a lot about humanity, just from a different angle. "That's ridiculous. Why should that matter?"

"I have no idea," Nightshade said. "Sex makes no sense whatsoever to me. Of everything you humans do, that is the most disgusting act."

Flynt ignored being called "a human"—to Nightshade, all humanoids were the same. "See, you don't fully comprehend human relations."

"I do not," Nightshade admitted as she drew up to the teleportation portal at the end of the passageway. The golden Aspect energy swirled in front of her, and Nightshade stepped through—there was a portal on each deck of the ship, each leading to the deck on the outside of the hull. If someone wished to go elsewhere on the ship, they needed to use the stairs or a lift. But first thing in the morning, Nightshade always wanted sun on her vines, nutrient-enriched green tea, and dirt when possible. That meant getting off the voyagecraft entirely.

Flynt followed her through the portal.

They emerged onto the bustling faux wood "deck" of the ship. If Flynt hadn't known better, the exterior of the spaceship would have looked like an old-fashioned pirate ship—albeit far too large for one. But she *did* know and saw all the little inaccuracies, the security panels, wires poking out, buttons, and the slight glimmer on the air that hung in a bubble over the flat-topped deck. This bubble was the line between the air outside the ship's invisible shields and inside. But still, she enjoyed the sound of the sails flapping in the artificial breeze created by heat-cycling fans from the core of the ship.

Nightshade stalked across the planks.

Several soldiers dressed in light armor and dock-boots stopped, watching them warily. Nightshade didn't react.

Flynt strutted out after, blowing a sarcastic kiss to one soldier from her bone fingers. He dropped his gaze. Screw them if they didn't have a sense of humor.

Screw them all if they thought she would hide on the voyagecraft, too. Though as Flynt followed Nightshade, she realized she hadn't brought her glove to leave the ship, and also that at that moment, she didn't care. Nightshade needed to feel the ground and sun; Flynt needed to stand in the open in her own way.

And after all, the natives might be freaked out, but they wouldn't know what the arm meant. Leaving the voyagecraft without her glove would just be a little clean fun. And maybe, just maybe, one of them wouldn't be afraid. Maybe she'd see acceptance in their eyes.

Chapter 2

A t the edge of the ship, Flynt looked to the dock and its network of twisting planks, scaffolding, and sturdy main thoroughfares. A few steps ahead of her, Nightshade started off toward an outdoor café partially hidden from view by two midsized leisure voyagecrafts. Once Flynt stepped off the Seer's Sword onto the gangplank, the gravity of the world slammed onto her. Her boots banged loudly against the metal gangplank. Just moving would become exhausting after a few minutes, and Flynt was happy that they weren't far from a seat.

No one looked at Flynt, but with her arm revealed, a jittery excitement ran through her. It was stupid to be out like this, but if she could find just one person to accept her as she was, maybe she could have hope.

The native Uvians all walked along jauntily, dock-boots adding propulsion to help them leap to higher levels where small ships hovered over the larger ones. Visitors stood out by their hunched shoulders, plodding steps, and narrowed eyes, as if each of them fought a headache. Undoubtedly, Flynt would have one of her own if she stayed out too long. On board the Seer's Sword, the gravity was kept to the Coil norm in public areas. Private areas could be adjusted.

There was, however, something she could do here that she couldn't while on board. Flynt reached up behind her ear and turned off the receiver on her comm device. She didn't want to hear from anyone right now.

Nightshade ducked into the café and trudged down two steps into the outdoor seating area. The chairs and tables were half a floor below the pier's level walkway, giving it a sunken feeling, despite the fact that they were still a few stories off of the ground. Still, the patio stuck out from the tiered portion of dock, leaving the sky open above the tables, which would be all Nightshade required.

Nightshade claimed a seat at a small table in the sunniest corner. The Diethyrian had chosen the chair with its back to the rest of the café and her face to the sun, leaving Flynt a chair that would leave her shielded from other patrons by the table. Kept out of sight, there was no chance of Flynt receiving that knowing look of understanding, that kind smile that said, "You're accepted just as you are." Flynt dropped heavily into the chair, more heavily than intended due to the gravity.

A pot of tea waited on the table, making Flynt wonder if Nightshade had called ahead. She usually tried not to be noticed unless she was ready to represent her people. Avoiding waiters was part of that.

At least Flynt would have Nightshade's company. For the time being, the Diethyrian was the closest thing to a friend that Flynt had, certainly the closest thing to someone who accepted her for who she was.

"After I am finished here, I'll be making a brief visit off the docks to a park," Nightshade said, stirring a spoonful of honey into her tea. "Do you want to accompany me?"

Flynt shook her head. Even putting the effects of gravity aside, parks were always full of kids, and kids made her nervous. She had been raised to give her life to bearing children. That had been her one duty to her people and the Coil.

"No. Parks are hard for me ever since I was declared unfit breeding stock," Flynt said. The words held an odd sting that she didn't wish to look into. "I never wanted to be a Mother, but I never wanted not to be a parent. Do you mind going alone?"

"You have an invitation, but your attendance is not required for my enjoyment." Nightshade positioned the tea below her face so the sweet steam rolled up to her and slid two fingers into the cup. Then she planted her feet firmly on the metal flooring and her palms on the painted metal table. With a deep sigh, she tilted her head up to the blue sky. She closed her eyes, which seemed pointless, as it wasn't like Nightshade saw through the stone balls tucked into her painstakingly formed eye sockets. But Nightshade had said humans tended to understand her actions better if she lowered her "lids."

Flynt ordered a drink from a waiter, who stood barely over five-foot. He had a beautiful gap between his front teeth, but once he spotted her bone arm, she didn't see the gap again. When he came back with her order, he didn't meet her eyes.

He half-turned away and then asked, "You're Captain Lem's new Death-magus?"

Safe assumption on his part, to go with the most common and least powerful of the Death-aspect manipulators.

"Magister, but yes," Flynt said. She wasn't a Death-magister, either, but that was at least closer to the forbidden truth. Once upon a time, her "kind," the Necro-equitems, had been revered. But she wouldn't rebuild that by terrifying civilians. Leaving her glove behind had been stupid. The waiter couldn't be more than a 1 on the Scale—meaning as far as value to the Coil, he was in the bottom thirty percent. He wasn't going to make a big difference anyhow. As a 60 on the Scale, her life was worth much more than his.

Unintentionally, her flesh hand lifted to touch her shoulder, where her Scale mark glowed just above the beginning of her bone arm. She dropped the contact as soon as she noticed what she was doing. Her Scale mark usually wasn't a great thing to call attention to when someone was already annoyed, unless she planned to pull rank, which she didn't.

"Magister... But how...?" The man only half-voiced the question. But she knew it by heart anyhow.

There was a way that all Death-magisters looked—sickly, old, and drained. Even the young ones had shrunken flesh and wrinkled skin. Death-aspect crushed them down into bone dust, usually within a decade. Flynt leaned across the table to the waiter, showing off the perfectly smooth skin of her face. "All the withering so far has been confined to one area of my body. Want to guess which one?"

He shook his head and scuttled off in the opposite direction. Nightshade hadn't reacted to any of the exchange.

Flynt shouted after him. "Oh, and lotions. You'd be surprised what a good lotion can do!"

Then Flynt lifted her cup with her flesh hand and drank. Not using her bone hand for the motion felt like giving up, but she just didn't want to face the fear anymore, not right then. Why couldn't she even have a cup of caffeinated soy concentrate with a friend without this barrage?

And yet she heard the whispers slowly growing at the tables around her.

"Death-magister—it's the colors, you can tell."

"She's not all shriveled up, can't be. You ever seen one like that? Think not!"

"I heard..."

"I heard..."

"I heard..."

They had all heard the same rumor and at the least had the wisdom to keep their voices low when they whispered it. Flynt hoped that Nightshade would finish before some jerk decided to come ask about what they'd "heard."

Every time Flynt lied, something invisible inside her shriveled up—just as all these people thought her flesh should have done. She was rejecting herself. Denying the core of her.

Soon she'd be dust inside.

Flynt was painfully aware that her excuse about her arm taking the draining wasn't viable. But luckily, most people didn't know exactly how Aspect manipulation worked. Normally, Death-aspect drained a bit of life with each Aspect manipulation performed. And Queen Milisade had impressed upon her that if Flynt claimed her true title, the act would endanger Flynt's family. Necro-equitems had been put to forcible extinction a thousand years ago and outlawed by the federation of Coils, the one law not even Milisade could flout. The existence of Flynt's type of link to the Death-aspect, to Ayal, might restart the dormant wars between Coils or prompt a new one with a particularly outraged queen.

Flynt grinned into her drink, thinking about a war being fought over her. At least in her mind, she could keep the whole thing pretty. And her connection to Death did add an allure to such battles. The war in reality would quickly lead to the deaths of the few people she actually gave a damn about. Because she'd hidden and protected Flynt, Milisade would be the first to die from that list.

A man sauntered up. Not a native—skinny build, green skin, and probably no more than four and a half feet tall. How could a creature like him even walk in this damn gravity?

"You Captain Lem's new Death-magus?" he asked in a scratchy, little voice.

Flynt had already been asked that question once and didn't feel like setting anyone straight again. She stretched her legs out beside the table, feigning ease and comfort. "Yup."

"You don't look like one," he said as he leaned in closer. He smelled like dead rats. And behind him, Flynt spotted a table of similar scrawny green people.

"Oh?" Flynt decided if this little bug wanted more, he could darn well work for it.

"I've heard rumors about you," he said, somehow managing to make the words seem dirty. Flynt *felt* dirty.

"Funny, I've heard nothing about you. I guess we can't all be newsworthy."

He glared. "How is it you still look like..." His eyes drifted down to her curves, pausing on the revealed cleavage. "This?"

"Good genes." Flynt waited until his eyes were back on hers to go on. "I guess that would be a mystery to you. What are you?"

"Less disgusting than you, necro."

He used the term as a dirty word, as the colloquial slang

to insult any Death-magus. She doubted he really believed the accusation was true in any deeper way. If so, he should have been more cautious.

All she wanted was the same freedom all these people had —to be able to walk down the street as herself, to have people around her who accepted her. Clearly, she'd been wrong to hope for that here.

Flynt felt the Aspect pressing outward, stretching, whispering. Below the table, she snapped the chain of her finger-cuffs tightly against her bone fingers, trying to keep her mind balanced on the living side of the veil and not slip into death's song. Obsidian ground against bone. The cuffs had belonged to the last Necro-equitem, Ieyil, and had been gifted to Flynt to help her navigate the tricky line between the living side of the veil and the dead. Balance, maintain balance.

People were listening. Flynt tried to calm down, to focus herself through the taut chain. She couldn't afford to prove the rumors about her true, even if this little fool dared to voice them.

Another person walked up, behind the man. A green-skinned woman this time, though you could barely tell the difference, other than the scrap of cloth she wore over her chest. "I heard you really are a Necro."

"From whom?" Flynt ground out. Her eyes flicked to Nightshade, who still hadn't stirred from her sunbath, who probably hadn't even noticed anything was occurring.

"Your captain calls you that," the woman said.

"Lem calls all of his Death-magi that. Easy mistake to make." Flynt stood, hip bumping the table. Her drink sloshed over the side of the cup. She needed to get out of the café before the Aspect forced its way out. If these idiots cornered her, they'd wind up dead, and that would only be the start of the issues for Flynt.

Lem would not appreciate her killing civilians on his homeworld. And Milisade would not appreciate her showing her powers in public.

"She's nothing," the woman said to the man. "Just another

Aspect moaner. The captain'll toss her away once the pretty skin shrivels. Let's go. This won't be any fun."

The man grunted, and they turned away. "Freak."

That was the second time that word had been hurled at her that morning. And she felt the Death-aspect around her, all the little lost deaths screaming to have their voices heard. Flies, mice, bird bones, and even a cat skeleton inside the café. Flynt's lips parted, a small puff of purple Aspect energy escaping. She didn't need to kill these stupid green interlopers, just show them Death's smile.

Flynt breathed in. Aspect moved between her fingers and several fly corpses rose in the air around them. She tasted their Deaths on her tongue, threaded with bright bursts of Life-aspect. She could drink them in...Nightshade's hand slammed over Flynt's, pinning it to the café table. "No showing off."

Flynt sighed. For a moment, she teetered on that internal edge between the veil and life. True death brushed against her. Then she gulped down the rest of her drink. The liquid on the outside of the cup made a sticky smear on her hand. "I was just going to play."

But Nightshade didn't even have to answer for Flynt to know a Death-magister didn't play—ever. Their powers were serious.

Hiding was torture.

As she walked out of the café's seating area, leaving the Diethyrian behind, Flynt felt eyes on her. A lot of eyes. *Way to draw attention*, she thought, and she doubted this would be the last she'd hear of the incident.

Chapter 3

As Flynt came back up the dock toward the Seer's Sword, all she wanted was to return to her little room and curl up under her covers. If she tried, she could pretend that almost unleashing forbidden Aspect in the café wouldn't come back to bite her.

Flynt used her dock boots to partially counteract the planet's high gravity and leap up a pier level. *Seer's Sword* was still two stories up in the winding maze of the dock's scaffolding. There were stairs, but using those would end up taking more time.

Her head was starting to pound, which was the first sign that the gravity was getting to her. Flynt took a brief rest then ascended the final two levels to the slip where they were docked. The *Seer's Sword* hovered ahead of her alongside several other large ships. She clanked along the walkway. *Seer's Sword* was large enough to carry over five hundred soldiers. It was lean for a war vessel but sported scars to prove its worth. Yet the quirky mast screamed this vessel was something more than just a military extension.

Flynt spotted Captain Lem standing near the gangplank leading onto the ship in front of a merchant. Several partially unpacked crates waited behind the merchant.

Captain Lem looked abnormally perturbed—even his near-constant smile was absent. He stood aggressively close to the merchant. On Uvus, Lem stood a head taller than many men, and that was the case with the merchant. This height combined with his large, muscular build and the three weapons he wore constantly under his Tempus-magister robes... He looked dangerous. In fact, everything about him made him appear dangerous, from his dark, shaved-on-the-sides and kept-short-in-a-military-style hair right on to his attire. Several buttons were undone toward the center of his shirt and a smear of ship oil streaked over one arm. The muscles of his arms and chest where revealed were massive, only adding to his intimidating nature. And the spark in his brown eyes gave his face an intelligent sheen... when he wasn't standing within inches of some merchant, glaring him down.

"Now," Lem rumbled. "I need it *now*."

Given better circumstances, Flynt could have drooled over him for hours, but Lem's temper concerned her. Why was Lem in such a hurry? She'd have to wait for Nightshade for any shot at an answer. But maybe, just maybe, it meant they could leave this dull world and actually do something.

She could have sat around being judged on the Coil without risking revealing herself. The whole point of traversing the galaxy was for Flynt to train her gift so that eventually, it could be of use to Milisade.

Aspect bubbled inside her and Flynt clenched her fingers, thumbing the finger-cuffs.

Flynt had to pass close by the merchant and captain to board the vessel. No chance of escaping attention, so she rested her bone hand on her hip and strutted up.

The merchant looked at her first and went white and then gray. She resisted blowing a kiss—if Lem was pissed at him, the poor man was already in for it. Then Lem turned, the anger in his face immediately dying. His eyes lingered for an instant too long, sliding over her body. He didn't even wince away from the sight of her arm.

The captain saw her, just her. And that was what made it so hard to forget him.

If they'd ever slept together, maybe forgetting him would have been easier—maybe he'd have disappointed.

Everything else in this life had disappointed her. Space travel thus far hadn't been thrilling; it had been long stretches of waiting, only to find out Lem and the queen still had no intention of using Flynt's skills.

Flynt passed by Lem and the merchant onto the ship, but before she could reach her cabin, her comm device automatically reactivated—there was no turning them off aboard the ship. The comm beeped. The neural display that projected in front of her eyes informed her she had received a new message. No one but her would be able to read it; they'd only see a light glow in her eyes to alert them she was interfacing.

The message was from the captain. Not good, considering she'd "misbehaved" at the café. Yet part of her hoped the message might be something more personal. It was timestamped from just a few minutes prior. She mentally accessed the message, pulling it up on the projected display in front of her eyes.

No personal message, just a set of coordinates on Uvus near their current location and two instructions.

> 1.   Go to the coordinates in place of your supervisory shift in the Magi library today. Aspect buildup does no damn good. You need *control*; power, you have. Move them without disturbing the dirt.

Move them? Move what? Flynt suspected that part of the instructions would make perfect sense when she arrived at the coordinates. Tasks helped her control her Aspect buildup. Any release was better than none and after nearly losing control with both her temporary bedmate and the jerks in the café, she needed a release. So she'd swallow the indignity of being handed orders through her comm like some Scale 1 nobody. She read on.

> 2.   Wear your glove in public. I didn't know this needed to be an order. It *is* an order.

Flynt wanted something to throw. Instead, she clenched her fists tightly. The worst part wasn't the commands. The worst part was that even with clearly personal commands, he couldn't be bothered to speak directly to her. She meant that little to him and the functionality of his crew.

His impersonal dismissal of her difficulties was too much. She couldn't go on like this, existing as nothing but an oddity gathering dust on a shelf. Denying who she was and still being excluded and shunned by the few people who knew her.

Something has to change, she thought. For now, that meant following Lem's directions and waiting an opportunity.

***

The coordinates from the captain's message belonged to a cemetery. Flynt hopped out of her transport vehicle and heard the dull thud of her boots against a stone walkway. The gravity in the vehicle had been adjusted for her, making her feel heavy and slow out in the natural gravity.

A cemetery spread before her behind a wrought-iron fence, the gate standing wide open. As the unmanned transport's wheels rolled along the paved road behind her, she stepped through the gate. This was nothing like the orderly cemeteries she'd visited before. Trees reached up from the soil, arching over graves. A few gravestones had been lifted by a root and rested at crooked, unstable angles.

What did Lem want her to do here? *Move them*, he'd written.

Unlike on the Coil and Flynt's homeworld, Terak, this dirt here wasn't transported off world—the trees' roots couldn't have disturbed the stones and ground in the six months that most Coil cemeteries allowed their corpses to sit. On the Coil's colony worlds and space stations, bodies were either burned or, for very important corpses, buried for a short time in designated cemeteries. The cemetery dirt and the corpses were all flown to the Bone Yard every six months. That was where Cyniel's body would have been now, on a planet-sized graveyard filled with century upon century of the Coil elite. But this place was different, as if pulled from another tradition. The bodies that were buried here had rested here without change.

Flynt wandered along a slender, stone path, cracked in many places where roots had pushed up through. She glanced at several headstones. The dates were ancient and there were no projected images to show the faces of the inhabitants. But she didn't need the dates or smiling holograms to tell her about the bodies underneath the soil.

Despite the heavy gravity, she felt light, resonating with awareness of each bone, each death remnant. Even the oldest ones still had a wisp of Life tied to them—a link to a spirit that had inhabited those bones. If it hadn't been for the satin glove climbing up her left arm and smothering her sense of self, she would have felt perfectly free.

The chain of her finger-cuffs clicked on her right hand before she even made a conscious choice to use Aspect. On her flesh hand, it wasn't as strong a tool—but she couldn't use the cuff through her glove. And even if there was no one in the graveyard at the moment, it did qualify as a public place, thus the glove stayed on. Deep in Flynt, Aspect energy already shifted. Both of her hands swept out in front of her. Velvet fingers and flesh moved with a cloud of deep purple, fading to black at Flynt's fingertips.

Lem wanted her to move the bones, she was certain.

Just move them. No more.

Flynt's fingers twisted—she could do so much more.

But she trusted Lem. If he said that control was the angle she needed to remain in her Magister costume, then that was what she'd go for.

That being said, Lem didn't know the ins and outs of her gift.

Closing her eyes, Flynt reached out with her mind and "saw" them. With each grave came a whispered story, a life remembered. With the oldest, most tired bones, she slid the blade of her Death-aspect across the air and severed their last remaining ties to Life. The spirits sang with their freedom from their former bodies and were gone. The other corpses she shifted, as Lem requested, turning their skulls to the side and bending their knees. Then she allowed their jaws to part and Flynt heard the song.

Death's beautiful song.

Purple mists swirled deep underground, calling her. The veil pulled on her, a gravity even more forceful than that of Uvus's.

And she saw another face in the Aspect energies. In her bones she recognized the signature energies of Ieyil; Flynt could almost see the other Necro-equitem in her horned crown. In life, Ieyil had slaughtered thousands and almost overthrown the Coil in a bloody revolution, during which she'd animated the body of Queen Sisha. And there was much of this violence in the Death-aspect rioting around Flynt, but also a smooth, calming feeling. What did it matter who the ancient Necro had killed or how many? By now, they all would have been dead anyhow.

The bones beneath the soil moved again, this time not at Flynt's command. Fingers crawled upward, scratching at long-rotted coffins. They whispered Ieyil's name and called for Flynt to join them in their rest.

Death was natural, simple, so much easier than life.

The weight of her finger-cuffs tugged her—the chain had gone slack, dragging her attention back to the physical world. It snapped tight as she righted her internal balance on the line between Life and Death. Someday, she would intake too much of the air on the other side of the veil. She'd either fall over into the chasm of eternity or go Death-mad, as they said the last Necro-equitem, Ieyil, had.

Death might have been beautiful, but so was Life. She couldn't forget that.

Flynt's eyes flew open. Ieyil's laughter seemed to echo on the wind.

Her body resonated with power, and she let her satin-clad fingers slide down her body. Desire swirled, making a magic all its own.

Flynt moved her flesh hand to run over the satin, then settle over the emeralds embedded in the glove's wrist.

23

Azucena's emeralds. And something of Flynt's dead friend twisted inside the gemstones, like a scream or prayer that only she could hear.

"I miss you," she whispered.

Azucena did not reply. Her bones remained far away on the Coil, floating in Bone River. Flynt had failed to protect her.

Tears stung Flynt's eyes. Azucena wasn't the only person she'd lost in the past year. Her husband's death had started her whole adventure. Cyniel's absence still snuck up on her at times.

Kneeling on the stone walkway, Flynt bowed her head. Cyniel would have been so proud of her if he were alive. She *hoped* he would be proud, anyway. She had broken free of their shared birthright. That was something they'd only dreamed of in quietest whispers in the darkest of nights.

Except that his death had been the currency her future was built on.

She'd saved the life of Queen Milisade, stopped an ancient foe from rising, and resurrected a dead order—but the balance of her soul still didn't equal out. Cyniel's death hung heavily, and Azucena's spirit whispered in that emptiness.

Once her knees began to ache, Flynt rose and activated her comm to call a transport vehicle. She requested one to return her to her ship. The ones on this planet didn't fly as the transports on the Coil did. They were slower to arrive as well, giving Flynt a moment to stare up at the deepening blue sky. How had it gotten so late? She wouldn't make it back to the voyagecraft before nightfall.

Plenty of time to stew. How dare Lem treat her like this? He'd promised her adventure, to see the universe. Instead, they'd spent six months ferrying dignitaries from their Coil's airspace into the realms of other Coils. The eternal wars that were constantly brewing between Coils were almost always inactive within Coil airspace—all the fighting was over unclaimed worlds or border worlds. Still, a military escort was normal for high-level dignitaries. But usually, it wasn't done by warships!

Even the few "missions" they'd had had been stealth

missions where she used her Aspect to help Lem navigate outside of the Galaxy-tunnel system. She could sense death in the void of space and guide them to inhabited worlds. But spending two months sneaking up to a planet, only to sneak away after a team of soldiers went down, wasn't exactly the adventure she'd agreed to.

And the truth was, she knew she wasn't needed for this. Any ordinary Death-magus could have done this work.

The transport showed up, and Flynt climbed in. The driverless metal pod knew where to take her without her needing to speak—her comm told its navigation system that she belonged to the *Seer's Sword*.

Which wasn't true. Technically, Flynt was a free agent. The queen had paid off her debts.

If her family's lives weren't at stake, she could just go off and find her own adventure. But doing that would mean either damning them to be hunted down for possibly carrying the Necro gene or Flynt never using Aspect.

Flynt sat back on the hard seat for the duration of the silent ride, gravity pressing down on her shoulders like a shroud. She hopped out on the docks. No one seemed to note her on her walk toward the *Seer's Sword*. But before she got halfway across the deck, her spirits flagged. The workers avoided her, carefully skirting her. There were almost five hundred people on this ship and yet Flynt was alone.

They had jobs and she was a useless nightmare they stashed in a cabin.

And it was Lem's fault. Did he really think communing with a few bodies in a cemetery would be enough to fulfill her? He couldn't have known the Death-aspect energies were disturbed. Even Flynt didn't fully understand what her breath of Ieyil meant. But the least he could do was supply a sympathetic ear.

Maybe she'd just *make* him listen. Especially given she'd felt Ieyil's spirit. That could mean nothing, it probably meant nothing, but dread welled up deep within her at the thought.

Without really planning, Flynt made her way through the voyagecraft to the bridge, where she hoped to find him. As a Tempus-Magister, Lem was not only a captain in the traditional sense, but also the one person aboard capable of using the Time-aspect inside the Galaxy-tunnels. Without his ability to manipulate the Time-folds inside the tunnels, faster-than-light travel wasn't possible. As it was, with him and a Galaxy-tunnel, the voyagecraft could be almost anywhere within days. That unique skill also meant that he was pretty much constantly in the navigation room when they traveled. But when they were docked, he was often in the bridge or his quarters.

Of course, Flynt knew his secret. He wasn't really a Tempus-magister at all. He was a Chaos-magister, but he, like her, had to live a lie. Using the Chaos Aspect was a crime punishable by execution. Fortunately, Time and Chaos were linked Aspects and Lem could pass as a Tempus.

Two guards stood outside the door and eyed her speculatively. Unlike the dockworkers and basic soldiers, these men held less superstitious fear of her "magic." In fact, most of the company she managed to find aboard the ship was from mid-level soldiers like these. Happy to take a place in her bed, but not quite willing to make friends.

"I'd like to see the captain," Flynt said, perching her satin fingers on her hip.

Chapter 4

Flynt's request to see Lem had barely passed her lips when the taller of the two guards at the navigation chamber door spoke, her voice practically overlapping Flynt's. "Not possible."

"He is not to be disturbed," said the other, a small man with a metallic sheen to his skin and gill-like markings where ears would have been on a pure-bred human.

"Does that 'not to be disturbed' order apply to anyone or just me?" Flynt asked, narrowing her eyes—well-aware the acid green flash from between her lashes would discomfit them.

"If... If you would like to leave a message?" the smaller guard said.

Oh, she'd like to leave a message, but she wasn't sure this fool would be able to repeat the message she wanted to impart to Lem. "Tell him..." She breathed in deep and mentally edited out the expletives. "That I met an old *friend* in the graveyard. And remind him that there is no contract on my head. I can leave this Aspect-ridden boat anytime I want."

The guard who had spoken last nodded. Wise choice. Flynt really wanted to strike someone.

Flynt shoved a flesh finger, pointed black nail first, against his chest. "Tell him that I am not a toy."

Then, before her temper got away with her, Flynt fled the hall and hurried back to her room, through the metal passageways and their stairwells.

Happily, when Flynt walked through the door into their

cabin, Nightshade was there, sitting cross-legged on her own bed, arms held out in a position that would have been tiring for human arms, as they certainly resembled the branches of a tree. The Diethyrian wasn't much for a friend, given she couldn't emotionally relate, but she was amazing to talk to.

Early on in species interactions, it became clear that Diethyrians made wonderful spies because they could not be broken as all human-derived species could. A secret was a secret, and they could be pulled apart particle by particle and never speak the forbidden. What laws they believed in were immutable.

"I'm so sick of pretending," Flynt snapped as the door hissed shut behind her.

Nightshade turned her face toward Flynt. "Costumes chafe after a time."

Flynt almost responded on a burst of pique, but something in Nightshade's voice stopped her. That comment hadn't been about Flynt. "Do you ever wish you hadn't been grown to resemble us?"

"In some ways. I serve my purpose, an ambassador between our people. But it means living between two worlds, never in one. I don't have your flesh, but I experience life as you do."

"Will you ever return to your people?"

"No." Nightshade bowed her head, obscuring her eyes— probably hiding the lack of emotion that made most humans nervous. "My seedlings will, but this is metaphorically where my roots have grown. I've never lived as one of my own kind. I wouldn't know how."

Flynt couldn't tell from Nightshade's voice how she felt about her life role. "I'm sorry."

"Don't be—find where to set your own roots and do so. Belonging means planting yourself and committing." Nightshade lowered one arm to motion at Flynt's muddy boots. "Despite your footwear, I sense planting roots is not a talent of yours."

Flynt walked across the room, putting her back to Nightshade and tilting her face down to her bed. "I thought I had. Lem and I fought together, and I belonged. Or I thought I did. But since then, all of our missions have been piddling things. We don't fight together. I serve no real purpose. How am I supposed to train my Aspect use if all Milisade gives us are fetch-and-carry and escort missions? In the six months I've been on this ship, I've used nothing but scraps of the power inside me. And Lem, who was supposed to be my anchor, hasn't spoken to me once in private—not since the night I first arrived."

"Which you spent imbibing poison." Nightshade let out a small sound, which Flynt tried not to hear as judgmental.

Flynt didn't recall much from that first night. Lem and she had spent it drinking the stars black and lying on the upper decking staring up at the Galaxy-tunnel's swirling Aspect. But apparently, Diethyrians didn't see the appeal in imbibing mind-altering products or agree with the resulting blurred memories.

"The captain meets with few of us personally," Nightshade said.

Flynt bit back on her natural retort about how Lem clearly *did* meet with people because he met with Nightshade. Without looking at her friend, Flynt gripped a lock of her own hair, twisting the black strands it into a knot around her hand. "I could deal with just being another of his officers. I'm not even that. I'm like a disease to the men aboard since they began to suspect what I really am. And Lem... he doesn't trust me. I can't think of any other reason he'd avoid me like this."

"You are in no position to assume what the captain feels. Focus on you."

Flynt lowered herself to her bed and looked over at Nightshade, letting her eyes trace the deep purple vines that curved gracefully to form a nose-like structure and high, sharp cheekbones. "He talks to *you*. Do you report on me to him?"

"I do not."

"What has he said about me?"

Nightshade shook her head. "I would not share what is

told to me in confidence. You know that."

Flynt sagged. She did know, and yet that didn't stop her from hoping. "I just feel so lost. He looks at me, and I see so much more in his eyes. He sees me. Me, not the robes, or the arm, or even the curves, just me. I came on this ship because he trusted me, and I trusted him." *I thought I could belong.* The memory of Ieyil rose inside her, the feeling of the Necro-equitem waiting just beyond the veil.

"The two of you are both very good at expressing your feelings," Nightshade said, dropping both arms to her side. "But I am the wrong creature to hear your confessions."

"He won't meet me!"

Nightshade sighed, an exaggerated gesture, considering she didn't breathe. "I enjoy you, Flynt, but you are dense. I should not understand any meat-creature better than you do. What is it that you want?"

Flynt touched the obsidian finger-cuffs on her hand. Recently, their weight was the only thing to feel right rather than like a chain. "To belong," Flynt said.

"No. You belonged in your old life as a Breeder, and you weren't happy."

"I was *accepted* in my old life because I looked the part, and they could pretend. I've only ever felt I belonged with a few people, and most of them are dead."

Nightshade stood and, crossing the room on silent feet, she leaned over Flynt and brushed one finger over Azucena's emeralds.

"Yes, Azucena, my mother, and my husband," Flynt said. Those were the people she'd loved, whom she'd belonged with. And Lem—or so she'd thought. Maybe that was the heart of the issue. She'd come on this damn ship for adventure, for battle, and to practice her newfound art form. But she'd also come because she'd believed she had a true place aboard the *Seer's Sword*. "I thought..."

"Being a crew member of the *Seer's Sword* isn't what you thought?"

"I can't live like this. I'm drowning." *And Ieyil is rising. I can't even make it to Lem to warn him.*

"Drowning? Well, that is a clear exaggeration. Why don't you go to bed?" Nightshade plucked her robes off the edge of her own bed and tucked them over her shoulders, folded the cloth over her stomach, and then tied the wide, yellow belt. "I'm going for a walk before my shift."

"Have fun watching over the Magi," Flynt said. When not on a mission demanding their skills, the duty shift for Magisters usually consisted of watching over the less potent Aspect users as they all practiced their craft.

Nightshade was gone within moments, and Flynt sat feeling the same weight pressing down on her. She pulled off her glove and tossed it onto her bed.

Her comm beeped to get her attention. A live call was coming through. Rather than take it on her comm's retinal display, she walked over to the wall and pressed the button to open the comm link screen. The call came from the bridge, so chances were it was Lem.

Her heart raced. Did he regret having his brutes send her away earlier?

Flynt activated the connection, not even bothering to smooth down her hair or wipe the cemetery dirt from her face.

He appeared on the screen, the wood-paneled bridge behind him. The bridge and the navigation chamber were the only internal rooms that stuck to the pirate theme of *Seer's Sword's* exterior. "Flynt, get up here. I need you."

"At this hour?" She'd come, but she didn't need to act eager, and it *was* late.

"Yes. Now," Lem said. "It's important. Get to the bridge."

The line went dead.

Flynt shoved her feet into her boots, trying to decide if Lem's command to join him was encouraging or just the opposite. He hadn't come off as in a friendly mood. She glanced at her glove hanging a few inches over the edge of her bed. She'd leave it—he had said to come now.

If Lem gave conflicting orders, she could choose which one to follow.

Chapter 5

As Flynt headed to the door of her cabin, she could practically feel Cyniel whispering to her that she was being foolish. She'd been ordered to wear the glove when in public just that morning. And really, deep down, she knew that wearing it was wise.

With a heaved sigh, she turned back and grabbed the glove. Before putting it on, she transferred her finger-cuffs to her right hand. The obsidian felt oppressive against skin, and she angrily yanked the glove on over her bone arm.

She immediately felt as if she were living in someone else's skin, pretending. No one seemed to understand that.

Flynt exited the cabin, head held high, but no one else was in the passageway. She took the portal to the upper deck and then walked down three flights of stairs. This time, there were no guards around the navigation room door. She marched up and the door slid open and stale dry air rolled out, carrying a healthy whiff of incense.

Incense was not a scent she associated with Lem. She associated the smell with many of his Magi, especially the Air-magi.

Disappointment curdled in Flynt's stomach as the scent of Magi rolled over her, overwhelming the smells of the control room. She'd been foolish to think she'd be alone with Lem—even just to get yelled at.

But at least he had to be pleased with her choice to wear the Aspect-forsaken glove. If she was going to shroud herself in the velvet lie, *someone* ought to appreciate her sacrifice.

Flynt took a step inside the faux-wood interior, an extravagant and strange concoction just like the upper deck. She was surprised Lem didn't have a wooden ship wheel akin to those installed on old seafaring vessels to navigate with. A large, glass tube, running from floor to ceiling, was the ship's true navigation system, filled with funnels of Aspect energy and electrical wires, along with bubbling gasses—it was through this that Lem could reach out to the Galaxy Tunnels. Displays of all sorts dotted the rest of the room, including a series of monitors that could scroll through security feeds from the ship's rooms.

As soon as the room's occupants came into view, the room didn't hold Flynt's attention.

Lem stood, hands clasped behind his back, facing two figures in Magister's robes. Not just Magi, but the higher-level Magisters who led the ranks of the Aspect-manipulators. Of course he'd called *all* the ship's Magisters aboard for some news. She should have known.

Flynt's mouth tasted bitter.

The two Magisters with the captain were the only Magisters stationed aboard the *Seer's Sword* other than Flynt and Nightshade. The Air-magister had a wan faded look to him that suited his calling but the Earth-magister was a frail elderly person who, by appearance, hardly suited the strength of Earth at all. Lem's crew included over a dozen Magi, but these were the leaders.

Then from behind the glass tube, Nightshade stepped out, her white Life-magister robes rustling. Which meant all the most powerful casters were in attendance, but no soldiers. Flynt had only taken two steps forward when the door behind her slid open again and the two highest-ranking military officers entered, looking brittle and serious.

Flynt's stomach clutched again. She'd never seen Nightshade so on edge.

Staid and slow in a way that implied his Aspect's curse was catching up to him, the Air- magister spoke. "I believe we are all here. What business do we have at this time of night?"

Flynt slipped behind the large, glass tube and moved to stand beside Nightshade. The air held less of the incense's smokiness near her. The bitter taste left as Flynt realized what this gathering meant. Lem wouldn't call this group together for a chitchat. Could it be the assignment she was waiting for? They'd had plenty of assignments and Lem always delivered them like this, but usually, there was more warning. This felt both sudden and important.

Lem smiled at all of them—bright and patently false. "I'll keep it short, given the late hour and that it will be our last night here."

"Last night?" one of the officers, a short man with a bald head, asked. He spoke in a dry, vacant tone that made Flynt instantly bored. "We're scheduled to remain five more days. The men have planned around it."

"Then they'll unplan," Lem said, the upward curve of his lips never wavering. Flynt thought that, in this case, that wide smile made him look crazy. "Milisade has sent us word. We're leaving tomorrow night on a special mission."

Flynt grinned and didn't bother to hide it. A special mission sounded promising. She picked at her glove absently, soon she might not need it. Maybe the queen had sent a private message for Flynt as well. Something to say this was her moment to prove herself, to earn her right to emerge from the shadows.

"What mission?" the other officer asked. She had a rasp to her voice that kept it from being as robotically dull as her companion's. Though the tight bun that held her deep blue hair did her no favors.

The Magisters each shuffled, eyeing both Lem and the military officers.

Apparently, Magisters were smarter than officers. They knew better than to open their mouths. Nightshade cocked her head slightly but showed no other reaction to anything happening. Flynt tried to absorb the Life-magister's calm.

Lem, however, allowed his smile to falter and his voice darkened, carrying a clear warning. "I will tell you what you need to know when you need to know it. I suggest you gather up the soldiers and get them aboard in a timely fashion. Make your announcements. We will leave tomorrow after dusk."

Flynt clenched her bone hand inside its satin cover. Queen Milisade was sending them on yet another mission. The queen had told her that hiding was temporary until Flynt knew her own powers. Only once she stood a chance of being able to protect her father and her vast number of siblings would she be called to step up as a Necro-equitem. But for any mission that meant a task worthy to prove herself and earn her freedom, she would also expect a private message.

This little excursion might be fun. She'd get to raise some skeletons and sic them on some of the Coil's enemies. Maybe even plague an enemy ship prior to their own people boarding to obtain some crucial information.

But it would be just another mission unless Lem called her aside to deliver that private message that could mean the first step toward freedom.

Lem rattled off a few details of the departure and a specific time for everyone to be aboard and a time in the morning for all the officers to meet for further instruction. The two officers left. Then the captain turned an eye to the silent Magisters.

"You are all dismissed." Lem looked at the gathered Magisters but seemed to only meet Nightshade's sightless gaze. "No special instruction, other than to make sure all the Magi are aboard. I'll be visiting my family tomorrow and when I return in the afternoon, I will meet with you and answer as many of your questions as I can."

Nightshade touched Flynt's flesh arm before stepping back and slowly approaching the door. Flynt remained still. The others turned away. The Air-magister was the first to leave, taking some of the spiced, smoky scent with him. Nightshade and the remaining Magister, a devotee of Earth, neared the door.

Before they could slip out, Lem finally met Flynt's daring

gaze. Her heart pounded. Was this when he called her aside for the message?

"Flynt, I appreciate that you recognize that this counts as public."

Flynt narrowed her eyes. What in Ayal's name was he talking about?

The Earth-magister slipped out the door behind her in a rustle of robes and a clack of heeled boots—more of the incense left and Flynt's breath came easier.

"Keep it on," Lem said. He levelled his eyes on her face, never moving to her bone arm.

The glove. Flynt's anger choked her. Her damn hand covering was what Lem chose to speak to her about? This! He'd decided it would be a lark to lecture her in front of others.

"We need you safe," he said. His voice had softened. "This mission... Just wear the damn glove."

Nightshade hovered inside the door.

Flynt forced a sickly-sweet smile to her lips and fastened her eyes on the captain. "Perhaps you should come to my room in the morning and remind me."

Mirth twinkled in his brown eyes. "I'm not your father. I already have two children; I don't need another."

Was he flirting or mocking her? Either way, this was the most personal he'd gotten in a long time. Flynt couldn't find words.

Nightshade grabbed Flynt's elbow and held up a finger to Lem, demanding silence. He huffed but didn't say more. Had Nightshade always been so bossy with Lem? Flynt had never noticed before, but Lem seemed to take it in stride. Nightshade firmly maneuvered Flynt out the door. The captain's gaze followed them.

Guided by Nightshade's constant presence at her back, Flynt headed toward their room. Neither woman spoke. Flynt held her tongue because she didn't know what she would say if she spoke. And she didn't know why Nightshade remained silent; Flynt was simply happy that the Life-magister did.

This was just another mission.

Flynt's glove seemed to entomb her arm, its breathless embrace threatening to take all of her.

Once inside their cabin, Nightshade went directly to her berth, unraveling her belt as she moved and dumping her robes at the foot. Flynt supposed the Diethyrian wouldn't have any understanding of the purpose of clothing. To Nightshade, Flynt supposed the cloth was no more than ceremonial decoration.

Flynt stormed halfway across the cabin before she noted the blinking light of a message on the cabin's wall display. It hadn't come through her comm, which meant the message had been sent internally. Something from Lem? Flynt couldn't think of anyone else who'd have any need to speak with her.

Flynt tried to access it through her neural interface on her private comm but couldn't. The message had been sent to her room, not directly to her. Which must have meant that Nightshade was cleared to see whatever it was.

Flynt jabbed at the button on the wall; she'd only just escaped the self-involved ego-bloated jerk. But the image that projected out was not a view of Lem or the control room. It was a recorded message, slightly fuzzy from being sent over a vast distance, of Queen Milisade seated in her private quarters. Milisade wore her platinum-blonde wig twisted and contorted in elaborate braids and dotted with gemstones. Her delicate features nearly disappeared beneath this overwhelming display of station. Yet Flynt caught something tight and worried around the queen's dark brown eyes.

"I fear I must ask for your help again," the recording said in Milisade's sweet voice.

This might be what Flynt had been waiting for. She took a step back. A real mission. Except nothing in Milisade's face or voice implied either calmness or happiness. If this was a time for Flynt to finally test herself, the situation was not one that the Queen wished to be part of.

"Necro-equitem Ieyil is not entirely gone," Milisade said. Her face seemed pale as she spoke the name. Milisade's unease made sense. Ieyil had nearly killed the queen mere months prior.

Now Milisade was claiming that Ieyil wasn't gone, which luckily didn't imply that the Necro-equitem had returned. Of course, the long-dead daughter of Death hadn't been entirely present when she'd drained the queen's life and nearly taken a hold of the living world. So "not entirely gone" could mean very destructive things.

The queen stared soulfully out of the screen. "There have been ongoing attacks of the undead on some of our smaller colonies as well as reported tears in the Aspect within Galaxy-tunnels. These tears very much resemble those that cropped up when Ieyil was trying to take over my body. And the undead attacks cannot be linked to any living Death manipulator. Two settlements have fallen entirely to the attacks, and we are warding off the rest as best we can. Based on her past efforts, it was determined these were likely traceable to Ieyil."

There went any hope for peaceful intent in Ieyil's return. Flynt pressed her lips tightly together.

"The Coil's mind, along with my Defenders and emissaries, have tracked Ieyil's energies to the source." Milisade's eyes fluttered down, shielding behind her lashes. "We hoped to stop her before she gained a hold on our Coil and reignited her war. However, I underestimated her. In our investigation, a team went missing. Defender Nekolai was among them."

Nekolai! If she didn't hear any more, maybe it wouldn't be true. Maybe she could hide.

Flynt lunged forward to stop the message, but her finger didn't touch the button. If Nekolai was in trouble, she needed to know about the situation. For her late husband's sake, for Cyniel, his best friend required protection.

"I am sending the *Seer's Sword* to the Bone Yard to investigate the disappearance."

The Bone Yard? *Shit.* The skeletons of an empire, century upon century, lay there. If there was one place that Milisade didn't want the ancient Necro-equitem showing up, it was there. And why had Nekolai been stupid enough to go?

Except Flynt knew the answer to that. Milisade had sent him. He'd gone. For him, the world was that clear-cut.

On the screen, Milisade went on, her voice evenly paced and modulated, but her eyes, when they flicked up, showing something of her inner turmoil. "You and your captain, along with your unique gifts, may be essential in achieving a positive outcome. It seems Ieyil is somehow manipulating the Death-aspect from across the veil—and given the planet she's manifesting on, this makes her nearly impossible to beat. Even if we knew *how* to beat her."

Which they didn't and Flynt certainly didn't. She wanted to turn away. Hide, hide, hide—that was all she'd been told. She wanted to escape, but this time, if she failed, Nekolai would be lost.

"I pray that your powers are enough. Between you and Captain Lem, I am hopeful we can yet stop whatever Ieyil has planned and rescue my advance forces." Milisade paused, perhaps wrestling with what she'd say next. "Please, bring Nekolai back to me."

The message ended and the screen went black, but Flynt continued to stare.

Her mind couldn't find a part of that message to begin parsing and instead attempted to process it all at once. Nekolai had supported her, been there for her when no one else had after Cyniel's death. Ieyil was dead, had been dead for one thousand years—she'd only been able to affect the world before because of a crazy Death-master and links to objects the Necro Queen had left behind. How could she be back? Milisade was asking for Flynt's gift—but the team the queen seemed to think she was bringing on board, Lem and Flynt, hadn't been functional since the *Seer's Sword* had left the Coil. Work with Lem? He'd have to *talk to* her for that!

But she didn't want him to *have* to. Lem was supposed to *want* to be by her side.

She'd been waiting for this mission, but now that it had arrived, now that it was real, fear crept in. What if she failed? Or even scarier, what would really happen if she succeeded? She'd wanted a mission, but this mission was personal and predicated on assumptions about Lem and her that weren't true.

Stopping Flynt's thoughts, Nightshade slid in front of Flynt and shut off the screen.

"I need a drink," Flynt said.

"You need sleep." Nightshade's flat voice showed a hint of disapproval. Flynt allowed Nightshade to lead her to bed and pull back her blanket. Flynt kicked off her boots and let her robes slide to the floor. Then she sank onto her too-firm bed. Nightshade crossed the room and settled onto her blanket.

Then, when they were both settled, Nightshade said something else. "You could run off and neither Lem nor the queen would ever find you. We are in a major space port. If you don't wish to be part of these events, you could simply step onto another ship and watch the *Seer's Sword* leave without you. Get your implant disabled on the next stop and just disappear."

Flynt gave a hard shake of her head. "They need me."

"What do *you* need?" Nightshade's painted eyes glowed. "You are under no contract. You're free."

Nightshade had a point. There were hundreds of voyagecraft in the harbor all bound for new places, and adventures that didn't involve battling ancient compatriots. But this mission would solve her problems with having to run away and hide. Now wasn't the time to run. Flynt closed her eyes and lay back.

A dream rolled over her mind, obscuring everything else like a heavy fog. Flynt knew it was a formation of mental images rather than reality, and yet she had no control over the blanket of thoughts—it wasn't her dream.

This was Ieyil's dream, and Flynt had been pulled along on these mental excursions with the long-dead Necro Queen before. This time, Ieyil moved with feline grace through a field of corpses. There appeared to be no end to the bodies, no horizon to set as a limit. Two Death-magi followed behind her. Flynt hardly saw them—Ieyil demanded her attention.

As before when Flynt had seen her, Ieyil seemed as much skeleton as woman, bones pressing against skin, cheekbones sharp enough to cut. Her ashy-brown skin like the silk of a dress over those perfect bones—she was the most beautiful thing that Flynt had ever seen. Obsidian dripped from her extremities: rings, necklaces, earrings, a belt, a cane, all glowing a slight purple at the edge. But she did not wear the horned crown that Flynt associated with her.

Without being told, Flynt knew this was because Ieyil had yet to attain the crown at this point in time.

Then Ieyil stopped and knelt beside one body among the thousands. This body was dressed in the robes of a Death-magus. Ieyil gently cradled the corpse's head in her hands.

"Left among the enemies," she whispered. "We will bring you home."

The two Death-magi behind her knelt as well, bowing their heads. Flynt, though invisible and aware this was only an echo, let her head lower in respect.

"Carry her bones to the river," Ieyil instructed them, sorrow a thick tar making her voice hard to comprehend. "We will see that she has the respect a child of Ayal deserves."

The two Death-magi leaned over the body, hands glowing until several nearby corpses rose and shambled over to carefully lift the fallen Death-magus and carry her away. The Death-magi followed the corpse. Once alone, Ieyil stood, then she turned and looked up, up directly at Flynt, as if she saw her there. And her words, now as angry as they had been sorrowful, were for Flynt.

"Our Magi die for people who don't see us, notice us, or value us. My children, Death's children, bleed and bleed, and it isn't right. I carried fifty of them inside me, fifty who with their bond to me are able to cast without their gift eating them. It wasn't enough. I had to save us all. But the balance between the pale world of the living and the veil is hard to keep... and harder to *want* to keep."

The wetness around Ieyil's eyes hurt Flynt. And she knew that balance, the way the veil tugged at her when she manipulated Aspect. How much harder it must have been while supporting so many other casters. From what little remained to educate Flynt on Necro-equitems, she knew on average, they had been able to support five Death-magi safely. This support saved the Magi from having Aspect manipulation drain the magi of vitality and life, but eventually doomed the Necro to Death-madness. For Ieyil to hold a steady link to fifty Death-magi inside her and have any sanity... Flynt tried to reach out and hold the other woman, but she had no arms.

Ieyil turned away, looking out. Columns of smoke plumed from between the bodies.

"The queen asks us to kill and kill more. She glories in Death and then shames us for touching the Aspect. I feel my people inside me crawling, screaming." Then Ieyil reached up, her skeletal hands stroking against Flynt's cheek. "You are never alone, sister."

Flynt woke to her dim shipboard room. Her cheek was cold where Ieyil had touched her.

Ieyil was like Flynt. The Necro Queen had served her entire life, bled herself for the Coil, and now she'd found the strength to reach out past the veil to try to reclaim some of what she'd lost. Who was Flynt to stop her *again*?

Why did no one ever question that Ieyil was the villain? Sure, she used some rather dastardly means, but so did Queen Milisade when it suited her. Maybe Ieyil didn't intend to restart the war to bring Death-magi into the ruling class. Maybe she just wanted another shot at life.

Ieyil wasn't good. But why did Flynt have to be the one to stop her?

She'd stopped Ieyil once already, cut her off from Queen Milisade and destroyed Ieyil's mortal instrument. How could the ancient Necro queen possibly call her "sister"? Flynt had chosen the side of the living.

Yet it was Death who loved her.

Nightshade's point about the other voyagecraft tempted her as she lay in the darkness. She didn't have to be part of this mess. Walking away would be so easy.

Chapter 6

Lem had once called his family home a "farm."

That statement became laughable the moment Flynt's transport came to a stop next to the sturdy, wooden gate and Flynt looked down the long, stone driveway lined with magnetic strips to guide personal transport vessels. This would be called an "estate" back on her homeworld. A vast, green lawn dotted with trees sloped upward to a thick treeline.

But Flynt had no choice. If she wanted to talk to Lem before the *Seer's Sword* left for the Bone Yard, this was her only chance.

The air hung heavy with dried grasses used as feed for animals and a sweet tang of overripe berries from the bushes near the fence line.

Public transports wouldn't run on privately owned land, so she'd have to walk the rest of the way if she wanted to get any closer. But looking at the small buildings that punctuated the lawn and the impression of a roof just behind the trees gave her pause. Flynt hopped out of the transport and watched it drive away but didn't walk beyond the gate.

Talking to Lem was imperative. Her dream the night before had not been her first moment shared with Ieyil. And her visions, her connection, whatever they were, certainly were not simple dreams. Each instance Ieyil showed her was real—everything she saw had occurred in some form and had come to Flynt like a memory—not wholly accurate, but also not a lie. They were Ieyil's memories.

If Flynt traveled to the Bone Yard, she would have to battle Ieyil. That was what it all boiled down to, and Flynt didn't know if she could bear to destroy Ieyil's connection to the living world again. But it was that or let Ieyil rise and live with the consequences. Flynt couldn't do that, either, not if Ieyil intended to wage war on the living.

Of all people, Lem might understand. He also belonged to an Aspect order that he couldn't claim. If anyone found out his truth, he'd be killed. Yet Flynt had never thought to tell him or Nightshade about the dreams.

Flynt made a fist, feeling her obsidian cuffs press into her flesh.

The truth was, she feared they would take the finger-cuffs from her. Ieyil's cuffs. They would assume that the object was somehow brainwashing her, allowing Ieyil to reach her. Flynt didn't think Ieyil needed any help.

They were connected. Sisters in Death.

Lem would just have to deal with her showing up at his family "farm." He'd have to talk to her because maybe he could help her decide if she could bear to travel to the Bone Yard.

But she doubted he'd appreciate her waltzing up to his home, where his children lived. So she'd wait—patiently. She'd waited six months already to be alone with him.

Flynt hopped up onto the fence and passed the time picking at the splintering wood with one black-painted nail. Lem would get out of his vehicle at the fence if he took a private vehicle to the edge of the property rather than walking—she'd always seen him arrive back at the ship on a public transport.

The heavy gravity pressed down on her shoulders and a throbbing started in her temples.

She had plenty of time to look over the property. It wasn't actually like the estates back home—there, she would have expected one large house and perhaps a smaller servants' quarters. Here, there were half a dozen small homes and five larger buildings scattered over the land, possibly more out of sight. She couldn't tell what lurked behind the trees except that the largest building was there.

Lem would live in the big house. Or would he? After all, he'd said that his wife had a new partner... Would Lem even be welcome in his own home?

This line of thought died when a man emerged from one of the smaller buildings and sauntered over to her.

He didn't appear angry—no pitchfork-wielding natives this time. Even at a distance, she knew that this wasn't Lem. He was too short and too slender, for starters. His skin was a cool brown with purple undertones. Even if not for all of that, she couldn't picture Lem in a wide-brimmed grass hat. Still, obviously, he was a native.

Having never left the dock area, except for her brief visit to the cemetery, Flynt hadn't really had much contact with the true culture of the planet, but he looked like a farmer. Probably not dangerous to her.

"Ho, there!" the man called out.

"May the Coil's waters run pure," she replied, only wondering if the polite greeting was appropriate here after it had passed her lips.

"Srike's eye be on you," he said—not a greeting she knew, but still familiar in form. He was being friendly.

The man drew closer. His wide-set eyes slid over her revealed thigh and then up to the intentional plunge of her neckline. "You waiting for him?"

Flynt lifted an eyebrow in an intentionally dubious expression. "I'll need you to specify 'him' with a name to answer that."

"Captain Lem," the man said, distaste momentarily taking over his voice.

Hmm. This native had just become far more interesting. She might as well chat with him while she waited. No grass-hatted fool could help her make decisions about her future, but maybe information about who Lem really was could prove an aid. "Yes, I am here for *him*. I figured it was best not to go up to the house... Where *is* his house?"

The man stopped about five feet from the fence and motioned back toward the trees. Exactly where she'd expected. "Just out of sight, if you mean the main house. The rest of the clan houses are scatted about, as you see."

Clan? How was it that hadn't come up before? "Oh, thank you."

Other people popped out of some of the houses, not approaching but watching. Flynt hadn't intended to draw so much attention, but she didn't mind it, either.

"If you're his new mistress, I'd suggest you leave," the man said. "Mags will walk him to the gate, and she'll be spitting fire at the sight of you."

Flynt snorted. "I'm not Lem's lover."

"Oh?" Now the man seemed suspicious. "Then who are you?"

And here it came. She resisted a sigh. "Lem's new Death-magister."

This time when the man eyed her revealed figure, he seemed to find her wanting. The colors were right, but the custom cut of the robes worked against her. "*You?*"

Flynt's satin-clad fingers curled over the fence. "Do you have a problem with that?"

"Only that no one will ever believe that one." He chuckled. "Magister, she says! Death-magister!"

Behind him, some of the people were moving. She didn't divert her attention to look, but she thought she saw someone coming from the trees. Two, even.

Flynt shrugged and brushed her velvet fingers over the fence. "I am who I am, whether you believe it or not. Who are you?"

"Someone who understands your predicament."

And what predicament did he see her in? The actual mess with Ieyil, forbidden powers, and imperiled friends hadn't occurred to him, that was a guarantee. Sometimes, fewer words worked better to draw information. "Oh?"

"I've been with Lady Mags for near four years now, and I

still get chucked from the main house when he comes home."

Flynt laughed, not even dampening her mirth at the man's insulted expression. And there it was. He was convinced she was Lem's new "sidepiece." She'd already denied it once—it wasn't worth a second go.

The man stood straighter, going rigid. "I don't see what's amusing."

"I didn't realize that Lem and Mags"—she tried out the name, up until then unknown—"were still together."

He shrugged, still looking offended. "That was his choice, not hers. He wanted to keep his family and bed pretty things like you without the stigma of cheating, I suppose."

Now that didn't sound like Lem. He'd turned Flynt down flat enough for her to have a decent idea of the moral code he worked with. But clearly, this man was an expert at believing what he wanted to believe. And anyone who referred to women as "things" didn't deserve an explanation. As the couple walking up from the distance was clearly Lem and a round-looking woman, Flynt didn't really have time to explain anyhow.

A girl, about eleven, popped out from behind the grass-hatted man, though it was hard to tell her exact age with the species difference. She was on the older end of childhood and before the changing pains of teenhood.

"Papa's coming, Dint," she said, "you'd better go."

Papa. So this was Lem's daughter. Flynt peered at her, but other than a skinned knee and bare feet, she was dressed in what Flynt's mother had called a "company dress." Too neat for the child it covered or her halo of auburn hair.

"They been fighting?" the man asked, his profile to Flynt as he looked at the girl.

The child nodded somberly. "Momma's steamed!"

The man in the grass hat tilted his chin at Flynt in what must have been a goodbye and retreated. The girl stayed and stared up at Flynt. Flynt stared back, enjoying the bravery of the inspection she received.

"Are you Milisade?" she asked after a moment.

"Nope. I'm Flynt." She tucked away that this kid apparently thought the Coil's Queen was likely to make house calls by perching on fences.

"Then... you're not Daddy's lover?"

Lover? What a word for a kid. "No. I doubt Queen Milisade is his *lover*, either."

The girl shrugged. "You look like you're his lover. You're pretty."

Just then, Lem and the woman, whom it wasn't a leap to assume was Mags, got close enough for him to yell. "Pris! Get home."

"I wanna say goodbye," the girl whispered to Flynt. "I'm not going."

Flynt kept her expression serious. As a child, she'd hated being laughed at. All she'd wanted was for someone to listen to her. "That may be unwise. I heard... from you... your mother is angry."

"Papa's leaving anyhow." The girl shrugged.

As the other two adults drew closer, Flynt nearly forgot the child. Mags was a plump woman, beautiful and rounded with a sturdy gait. Her soft, auburn hair looked exactly like her daughter's. But the ice-dipped expression in her eyes belonged solely to Mags.

Lem looked... amused? And there was half an arm's length separating their bodies.

"Flynt, how did you even find this place?" Lem asked.

"Comm links. You don't hide as well as you think," Flynt shot back, twisting on the fence so she could get off in a hurry if required.

The woman glared, and the girl, despite her protestations, ran away before the adults got within arm's reach.

"Why is one of your women here?" Mags asked. Her voice, in comparison to her eyes, was not cold. It was hot as acid.

Lem started to respond, but Flynt cut him off. She could speak for herself.

"I'm not *his woman*. I'm a Death-magister... and if one

more person tells me how much I don't look like one, I swear to Ayal that I'll—"

"*Flynt.*" Lem's voice darkened. "Don't threaten my family."

Mags sniffed. "Well," she said, though the word had no obvious meaning.

"And why are you here?" Lem asked, amusement drifting back into his eyes as they took in Flynt's perch. He stopped a few yards from the gate.

"You won't talk to me." Flynt pulled her knee closer to her chest, fully revealing her leg from thigh to ankle. "I figured here, you'd have to."

"I don't want your little—" Mags started.

Lem lifted a hand to cut her off and turned away from Flynt toward his wife. "Whatever you think is happening here, it isn't. Flynt is my Death-magister. She may be unorthodox, but if you insult her, you are insulting her order along with her. Back down."

Flynt felt a little lighter despite the planet's gravity.

Lem pivoted away from his steaming wife and strode up to Flynt, leaving Mags a few yards back. "Flynt, do not come here again. Ever."

"Six months, Lem. I couldn't wait longer—not with where we're going from here." Flynt didn't want to come out and say the Bone Yard in case Mags didn't know.

Lem nodded once, folding his arms. "You watched Milisade's message."

"And we need to talk about what it said."

Lem glanced back at his wife, then reached over and touched Flynt's hand, his fingers running over the satin. "Not here."

Flynt folded her arms. "I'm not leaving."

"Let me say goodbye to my wife."

Flynt nodded and hopped down from the fence. She pointedly didn't watch his goodbyes. One thing was clear from this visit: His relationship with his wife wasn't as clear-cut as he'd let on. How much of Flynt's reason for sticking with the

Seer's Sword was for Lem? Because if it was a high percentage, she really should rethink the choice; he was a stupid reason for her to stay.

Nightshade's suggestion rolled through her.

She could just walk away.

What kept her here? Why keep running after Milisade's goals? Even the queen had once mentioned that it might have been better to let her die than to let her use Necro-equitem powers.

Flynt could go off someplace outside the Coil system and enjoy a full life. Getting rid of the chip in her spine that connected to the Coil and its spaceships would make her impossible to track, even if someone wanted to. Sure, it would take time to build a new community, but maybe she could do it and leave behind all the baggage that came with her gift. Stop hiding.

Lem was hiding too—his powers were even more illegal than hers. As a Chaos-magister, he had to pretend all the time to be something he wasn't.

His Tempus-magus disguise was more socially acceptable than hers, but it had to weigh on him. But just because he'd chosen to live within the Coil's restrictions didn't mean that *she* had to.

Only there was Nekolai to consider. Flynt nibbled at her lip thinking of the blond Queen's Defender. If she were in trouble, she knew Nekolai would aid her without question. But Milisade had no way of knowing if he was actually in trouble. Perhaps he was just held up.

She jumped when Lem leaned against the fence beside her. "Did you ever consider just sending a message to me?"

"No," she said. Mags was marching back up the hill.

"Or that I might have reasons not to meet with you?" he asked.

"For six months," Flynt said, then she gave an intentional snort to show how stupid that idea was.

"What do you need, Flynt?" He glanced after Mags and

then at Flynt, the casual smile on his face seemed strained.

"A reason to keep going. I'm so tired of how things are —I'm tired of hiding, I'm tired of the prejudice when I enter a room, and I'm tired of being alone."

"This is what you signed up for."

Flynt clenched her fists and glared. "I thought you and I would be friends. I thought..." She swallowed. She'd pictured everything so differently. "I thought that I would be accepted into the social structure of your ship, but I'm not."

Lem nodded. "You've screwed enough of them."

"Oh, were you counting?"

Lem smiled, almost laughing. "Good point. But more important than that, we get to kill things—that's what you wanted most of all."

Flynt shook her head. "Nekolai is in trouble."

"Yup. I thought you'd want to run in and save your paladin."

That was actually a sadly accurate description of the Queen's Defender. "I do, but..." She didn't want to fight Ieyil. He'd never understand. Why had she come? Talking to him wasn't helping.

"Think of it this way: Being part of team means not always getting what you want. It means following orders."

"You, of all people—"

"Understand the need for order. Flynt, I live on an edge and the only things that keep me from tipping over are rules and order. Steady, rock-solid things to keep the Chaos at bay. What is it that you want from me?"

"A friend." And more. But a friend would be enough.

"I can't be that. Look elsewhere." Lem smiled that smile, the one she fell asleep thinking about: mischievous, warm, open. "One thing, though."

How could she move on when he smiled like that? "Yeah?"

"Thanks for showing up here."

Flynt jabbed her hand into her hip. She'd been certain he didn't want her here. Hadn't he forbidden her from coming back? "What? Why?"

"Mags needed a pretty face to hate—the man she'd been living with throws a fit every time I come home, accusing her of being unfaithful." Lem's comm blinked, summoning a transport. They wouldn't have much longer to talk.

"Maybe I'm being dense," Flynt said. "I don't follow your logic. What are you thanking me for?"

Lem's eyes twinkled with mischief. "Mags told me she was sick of it and thinking off calling things off with him. But she's unbearable when she's single."

"Unbearable. Define your terms." Flynt swung her legs down from the wall to dangle beside his chest.

"I shouldn't be talking about this. Let's get to the ship."

Flynt felt a driving need to prod at this. "Unbearable like mean? Like she hits the kids?"

"Ordioch's balls! Stop."

"Tell me what you meant."

"She starts to hint at getting back together and me giving up the space-travel. It isn't happening. But she thrives on a man's attention. So as long as that sap sticks around, she's happy. And —seeing you, he's not as likely to worry about what I'm doing with 'his' woman. If he stops complaining, she'll forgive him."

Flynt perked up. She thought she saw where this reasoning was originating from, and she'd take a compliment. "What does that mean?"

"It means no one buys that you are a Necro. And you look... You know how you look."

Flynt grinned. "You could still say it."

"But if he thinks I'm screwing you, maybe he'll believe Mags that we haven't shared a bed in ten years." Lem looked up at the road. A transport was within sight. "Now, back to the ship."

Only Flynt hadn't fully decided what ship she intended to be aboard that evening.

Chapter 7

F lynt watched Lem head directly for Seer's Sword. She paused, staring at the vast array of ships.

Boarding felt wrong. Something inside her whispered she shouldn't.

And as a perfectly timed distraction, her comm alerted her to a new message. Flynt opened the message, and the words scrolled in front of her eyes. It was from her father. Normally, she'd want to read it in private, but right at the moment, she needed the delay.

Flicity,

Good news! Grizzeld has given birth to twins. It is hard to tell this early, but the elders believe one of the boys will be a Breeder. Grizzeld is beside herself with joy.

I hope all is well with you. You will always be my first child and you know you can come home if you want to. Grizzeld and I would happily find a place for you. But if you are enjoying your excursions through the stars, I am happy for you.

Flynt closed the message. She wasn't happy, but going home had never been an option. Her father's house wasn't home anyhow. She touched the emeralds in her glove and thought of her friend. The last time she'd felt like she'd had a home was when she'd been bunking with Azucena.

Flynt checked for a message from the mercenaries she'd hired to find Azucena's missing arm bones: nothing new. This was the second team she'd contracted with. The first had quit, stating that the bones couldn't be found.

Then, with nothing left to do to put her destination off, Flynt boarded the *Seer's Sword*.

Back on the deck, with Lem over by the portal discussing something with one of his officers, Flynt realized the truth stirring in the back of her mind. Having to battle Ieyil again was a complication, but it wasn't what bothered her. She could deal with the soldiers and ignorant natives. That wasn't the real problem, either, though it added to her issue.

Her real problem with staying and going on this mission had nothing to do with the mission. The real trouble was Lem's damn smile.

She had never been in love; she'd loved Cyniel, but never romantically. They'd never claimed that deeper bond of *in love*. Lovers came and went. Sex wasn't love. But something about the captain hit her hard and had wormed in deep—she couldn't let go. She was obsessed. If this was love, she wanted out. It hurt.

And she didn't like the person it was making her into.

She'd never needed someone's love or approval before. The pining, the waiting, the longing—those things weren't who she was.

No man could fix her life, and somehow, the idea of Lem had imposed itself in her mind as what she needed to survive.

Maybe it would be best to leave just to escape him.

Nekolai was big enough to take care of himself. Just because Queen Milisade was worried didn't actually mean he was in any dire danger. Or was she just telling herself that?

These thoughts plagued Flynt in a loop when she went to the Magister meeting. Lem didn't pay any particular attention to her, but he was fielding a series of questions from the Air and Earth Magisters. Nightshade remained silent, hands folded over one knee as she sat and watched, detached from their emotional connections.

It must be soothing to be like Nightshade, Flynt thought. To not feel the constant tug and pull of hormone and body-chemistry-driven emotions. Nightshade could be logical—and Nightshade had suggested that Flynt leave.

When Lem dismissed them, Flynt was first out the door. She hadn't been able to concentrate on a word he'd said about the mission. Her only question was if she intended to go along for the ride. And she needed to know by sunset.

She went back to her room and watched Queen Milisade's video again.

And checked for messages from her hired investigator or anything from Nekolai. If she could just fulfill Azucena's last wish and prove Nekolai was safe, she could flee with no compunction. But there were no messages. She messaged Nekolai, but with the distance, it wouldn't even reach him, let alone prompt a reply before the *Seer's Sword* left for the Bone Yard.

Nightshade hadn't returned to the room.

Flynt grabbed a bag and shoved her few belongings inside. Azucena's emeralds glittered on her wrist. Azucena wouldn't have approved of Flynt fleeing—she was certain of that. The other woman had given everything for the Coil... She'd let people cut off her arm and eat it.

No way Flynt could let those arm bones stay missing.

"I'm not as strong as you were," Flynt whispered to the glittering stones. "And you ended up dead."

The emeralds made no response.

"You fought so hard to get here," Cyniel's voice whispered in her mind. Even knowing that she was entirely imagining him, the voice irked her. Why couldn't he speak up when he had something nice to say? *"Giving up is stupid. It's emotional. It is exactly what a female Breeder would do."*

"Screw you," Flynt hissed at her imaginary husband. She stalked out of the room and up onto the upper deck. The sky above was gray—angry clouds that promised a storm. Odd to have natural weather that simply changed like that. She was used to the Coil's weather, which was strictly controlled by Magi.

Flynt lifted the hood on her robes and darted down to the docks. The tiered railings made the descent easy as her dock boots allowed her to navigate both vertically and horizontally.

Once on the main walkway, she refused to glance back at the *Seer's Sword*.

Along the docks, several military vessels were stationed, but most of the occupied spots were taken by voyagecraft. The smaller ones would be independently owned—her father owned one.

The thought of him stung. If she ran, she'd never see him again. She might never meet his new twins. Flynt wasn't close with her father, but she cared about him. However, if no one ever learned she was a Necro, then no one would try to hunt down her relatives to see if they had the gift. Maybe her leaving would actually be better for him, but her heart didn't agree.

All he'd ever wanted for her was for her to have a place in society, to matter and to contribute to the give and take. This act of cutting and running would shame him.

Flynt tightened her velvet fist into a ball. She couldn't live her life for him. Or her new half-siblings.

Flynt made her way over to one of the larger voyagecraft vessels—judging by size alone, it had to be a vessel that sold passage, and this world was not the largest. She suspected the craft wouldn't be full. Sure enough, when she walked over to look at the occupancy display near a glass-paneled doorway in the gunmetal-colored hull, they were still selling passage.

All she'd have to do was touch her Scale mark to the panel. Travel was covered in her class, so technically, she didn't need credit for passage. But if she didn't want to be tracked, she'd have to disable her comm device and spinal chip.

This first purchase she might as well make using her Scale ranking.

Flynt ran a finger over the gray hull, nothing like the expensive and silly faux wood of the *Seer's Sword*. Stepping on board this vessel would change everything. And nothing held her to the Coil, not really.

She could leave.

Again, Flynt searched herself for her reasons to stay.

The first thing to come to mind was that smile. And she

needed to get herself galaxies away from that smile. He didn't want her. She should move on, but she couldn't.

Flynt fished a few credit chips from her boot. Enough to hold her over for a while after she had her spinal implant taken out.

Her hands shook. She slid her wrist across the panel and watched it alter color. Her money was good. The glass-paneled door slid open and Flynt took a step toward it. The air from inside the ship smelled vaguely of vanilla. Her flesh hand wrapped around the door edge, and she peered inside.

Then she stopped.

It was true that she could run away from Lem.

And Queen Milisade.

And Nekolai—though the idea of him in trouble made her heart clench.

She couldn't run away from herself. Death-aspect was awake in her blood and there was no way to run from that.

If she did, she could never use her Necro-equitem powers. The Coils would hunt her just as they had hunted Ieyil and Ieyil's contemporaries. Just as they had exterminated the few who'd risen up since.

If being on the *Seer's Sword* was the only way to earn the right to use her gift, and her place in society, that was her only real choice.

Flynt spun and stalked back to the *Seer's Sword*, trailing her velvet fingers along the magnetized railing as she went.

Back aboard the ship, Flynt stood on the main deck as rain splattered, large drops striking the invisible shielding above her head and rolling off, smearing the outside world with wet wiggles. She stood there until the ship detached from the dock less than an hour later, and then until the stars arced overhead unobscured.

Somewhere in the time that followed, Nightshade moved up beside her.

"I knew you'd be here," the Diethyrian said, her painted eyes staring eerily out at the stars.

"You didn't think I'd leave?"

"No, that is not a strong enough statement. I *knew* you wouldn't."

Flynt looked at the 60 Scale mark emblazoned over her satin glove. When she didn't wear it, the mark moved to her shoulder. "I almost left."

"You would have found your way back."

Flynt pursed her lips. Nightshade made no sense. "So why suggest that I could leave?"

"I voiced the idea, no more than that." Nightshade's voice was flat and even, but there was something in the tilt of her head that implied interest to Flynt. As the Diethyrian spoke, she watched for Flynt's reactions, even with her face tilted to the sky. "Captain Lem wished me to pose the idea to you. I merely did so."

That sucked the breath from Flynt's lungs. Did Lem want her gone? "What? Why?"

Nightshade did not glance away from the starscape over their head. Metal shielding was folding up and would soon obscure the view. "His reasons are something you should discuss with him, not with me."

"No. I'm done with chasing him. I've spent too much mental energy on Lem. He knows where to find me." And if he wanted her gone, he could have the guts to ask her.

Somehow, she suspected that wasn't what motivated him.

***

Within the first six hours of flight, Lem proved that he did indeed know where to find her.

Flynt was on her shift in the Magi Library, which held only a few books and was really a small, insulated chamber meant for safely tossing Aspect about. Being "on shift" for a Magister entailed supervising the Magi who wished to practice manipulations. For most Magisters, this meant time to practice with the Magi. But Flynt had to pretend to be a Death-magister, and when every spell drained life, practice wasn't done. A Necro-equitem might practice, but a Death-magister never would. So Flynt would sit and watch as the Magi threw about Aspect manipulations and read through the ship's small selection of Magi-related history.

Most shifts bored her intensely.

This time, Nightshade and Lem waited for her, huddled together in the insulated center of the chamber behind clear, curved walls that resisted heat, cold, and pressure. All books and seating clustered in a ring around the center chamber, leaving nothing to do inside it except manipulate. She knew the shift would be interesting. No one else was in the chamber—not a single Magi in a chair reading or prepping a manipulation. Lem looked rumpled in his Tempus-magister robes and his hair seeming untended. She couldn't tell if he looked more like he hadn't slept in ages or if he'd simply rolled out of bed and headed directly here.

Nightshade might have crawled out of a bottle of starch she was so stiff.

Flynt froze in the doorway. "Should I leave you two alone?" She'd meant the question to sound like a playful tease, but the tremble in her voice gave away the surge of fear inside her. This was an ambush.

"Come in," Nightshade said.

Flynt folded her arms and stood still. "Nope. What is going on?"

"What usually goes on in here?" Lem seemed honestly relaxed. "Training."

"Come inside and we'll explain," Nightshade said. The dark purple of the vines that twisted to make her lips seemed to sweeten the words. Like the taste of berries in an otherwise tart sauce.

Flynt didn't like that "we," no matter how prettily Nightshade spoke. The statement rang of conspiracy. But she wanted to know, so she stepped in and let the door hiss shut behind her. The air seal gave a sharp sound as it completed, and a high beep cut pierced her ears. The panel on the edge of the outer doorway went orange—indicating the room was occupied and locked.

So they were to be alone for this.

Nightshade leaned against the clear wall at her back, propping one leg behind her. Lem took a few steps in Flynt's direction. For a long moment, all Flynt heard was her heart and her hurried breath.

"Once we reach the Bone Yard, it will be just the three of us traveling together," Lem said, stepping into the center of the inner room, then waiting for Flynt to come to him.

Grudgingly, she did so, keeping a few feet between them as a buffer. "There's a whole ship full of soldiers. Why would we travel alone?" And not the good, sweaty tumble kind of alone. Even now, Nightshade's presence spoke to that.

Lem smirked. "None of them can see me cast. If we're going to survive down there, I can't play the cute, little Tempus-magister. Thus, only the two of you can accompany me."

Flynt looked over at Nightshade. "Moving past the fact that I'm not sure anyone thinks of any Magister as 'cute, little'... Nightshade knows about you?"

Lem laughed and Nightshade's mouth quirked up at the corners.

"Of course," Lem said, moving to stand beside Flynt and look over at the Life-magister. "Nightshade is Milisade's spy—here to make sure I stay on my leash."

Nightshade didn't visibly react to this statement.

Flynt waited just long enough to feel discomfort in the delay for Nightshade to explain or deny. Then Flynt spoke. "Spies work best if you don't know who they are."

Nightshade flicked her fingers into the air, as if dismissing the thought. "I don't find that to be the case. I have been supervising the captain since the start of his career with Milisade."

The start? Flynt looked between them, propping her velvet-gloved hand on her hip.

Lem leaned toward her and spoke softly. "Nightshade was a Queen's Defender until Milisade sent them to this job," Lem raised his voice to its normal boom. "And our sweet Life-magister has resented me ever since."

"I do not," Nightshade said. "I serve as I'm asked—as I am needed. Your inability to control your emotions does not dictate my abilities."

Flynt swallowed and took a step forward, past Lem into the center of the room. He followed after her, close enough that she felt his movements.

"Okay," Flynt said. Nightshade being a Queen's Defender made sense. To a Queen's Defender, Milisade's word was the only law, her life the only life. Nekolai was a Defender, and Nightshade sometimes reminded Flynt of him. More, Nightshade was loyal to the Coil and Nightshade could keep secrets. "But coming back around to the Bone Yard—the three of us will die on our own if it's as bad as Queen Milisade made it sound."

"We're the only ones who have any chance," Lem said, passing by her, then rounding in front to stare into Flynt's face. Once more, he and Nightshade stood together, and Flynt was on her own. Except now she knew Nightshade wasn't on his side at all.

Lem smiled. "Come on, Flynt. It'll be fun."

Flynt took a step back. She didn't need his mixed signals.

"And even then," Lem said, his smile seeming to falter a little at her backward movement, "we only stand a chance if we work together. That's why we're here." He pointed to the floor of the training enclosure. "There isn't time to train as a real unit. But even one session to feel out how we each handle Aspect will help."

Nightshade nodded. She wasn't inserting herself between them, just waiting, watching. Maybe she *was* a good spy.

"But," Flynt said, trying to gather her thoughts into words, "I'm the Necro. Why do I need you?"

Nightshade chuckled. "Confidence isn't your problem—either of you."

"You are the only one of us who can raise skeletal critters," Lem said. "But tell me: Can you control a critter another has raised with Death-aspect?"

Flynt shook her head. Her stomach clenched. He had a point.

"Can you kill a critter you don't control with your Death inflictions?" Lem asked.

Nightshade cocked her head, remaining silent.

Flynt shook her head again.

Lem leaned in toward Flynt. "Can you actually do *anything* against an army of the dead under another's control? *Anything*?"

Flynt glared, refusing to shake her head. "Fine. If I'm useless, why bring me at all?"

"Not useless." Nightshade cut in, still reclining against the glass wall. "You are part of a team."

"One of Chaos's prime powers is deconstruction," Lem said. He shifted nervously on his feet. Given that he'd be killed for just the hint of being a Chaos-magister, his nerves made sense. "I can pull apart the Aspect binding the critters and manipulate time to let you do your work."

Flynt felt a surge of Death energy inside her. It pooled and twisted in the bones of her fingers. "So you break Ieyil's hold on her undead. And then I confiscate the critters and take over control. We won't be able to take down an army that way."

"We only need to carve a path," Lem said, leaning eagerly toward her.

"And her?" Flynt motioned to Nightshade.

"They boost us." He used a gender-neutral term for Nightshade, and it jarred with Flynt's self-created identity for the Life-magister.

"Like a reservoir of power?" Flynt looked between them. If that was all she could do, then bringing Aspect vials to give them extra juice made more sense. And taking a spy really didn't appeal to her.

"No," Lem said. "They'll show you the difference between an Aspect reservoir and a Life-magister shortly, but first..." Lem reached out and took Flynt's right hand.

Flynt pulled her fingers free. "You can teach without

touching."

Lem frowned. He had the nerve to look insulted. "I can."

"Then do," Flynt snapped.

Nightshade dropped her foot to the floor, watching them carefully... or seeming to with her painted eyes.

Lem moved between Flynt and Nightshade and backed away from her. "Okay. Cast at me."

Flynt winced. She was annoyed and confused by him, but she didn't want him dead. "My powers kill."

"And if you manage to hit me, then I'm too old and useless to be on the field anyhow. Cast."

Flynt's gloved fingers reached up to comb through her black hair.

"You have been holding back too long," Lem said. His arms dropped to his sides, but the curve of his fingers suggested he wasn't relaxing, more like lying in wait. "You'll need to speed cast out there. Come on, get the kinks out."

Flynt hesitated, though she felt the Aspect tingle in her fingers.

"Come on—plague me," Lem said.

Flynt lifted her right hand, and the finger-cuffs clinked. The abyss opened inside her, yawning, hungry. Her soul perched on the edge above the endless, billowing death. Life pumped inside her, hot, fresh, and just as hungry as the abyss. Flynt breathed out, sweeping her hand through the air—a dark mist hurled out, seeming to writhe with a tangle of screams. Suddenly, she didn't care if she killed him. Death was nothing to fear. It was a gift.

Lem disappeared—and reappeared beside Flynt. The Death cloud evaporated against the wall a few feet from Nightshade's shoulder.

Flynt groaned. That was it? That was all he was going to do? Time folding and Time bubbles were something any Tempus-magi could do. She wanted to see some Chaos. "I've seen that trick before. It's a Tempus trick."

"I can't use Chaos on this ship, Flynt," Lem said. "We're in a hunk of metal floating on the abyss—too much could go wrong."

"Then how does it help to practice with you?" Flynt struggled not to hurl more Death at him. He'd make a beautiful corpse. But she knew those feelings came with balancing between Life and Death. Those thoughts meant she was tilting toward Death madness. Flynt stretched her fingers and tried to rebalance.

"There's a rhythm to casting," Nightshade said. "I've heard it compared to sex. You mammalian types can sleep with a stranger—but it isn't as satisfying. The act works better when you know the other person, their rhythm, their desire."

Flynt was certain Nightshade had used that example on purpose. Diethyrian bodies weren't even capable of sex; they procreated with seeds. So why use that example? Life was hard enough.

"Flynt wouldn't know about that," Lem said, folding his muscular arms in front of him. "Not sure she does repeat business."

Without thought, Flynt reached out and shoved him, her fingers still glowing with Death. Then, glaring at both, she said, "Let's get back to Aspect."

"Nightshade," Lem said. He rubbed his arm where Flynt's touch had left a residual gray mark. "Your turn."

Nightshade left the wall, and Lem retreated to one of the chairs at the edge of the room, outside the protected circle. Flynt's stomach tightened. She'd never used Aspect against a Life-magi of any level, let alone felt their Aspect powers.

"Stay calm." Nightshade stalked forward with purpose. "Hold on as long as you can."

Flynt had just started to speak when she saw a golden glow ripple over Nightshade. Then the light, like condensed starlight, ran off of her, trickled over the air, and struck into Flynt.

Using reservoir power from power vials had felt like a deepening, a well inside her. But the power itself had been the same, just a steady flow. This was a not a deepening, but an expanding, a swelling inside her veins. She didn't have access to more Aspect. Instead, she felt intuitively how to use the Aspect better, quicker, longer. Holding the Aspect was easy and light. She could have danced on the edge of the veil.

Then a second wave hit her. She didn't know how to contain the power. It shoved against her, forcing its way out as if she were a sieve.

"Cast at me," Nightshade said. She glowed again.

This time, Flynt didn't hesitate—couldn't. The Death demanded to sing. She pulled the Aspect from the air and deep purple rolled off her fingers. A canopy of green vines shot up from the ground and arced over Nightshade. Death hit her vines, and they shriveled and died.

Nightshade was no longer behind the shield, but rather stood off to the side, leaning on Lem's arm. She swayed on her feet but pushed out of Lem's grip.

"I do not need to be rescued."

Lem looked doubtful. "The push of that cloud got through your shield."

Nightshade looked exhausted. "Enough."

"You tire quickly," Flynt observed. Power still flooded her, but enough had drained off that she could see and think clearly with the aid of her finger-cuffs.

"Life-aspect is slim in space—I have far less to draw from than either of you," Nightshade said. "Good night."

Flynt watched the Diethyrian leave, wondered if she should follow. Lem answered that question for her by heading to the door himself. He paused before stepping through and looked back at Flynt.

"There are four living colonies on the Bone Yard. The others on the *Seer's Sword* will all be assigned to one of these and tasked with keeping the inhabitants safe from the roving hordes of dead. We will go with a small escort to where the lost Queen's Defenders were stationed. Be ready. Get some sleep."

Flynt bristled at the order and at him leaving like this. He'd called her here, acted all friendly, and then the minute

Nightshade had left, he was fleeing. "You're running away from me?"

"Yes," Lem said in a flat tone. As he said the word, he seemed truly exhausted.

"What? Scared to be alone with me?"

Lem lowered his eyes so she couldn't see his expression, except that he wasn't smiling. "Yes."

Chapter 8

Sleep didn't come easily. With the pulse of Nightshade's Aspect boost inside her, Flynt found herself walking the passageways of the Seer's Sword until her legs ached, but every time she stopped, her mind picked up the pacing—running loops between Lem, Nightshade, Milisade, Ieyil, and the Bone Yard.

What had Lem meant when he'd said that he was afraid to be alone with her? She couldn't think of one thing that man had to fear from her other than her spilling his secret—and they didn't have to be alone for that. He'd made it clear why they couldn't be lovers, but not why he seemed to feel driven to run away anytime she came near him.

And for once, Lem was the absolute least of her worries. He was barely worth mentioning amid the other concerns.

Flynt's boots clanked against the metal floor, then thunked onto a rug.

No, Nightshade was a bigger worry. She was a spy for Queen Milisade, albeit a spy specifically to watch Lem. But it was possible she was also reporting on Flynt. Flynt ran through everything she'd ever told the Diethyrian, searching for the most damaging confessions. This would have been even more worrisome, except Nightshade couldn't betray a confidence—that would be impossible for her species. So what did she report exactly? Had she at some point at the start informed Flynt that she didn't keep secrets from the Queen? Was that sort of loophole open to her kind?

As infuriating as the thoughts of her two companions and the queen were, what was to come in the Bone Yard was worse. Lem was putting them all in danger by using his powers. She wanted to see Chaos manipulation, but Lem seemed scared of even using Aspect.

Flynt rounded a corner in the passageway and passed a small communal room where several soldiers reclined, drinking and goofing off. Flynt passed them. She didn't belong there. Only a few people had ever been that comfortable with Flynt, or she with them. Cyniel and Azucena were both dead. So drinking and chatting with them was out. Nekolai might be dead soon if Flynt couldn't rescue him. Nightshade and Lem were both present, but she doubted how much she should really be trusting them.

And Ieyil... Flynt sighed. She'd learned a lot about the Necro-Equitem queen since their first encounter. Much of her knowledge was from the dream-memories, but she'd also been studying ancient books and histories.

Laughter rang out from the room behind her. Flynt walked on.

It was not clear from the histories why Ieyil hadn't been killed the instant the Coil had realized she'd lost her mind to the Death-void. This Death-madness had led to her attempt to take over the Coil by killing and puppeteering the Coil's queen.

What Flynt could never understand in this account of history was how Ieyil saw the coup ending. Only a queen could rule a Coil because only a queen could read minds and thus speak with the Coil's heart and hear the voice of the living space station. The Coil itself was the true ruler; the queen was its voice. But she was the perfect voice because a queen could access her closest advisors' minds and see treachery and loyalty. Ieyil never could have ruled—even if Milisade hadn't rode in and killed off the Necro and her followers all those years ago.

The ancient Necro's grab for power must have been a symptom of Ieyil's madness—her mind's plummet over the edge of the divide between Life and Death, the full joining with the Death-aspect Ayal. Yet no one seemed to see this. They saw Ieyil as a monster, not a victim.

Flynt just couldn't see the same thing.

Ieyil had meant to save her people—the Magi of Death. She had meant to lead them to a better world and a universe that they could live happily within.

And now Ieyil wished to return.

Stopping her before had been easy—because Queen Milisade and the Coil had been in danger. Now, could they give the ancient Necro-equitem a second chance? If her destructive impulses could be controlled, then all that would remain was her goal to help.

And these were questions that Flynt couldn't ask anyone. Not without admitting how strongly she identified with Ieyil.

People already feared Flynt enough without her showering them with reasons.

When Flynt finally returned to her room, Nightshade sat in bed, legs crossed, and head relaxed back against the wall. This was her "sleeping" position.

Flynt took off her boots in the doorway and held them in her right hand. Then she hurried over to her berth, trying to be quiet.

"I believed you would wish to talk when you returned," Nightshade said.

Flynt glanced over and Nightshade hadn't moved. Flynt wanted anything except chitchat with the spy.

"No. Just sleep," Flynt said, dropping her boots to the floor and then nudging them against the wall with her toes.

"You can talk to me. I imagine this situation and its revelations are difficult for you."

Flynt spun away from her bed, hands jabbing into her hips, and glared across the room. "You are a spy; I can't trust you."

"Is that what is bothering you?" Nightshade's head cocked to the side, but otherwise, she remained still on her mattress. "I think you may be misunderstanding my purpose."

"To report back to Queen Milisade."

"I do that on occasion, yes. But no more than Lem or you."

"Then what *is* your job?"

Nightshade shifted, lowering her feet to the floor and leaning forward so the painted whites of her eyes glowed out in Flynt's direction. "To kill the captain."

Flynt plopped on her bed—hard. She couldn't have heard that one right. "What?"

"My job is to watch Captain Lem and kill him if I see Chaos taking over or if one of his manipulations starts to spiral out of control. My duty is to keep him from detonating."

"Lem knows this?"

Nightshade nodded. "It reassures him."

"But..." Flynt rubbed at her temples.

"You are blind when you wish to be." Nightshade leaned back again, resting her head against the wall behind her. "Lem is a bomb, Flynt, and one day, he will go off. And our only hope is that he doesn't take too much out with him."

"That's not fair." Flynt heard the childishness of her statement but couldn't pull it back. She didn't even want to. "Aspect powers can *all* be deadly!"

"Yes. You and I are deadly, too. But it is not the same. He realizes this. You believe you are powerful—and that's true—but the danger you pose is nothing to his power unleashed. People like him are why Chaos Aspect manipulation was made illegal. He lives *only* because Queen Milisade believes she needs him and that she can mitigate his damage."

"I am the same. My Necro manipulations are illegal... Will she send an assassin after me, too?"

"No. The difference is your power is in your control. His Chaos link is not within his capacity to control. Most of his Aspect use is relatively safe, but should he slip and use 'wish-magic,' he could do unbelievable harm."

"Wish-magic?"

"One of Chaos's most potent powers. A Chaos Magister needs only wish for something, and the Aspect will go serve that wish... but the Magister is not in any control over how the wish is fulfilled. If he begins to use Aspect in that way, I am permitted to make a judgement call to kill him regardless of the actual damage done. Anything to stop him."

"Why you?"

"I represent all Diethyrians. I cannot afford to make mistakes or it will affect all future relations with our people. The queen knows she can trust me not to hesitate when the deed needs to be done."

"You speak as though Lem's this horrible monster." *The way they all speak of Ieyil.*

"I fear him," Nightshade said, and the fear echoed in her voice. "I do not think *he* is horrible, but that doesn't make him less fearsome. And Flynt—hear this because it matters— he fears himself. There is nothing that terrifies him more than himself. Imagine knowing that you were a bomb and that you could detonate at any time, killing those around you. That is his reality."

Flynt shook her head. She would not imagine that. And she was glad for the dim lighting that would hide her pallor as the thoughts and fears drained her. "There is enough pain already. Please stop. He may not care about me, but I care for him. I won't let you kill him. Do you hear me?"

"I do." Nightshade pulled her legs back up onto the bed and folded them. "Now sleep."

Flynt curled up and checked her comm again for any messages from Nekolai, her father, or her hired mercenaries. Nothing.

***

Ieyil came softly to Flynt's dreams this time, like a mist settling slowly over the normal spinnings of her mind. This time, Flynt walked as Ieyil through a stone hallway adorned with glowing panels that spoke of hidden tech and came to a doorway surrounded by two slumped corpses and a Death-magus who bowed her head under a neon green robe to Ieyil.

The corpses wore odd uniforms, military but not resembling any from Milisade's Coil—even the historic uniforms that would have existed nine hundred years ago. Cyniel would have loved to see these, but Flynt's consciousness recoiled from that thought. All his obsessive study of the past had led only to an early death.

"She is within," the Death-magus said. "I've left her for you."

Ieyil settled one thin hand on the other woman's shoulder. "I felt your kills. You're becoming stronger. But it is good you left the queen for me to deal with. She will be different, and no one should bear the burden but me."

The queen? Flynt wondered. Was that Sisha, the queen who'd ruled before Milisade?

The Death-magus ducked her head again, and Ieyil passed by her into the room.

A woman, with spiked horns coming from her head and ridges along her skull where hair would have been, sat amid the tatters of an opulent room. Her gown was of indigo and shimmered against the cool purple tones of her iridescent skin. This woman, apparently a queen, though not Sisha or any other queen from the history of the Coil that Flynt knew, watched with shimmering, violet eyes.

Ieyil crossed the floor silently despite the heavy, black boots on her feet and the layers of acid-green robes, despite the onyx head cane, and the beads dangling from her ears. She reached out one skeletally thin hand, toward the foreign queen. Obsidian finger-cuffs glittered on her fingers, the chain dangling loosely.

"My queen has ordered your death," Ieyil said.

"And you are Sisha's executioner," the queen said, sitting on a decaying chair of brocade. Stuffing spilled from slashed holes. Her body trembled, though her voice was calm.

"I am Death," Ieyil said.

"Then take my life—for all the good it will do you and the power-mad fool you serve."

Ieyil planted her hand over the woman's head and Death stirred inside her, but she hesitated, watching the violet shimmer in the foreign queen's eyes.

"Killing a queen is not as easy as Sisha believes," the woman hissed.

"Sisha is my queen. I obey." Only Ieyil didn't. She continued to wait, Death-aspect singing inside her. To kill a queen was a line she'd never even seen, let alone thought to cross. This queen troubled Queen Sisha. As such, she must die. That was the order—a simple execution. But just getting here had released Death to walk the halls of this Coil. It was not home, but a Coil nonetheless. Ieyil's Magi moved in her veins, sliding with their own mistakes and threatening to pull Ieyil with them.

Only Death made sense to her anymore—but she was still sane enough to recognize this as the start of Death-madness. Would this kill be her step over the edge?

"You're slipping," the queen hissed. "Sisha shouldn't still be using you. Take my advice, Necro. Don't let her use you up, as she does all the others, and then throw you, bones and all, to her Bone Yard."

Ieyil tugged at the Death-aspect and shoved it into the yapping queen. The queen shivered and flopped back against the brocade. That should have been it, should have silenced her, but Ieyil allowed herself a small reach, a sip from the well of the queen's Life-spark. Even as that spark sputtered, she drank deep. Wanting to remember Life, she tasted it like a heady wine.

Her fingers wrapped around the queen's horns, and she held the body up as Death filled the flesh and the Life-spark disappeared. A voice rang in her head.

"All gifts are a curse in a fashion."

Flynt was shoved back, out of Ieyil's mind. It took her a moment to remember herself; she'd never been so lost in a dream before. Ieyil collapsed to the floor at the dead queen's feet and screamed. Her shrieks pierced the barrier of the dream, and Flynt knew that she was screaming too, but she couldn't wake, couldn't pull herself free.

The Death-magus from outside burst into the room and Ieyil, still sobbing, lifted her face. Then Ieyil began to laugh, a

sound of deep sorrow. "Take the queen's head. I want her skull...
I will have a crown."

Flynt woke to a dark room and Nightshade faced her,
kneeling beside the bed.

"A dream," Flynt croaked. Then she lay back, refusing to
look over at the assassin-spy. What had happened to Ieyil in that
room? With that queen? Flynt had seen portraits of the Necro-
equitem in her crown—a horned skull worn over her black hair
and dipped in obsidian, dripping black stone like icicles.

Queen Sisha had been dead for a thousand years—she had
ruled the Coil before Milisade had taken it over. Anyone who
had answers to what had occurred in that moment was long
dead. But one thing seemed terrifyingly clear to Flynt as she lay
shivering in her bed:

Ieyil had worn the slain queen's skull as a crown.

"You should get up. We have arrived," Nightshade said.
Flynt was glad Nightshade wasn't showing concern. Flynt
couldn't handle concern.

She sat up and heard the proximity alert buzzing. They
were approaching the Bone Yard. The place where all important
dead were sent. Flynt wondered if Ieyil's bones lay there—then
she knew they did.

This was Ieyil's playground.

History called her "the Necro Queen," and she'd crowned
herself in Death.

And now they were approaching her playground, and they
hadn't come to play.

Chapter 9

An invisible barrier protected Flynt and everyone else on the main deck from the ravages of space while allowing them a perfect view of the mid-sized planet.

It didn't look like a Necro playground.

A uniform gray color blanketed the Bone Yard with slight variations for gray-blue water patches and gray-white at the colder poles. Most occupied planets glowed with bright lights, but Flynt doubted a planet with under five thousand residents could be called "occupied."

Flynt felt in her blood who really occupied that world. Even from orbit, Death sang to her. She searched those energies for one in particular. She searched for Ieyil.

There was no visual sign of the ancient Necro. No logical part of Flynt had anticipated finding one. Yet somewhere inside, she'd expected to feel Ieyil stirring in her waking mind. They had come to steal back the lives Ieyil had stolen and to circumvent whatever her plot was to rejoin the living. Flynt stroked her thumb over the obsidian finger-cuffs.

The *Seer's Sword* pulled into an orbiting space dock. Typically, she'd been told, filled with pilgrim vessels and hearse ships. Now, due to Milisade setting up a military block, the entire dock was empty except for the *Seer's Sword's* bulk.

Nightshade stood beside her in a gray-and-black soldier's uniform—only sporting her Life-magister colors on her leg patch and the wide cape that swaddled her shoulders and head. Flynt kept a purposeful space between them, but she had no one else to talk to. After half an hour of observing the planet, she turned to the Diethyrian.

"Have you been here before?" Flynt whispered.

"No," Nightshade said, turning her back to the Bone Yard and observing the walkway behind them as if waiting for something. "I see no purpose to this planet."

Flynt shrugged. "I expected to feel the Death even from orbit, but... it's not what I thought. I'm used to fresh death, but this is all so old, it bleeds together. There are no large single deaths, only small organisms dying across the planet and residuals." Flynt kept the rest to herself. She didn't feel the energy she'd expected, but sensations she hadn't expected reached her. The Death-aspect down there seemed to curve in cold patches where another's control froze her out. While that had to be Ieyil, Flynt couldn't feel her energy... It was just empty space.

Before Flynt or Nightshade could either say more or choose silence, Lem sauntered up. His uniform looked neater than usual—almost as though he hadn't slept in it for a change, and he'd combed his short hair into one unified mass. Flynt wanted to reach up and muss it.

The clean-cut look didn't suit him.

"Time to go," Lem said.

Okay. No pleasantries, then. "Where exactly?"

"This way." Lem motioned toward the stairs leading deeper into the ship.

"You're nervous," Flynt said.

"You should be," Lem replied, then he started walking away.

Nightshade and Flynt followed. They made their way without further talk to the large transport chamber—not the private portal in the Navigation Chamber. The reason for the locale was evident from the two dozen soldiers standing around.

This was a *small* escort? Flynt didn't want to see the other four teams he was planning to send down.

Nightshade moved confidently into the room, standing at

Lem's side. Flynt forced herself to follow even as the eyes of soldiers avoided her. Something about not being watched when in a crowd irked her.

Lem tapped a panel on the wall to pull up a map of the world below. Six points were marked with names and then a series of dots between the settlements representing the established portals over the world's surface.

"When the Bone Yard was founded, there were six settlements," Lem said as he jabbed his finger at the main points.

The soldiers stood at perfect attention, and Flynt nibbled at her lip. She didn't want explanations. She wanted to go. The land below called to her—Death called to her.

"Over the millennia, two of these colonies have faded and fallen into disrepair, and the Coil has chosen not to rebuild." Lem motioned to the two settlements at the poles. "Officially, today, four teams are going to the Bone Yard, each to a different settlement. We are the fifth—and we travel here." He jammed his finger hard at a portal dot close to one of the fallen settlements.

Flynt leaned in to look, hoping to see something special, but she didn't.

"Officially," Lem drawled, "we don't exist. If we go missing, no one will come looking."

"Why?" Flynt asked. No one else was going to speak, but she'd be damned if she was going to swallow her questions. "I mean, why are we going there?" she clarified; she did understand why no one would search for them. They were the rescue party. Throwing one rescue after another made no sense. But why there? Surely, the Queen's Defenders hadn't landed outside a settlement.

"The lost troops had a base-camp there," Lem replied. "That was the last place they were in contact, and the remainder of their party is still inhabiting the camp and in contact with us. They don't have the manpower to do anything but hold the camp, but they will await our arrival and give us whatever information we need."

Flynt didn't say more. The weight of the soldiers' gazes

moved to her, froze her under their expectations. She just wanted out of this room.

"Let's get moving." Lem activated the portal and the hum of Aspect twisting in the air buzzed through Flynt. The soldiers marched through first, leaving Flynt, Nightshade, and Lem alone.

"You two go first. I'll follow you in a few minutes." Lem motioned for them to move to the portal. "Enjoy your evening down there, if possible. The three of us will set off alone at sunrise."

Flynt quirked an eyebrow. "Why?"

"We have to get away from camp where everyone can see us."

Nightshade shifted, seemingly impatient.

"Then," Lem continued, "we will create a temporary portal to wherever the camp's inhabitants think it's most likely the lost troops disappeared. Questions?"

"Temporary portal?" Flynt asked.

Lem's eyes narrowed. He clearly didn't want more questions from her.

Flynt didn't take a single step toward the portal. "What are the soldiers coming with us doing, then?"

"They are holding that camp," Nightshade said. "We'll need a location to fall back to. You have never done this before, but your brain isn't rotted yet."

Flynt snorted. "We're not being told the half of this story."

"That also is typical," Nightshade said.

"I don't give a damn for *typical*," Flynt snapped.

Lem grinned. "There's my Necro."

"Maybe you shouldn't be so proud of your secrets," Flynt responded, wanting to slap him. She took a step toward the portal, then paused with the Aspect from the portal warm against her face. She shot him a look over her shoulder. "And I'm not *yours*."

His laughter followed her through the portal.

Flynt belatedly realized she had lots of questions. Like

how would the camp's people know where the portal should go? And given that Lem wasn't really a Tempus-magister, could he even create a portal? And why couldn't they build a portal in the camp? But she'd have to save her questions for a private audience... which she wasn't likely to receive.

Cold air smacked her in the face and overhead hung a dark, cloudless sky.

The base camp she stepped into didn't live up to the name—this was no base. A dozen tents and a fence of bronzed metal that buzzed with electricity made up the entirety. The two dozen soldiers who had preceded her stood in the mud-churned ground at the center of the tents, and to one side of them was an electric firepit, surrounded by tables and pots. Dotting the fence line were heating units to warm the air.

Flynt acknowledged that this was a camp.

But a base?

Then she saw two bedraggled soldiers with the queen's blue emblazoned over their uniforms and between them stood a Defender—not one of the queen's, possibly a Prince's Defender. Flynt didn't recognize the colors. She did know the fanciful scarves twisted over the woman's torso and the white hood that fell to cover her face to her nose, leaving her mouth in full shade. Only Defenders dressed like that.

More, this woman was well over six feet tall with gray-white skin that would have made Flynt suspect she was a risen critter except that Flynt didn't feel the concentrated Death energy that went into creating one of the undead creatures.

Flynt's eyes flicked over the rest of camp, automatically searching for Nekolai, for his golden-blond hair and sun-browned skin, his stiff, formal posture. Nothing. No sign of that annoying and utterly precious man. Outside of the camp was a bland tundra, sparkling with ice, which dripped from stunted, gray-branched trees. An icy breeze blew dry air with undertones of ash and a bitter lemony scent that must have originated in the trees.

Nightshade slid out of the portal behind Flynt and

without pausing, rushed over to the dead-pale Defender. Both touched their hearts and bowed their heads.

"The captain?" the Defender asked.

"He enjoys an entrance," Nightshade said.

A soldier chuckled; Flynt couldn't see who.

The Defender's gaze settled on Flynt. "*This* is the Death-magister?"

At least she didn't directly say that she didn't buy that story. Flynt moved through the soldiers—their uneasy looks did more to prove who she was than her words could. "I am. I am also Defender Nekolai's friend. Where is he?"

The Defender paled, now ghost-white instead of corpse-pale. She pointed out toward the horizon, past the fence toward… Flynt's gut figured out the truth before she did.

Death-aspect here behaved oddly. Out where the woman pointed, the Aspect was not free-floating but bound to a will, distant but throbbingly pure. Any beings out there were with Ieyil for certain.

Without thought, Flynt's right hand flew to her heart, and she bowed her head. Ieyil waited out there. Flynt stretched her hand out. Clink.

The chain drew tight and through her fingers, Flynt witnessed the storm of purple on the horizon. She blew through her fingers—a tiny puff of purple—Death-aspect not bound to a manipulation pulled tight and sent out, a kiss to be borne on the lemony wind.

And an echo returned to her. A nod. Ieyil acknowledged her presence.

Flynt turned back to the camp to find all eyes on her. Even Nightshade's painted orbs were turned in her direction.

"She is waiting for me," Flynt said.

Everyone stared, wide-eyed at Flynt, except Nightshade, whose slight stiffening implied annoyance.

Lem sauntered through the portal, not seeming the least disturbed that no one looked at him. Instead, he approached Flynt, placed a hand on her lower back, guiding her away from the edge of camp, and leaned in to whisper. "I figured you'd make an entrance to remember."

Silence reigned in the camp.

Lem and she made it into a large tent positioned near the center of the camp. A desk filled one end of the sloped space and several chairs along with a single cot crowded one edge, partially hidden by a beige curtain. Lem dropped his hand from Flynt's back. Moments after they entered, the Defender burst in.

Flynt turned to face the woman.

Once the tent flap had fallen shut behind her, the Defender said, eyes on Lem, "She's not a Death-magister! She's—"

"Yes." Lem cut the woman off. He stood between them and adjusted himself so his bulk formed a solid barrier. "And if we survive this, Queen Milisade will announce that. If we die, there is no point."

"But she's—"

"A Necro," Flynt stated in a flat voice. She pushed forward to stand even with the captain; she didn't need his protection. "What I'm not is Ieyil—so if you want your friends back, you'll work with me. Ieyil's had a millennium to build her powers— she's a goddess. You want me to stop her plan?" Flynt moved very close to the dead-pale Defender and set her velvet fingers on the woman's face, "Then shut up and play along. This is my game."

"Take it off," Lem said, his voice low, thick. His eyes were on her glove.

Damn, that sounded sexy. But she couldn't really have heard it. She looked over at him, unsure.

Lem reached across the distance between them and flipped the latches on her glove. Then, when she didn't move, he reached up, moving her fingers from her flesh shoulder down to the velvet. The glove came free in his hands.

Flynt pulled her arm back, enjoying the feel of her bones in the air, touching the threads of Ieyil.

The Defender gave a choked gasp. "Aspect's thread... That..."

"Is beautiful," Lem said, admiration in his voice and eyes.

Flynt couldn't look away from him. "Flynt is perfect."

Flynt carefully set a finger on his chest. "You said to keep the glove on."

"And now," Lem said. "I'm saying the opposite. Now isn't the time to hide. Now you get to go out there and terrify them, lure them, bind them…" He stopped, sadness washing his features.

He'd never be able to do the same, she realized.

"I'll bring Nightshade in," the Defender said, then she fled.

"Lem… I…" Flynt turned and flattened her hand so her fleshy palm rested on his chest. "You confuse me. What do you want from me?"

Lem avoided meeting her eyes. "I want you to get us through this alive. I suggest you forget the rest and look for the same from me. Anything more is a distraction."

"Fine," Flynt said, dropping her hand.

Nightshade entered, ignored them, and moved to the table at the back. The green-and-purple vines of her skin were hidden under her white robes and hood except for her bright hands. "Let's plan our movements for tomorrow." She jabbed a finger onto a display on the table.

"There is an old temple near a series of tombs. I'm told the last group had a Gate-stone, so with one of our own, we can track them. We should be able to walk close to this temple and set up your gate."

"If they have a Gate-stone, why do we need to go to some temple?" Flynt asked. Gate-stones were the devices used to create new portals. It made sense that the team of Defenders would have used one, but if they'd activated it, then any on-planet portal keyed to on-planet transportation would suffice. "Why not use the portal here to reach theirs?"

"Can't," Nightshade said.

Lem smiled softly at Flynt. "Activating the link between the two portals would make the connection stable. Which means anyone can use it. Right now, we are the only one with the key to use their portal. We are not giving Ieyil's minions a direct line inside the camp's defenses."

Flynt sighed and eyed Lem. "Can *you* create a portal with a Gate-stone? That uses Order, not Chaos."

"Tomorrow, you can see for yourself," Lem said. "We're going there. And for now... have some fun."

Chapter 10

Apparently, by "let's have some fun," Lem meant he would go off and supervise his workers. Nightshade would move to the edge of camp and dig her toes into the frozen ground outside the heated area. While Flynt paced the camp looking to feel something clear from the dead roaming the tundra.

Finally, Flynt went to bed—a cot in the general tent—and closed her eyes.

The dream came slowly, with sounds from the camp outside filtering in. Flynt heard Lem's laugh and the click of Ieyil's heels at the same time, blending the waking world and the dreaming one. Then Ieyil walked past her over a dream-blurred walkway. The ancient Necro-equitem wore her robes, but now bones of her victims curled over the cloth, a cage of ribs over her chest and a spinal cord running on the outside of her silk-clad back. Her staff clinked against the stones, its onyx head glowing a dim purple.

Most notably, she wore her crown, horned and dripping Death-aspect. Ieyil moved like a goddess. Following the current of the dream, Flynt stood to trail after.

They entered the Coil's throne room, blurred by Ieyil's fading memories of it. Only the glowing pool of water in the center and the queen on the throne were clear. This was the same throne room in which Flynt had previously met with Queen Milisade. But in the dream, the figures of the Queen's Defenders flanking sides of the room were only menacing shadows and a different woman sat on the throne.

Flynt stuck close to Ieyil and watched Queen Sisha, who was painfully thin, but unlike Ieyil, did not carry the look with grace. Her long hair had grayed with age and fell thin and scraggly down her back—even queens aged, eventually.

"May the Coil's waters run clear," Ieyil said. Then, her tone darkening, she added, "You called me here?"

"To see if the rumors were true." Sisha stood but did not approach.

"You asked me to kill the queen. I did so. The consequences were not my choice," Ieyil said, but something in her eyes was hungry. She did not want peace. Death-madness burned in her along with some unnamed truth.

Queen Sisha gave no visible sign, but two of the Defenders launched themselves at Ieyil. What they intended to do was only clear in the desperation of their movement because neither got more than a step before Death-aspect snapped out from Ieyil's cane and the Defenders dropped to the ground, writhing, flesh withering.

They'd moved without warning… How had Ieyil reacted so quickly?

"This will be Death's Coil," Ieyil said softly, and her arm lifted, the finger-cuffs on her hand snapping tight. "I will be the queen."

Death-aspect spiraled over the room, screaming, tearing, and when it howled back to Ieyil's hand and settled inside her skin, the Queen's Defenders all lay dead, and the queen fell to the ground with a sick thud.

"Rise, my puppet. Rise and obey," Ieyil cooed.

The queen did rise, eyes clouded with Death.

Ieyil inspected the risen body for a moment, then with a tug of a smile on her lips, she spoke. "You must remain on the throne for a time—not long, my pretty dead one. I'll free you."

Flynt took a step back, admiring the Death surrounding her, feeling the peaceful cleanness of it and the depth running beneath a river that ran the length of all existence.

Ieyil looked back at Flynt, eyes still glowing red with Aspect. "My sister, my dearest heart. You've come to me. What beautiful worlds we could create together, you and I."

"Please let my friend go, or I must stop you," Flynt said.

"Must you? I'm afraid I can't allow that."

Flynt sat up in the camp cot, sweat sticking her hair to her forehead. The glow of Ieyil's eyes still flickered in her mind's eye. The ancient deaths in that throne room echoed like the most haunting melody in her soul.

So beautiful. But Flynt was still sane enough to know death shouldn't be beautiful, at least not deaths that came before their time.

Kicking free of her blankets, Flynt stood from the low cot. Nightshade had retired to the tent and reclined on the ground, legs folded and head tilted back. Lem's cot was empty.

Flynt moved carefully over the floor, not wishing to speak with Nightshade. Who knew what the Diethyrian could figure out, and Flynt definitely didn't want her knowing about the visions of Ieyil. Out in the night, the freezing air brushed over her damp forehead and the starlight danced on her skin.

Lem stood at the edge of camp, facing out, hunched in the bone-dry wind.

Her impulse was to go to him and offer comfort.

But Flynt resisted. The things Nightshade had said about him lingered inside her. She knew very little about the man. And the only thing she knew of him lately was that he didn't want her around. If she was not a balm to the captain, then there was no point, especially since their interactions always served to confuse her.

Flynt was confused enough.

She turned away, walking toward the other side of camp. A suspicion moved under the surface of her mind, and she wasn't willing to share it with Lem anymore than with Nightshade.

Ieyil had killed a queen and drunk her life.

She'd done so on the command of Queen Sisha, whom

she'd served. These were facts that Flynt trusted from Ieyil's memories.

But whatever had driven Ieyil's revolt had happened after that. And it had happened in the throne room where Ieyil had seemed to sense what the others had been doing before it had happened. What if her coup made more sense than the histories told? What if Ieyil had consumed the queen's ability when she'd drunk her life?

Flynt had never heard of that ability, but Ieyil hadn't just been a Necro-equitem. She'd been Ayal's Haeres—the heir to the Death-aspect. Haeres were titles of legends; Flynt had never heard of a living one. Ieyil might well have had abilities beyond the known.

And there were clues other than how instantaneously Ieyil had responded to the Queen's Defender's attack.

They'd called her the "Queen of Necros." Maybe it wasn't an idle title. She could have been living in Milisade's place—the Coil would be different under a Necro queen, but it would still exist. Ieyil could have led the Coil.

She had tried to build a better future for the Death-magi. She'd tried to create a place where Death-aspect was seen in all its beauty, not simply as a horrid thing.

Ieyil was the one woman in all creation Flynt could truly believe was her "sister." They were connected in a way Flynt had never been with any other being. If Ieyil had been in power, maybe Azucena never would have died in the Bone River trial.

And Flynt was fighting her, working against her plan.

Flynt wrapped her arms over her chest to block the chill. Maybe Ieyil hadn't been wrong—this governmental system deserved to burn. Who was Flynt protecting? Her father, whose life was no more than a desperate grab to create more and more life? Milisade, Nightshade, and Lem, who were happy to use Flynt but just as happy to push her away? Nekolai? Who was to say all of them wouldn't be happier dead?

Only that was madness. Ieyil had been insane and trusting her was a mark of insanity.

Still, choosing the current way of things over the ideal world of her sister felt equally mad.

Chapter 11

F lynt's feet were sweaty and sore inside her boots, and it felt like the cold air was scraping the skin off her cheeks. They'd gone on foot and with their comms deactivated to make tracking them nearly impossible. But after hours of walking, the sun was sinking in the sky and she questioned the need to travel to the specific destination chosen.

Nightshade walked ahead with Lem. Flynt lagged behind, often zoning out until all she saw was the white blotch of Nightshade's robes and the yellow glow of Lem's jacket.

The lemony spice of the air barely covered the scent of death, old and moldering under the soil.

"Why are we still walking?" Flynt complained.

"You need to rest?" Lem asked, pausing and half-turning back to her.

"No," Flynt snapped. "We could start the portal here, or have erected it an hour ago... Why, by the Aspect threads, do we need to reach those ruins?"

"We'll get there by nightfall. Sooner, if we make good time," Lem said. The deserted landscape whispered behind him. Trees with tight, brown-yellow balls waved their branches to her like old friends calling for her attention.

"Once we get the Defenders, won't it be better if the portal is located closer to the base camp? They won't want to walk a whole day."

Lem adjusted the gun at his belt, taking care not to look at her. "There should be a portal set up in the last camp that the

Defenders used before they 'got lost.'"

Flynt groaned. "I know that. So?"

Lem went on as if he hadn't heard her. "I'll create a gate tonight and tune it to the portal they set up. There won't be any others here running off of Gate-stones." He fished in a pocket and pulled out a Gate-stone. She hadn't heard of a Gate-stone before, but the small circle of metal held Coil stones—tiny, crystalized bits of Aspect—around the edge. One fleck of stone for each of the seven Aspects of Creation—except Chaos.

Coil stones were rare and incredibly valuable because they allowed those not gifted in Aspect manipulation to use the Aspect contained within.

"What is it exactly?" And why was it called a "Gate-stone," not a "Portal-stone"? Gates were essentially portals anyway, just impermanent kinds.

"Creating a portal requires use of all Aspects. Predominantly they use Time, but you must have felt it—inside the tunnels, all the Aspects twist together. The only way to use Chaos, unless you are me, is with a stone. Which is why new portals don't often get built these days."

"Seems shortsighted to outlaw something we need," Flynt said. The wind sighed as if in agreement.

Lem shrugged and pocketed the Gate-stone. "The physically condensed Aspect in the stones helps for smaller work. But such stones get rarer and rarer. A Gate-stone doesn't use a Chaos gem because it's meant to be used by a Chaos-magister."

"How much is that thing worth?"

"A lot, but a lot less than the ones that *do* have a Chaos gem." Lem picked up his pace a little. Was he trying to distract her with shiny facts?

"Why not use it now?" Flynt asked, darting ahead to keep up. He was avoiding her question, which really shouldn't have been a surprise.

"It's not a choice, Flynt." He held up the stone. "This is the fastest way to get to our lost Defenders. Nightshade made a judgement that the safest place is at the temple we're heading too."

"Safest place to make a Chaos-portal?" Flynt gripped his arm, pulling him closer to her and giving one nervous glance toward Nightshade.

"Gate. They're called 'Chaos-gates.'"

"Lem, is that safe?"

"Chaos is never safe—but I don't have the ability to create a portal any other way. Chaos structures don't last long enough to ever be considered portals. The only crossover Order skill I possess is bending Time. For building the gates, it has to be Chaos. The one benefit to this method is that it's faster. A Time portal takes weeks to set up. With a superb Order-magister, maybe four days… We don't have that time to waste. Chaos-gates aren't stable, and they don't last long, but I can create one in an hour."

"Don't last?" Flynt had a bad feeling. The gray trees moaned in the distance. The yellow orbs on their limbs waved in the cold with a few lone bones singing from the soil. "You mean the Aspect disconnects? What happens if someone is using the gate?"

"Best not to think about that. I can easily create one fit to last the twenty-day moon cycle here… and if we need longer than that, we're dead anyhow."

Flynt wiped at her forehead. "So why not set it up here?"

"I already answered that."

"Not to my satisfaction."

"If anyone finds the gate—they'll know it isn't a portal. Chaos doesn't feel like Order. Someone will guess. So we have to be far enough away for secrecy."

"And if the Defenders back at camp find our actions as suspicious as I do?"

He grinned. "Suspicion isn't proof. Plus, they think we're walking to our destination."

Nightshade had paused ahead and waited.

Lem brushed Flynt's hair back from her face, letting both

the touch and his gaze linger. "It's too quiet. You haven't felt anything?"

"Nope." Flynt tried to keep her voice light, but between his touch and the pure wrongness of the empty walk, she was entirely off-balance. There should have been bodies buried all over the land. This entire planet was a graveyard, and yet she had found only a few corpses as she'd walked, most of them incomplete. She didn't have time to figure out her own mind, though, because Nightshade called back to them and Lem turned away, marching toward Milisade's spy.

For the rest of the journey, Flynt gathered the corpses she located, creating a trail of a dozen risen critters to click and clack behind her. She could probably have asked them to carry her— but figured it was better to save her inner energy pools rather than her calves.

Neither Lem nor Nightshade spoke much for the rest of the evening. The critters had the effect of keeping Nightshade well away and drawing Lem closer. He inspected Flynt's creations with open interest.

"Can I dismantle one?" he asked as they stopped for a drink. His nose was reddened with the cold and cheeks equally frost-kissed.

"Another time," Flynt said. She stretched her flesh fingers, trying to bring warmth back to the extremities. "The stillness out there scares me. I don't know what's coming, but I'd rather have an army... even a small one."

A frosted Nightshade paced nervously, watching them talk, her hand playing at a woven bag she wore over her shoulder to rest at her hip. She muttered about the air being wrong and gave the critters and their mistress a wide berth.

As the sun neared the horizon, they spotted the temple ahead. It displayed a series of columns that ringed a small center building. It lay in the center of a natural formation of rock and Lem led them to the side into a semi-protected section of stone rather than to the temple itself. The spot he'd chosen was like the rest of the landscape, dotted with snow and ice-hardened soil as firm as the rocks that jutted from it. Small, grayish trees with limbs that bent at odd angles made a loose ring around them. The lemony scent was heavier in the enclosed area. Lem placed the Gate-stone at the base of one of the longer rocks—it towered over them with the height of at least three humanoids.

Nightshade reached into her bag and, dropping what looked to be seeds, created a ring around the area. She avoided the ancient temple, which, on closer inspection, was clearly a temple to the Life Aspect. Stone woodland creatures were carved as if wending through the columns.

Flynt used the moment to reach out with her mind. There were more bones now. But most out of easy reach. Still, she pulled at the most complete corpses she could find, raising several four-legged creatures in various states of decomposition and a few human remains that were little more than skeletons with flesh hanging from their ribs. She sent them to ring the area just outside Nightshade's seed-ring.

But she kept them back from the temple—Death's creations did not belong there.

With her critters "on watch," Flynt had nothing to do but wait. She turned to the horizon. Ieyil was watching them, but she didn't speak or act. Lem had stationed himself along the slope of the rock wall to the east. And the temple sat to the north. But the area to the west was fully exposed. Flynt walked just outside of Nightshade's circle to the west and, standing beside one of her critters, she closed her eyes, fingers reaching out.

"Why isn't Ieyil trying to stop us?" Nightshade asked.

Flynt jumped. She'd been wondering the same thing. But she doubted their reasons were the same. Rather than get into her own worries, Flynt lied. "Maybe she doesn't know where we are yet."

Nightshade cocked her head so her white-painted eyes gleamed in the moonlight. "You've been using Death-aspect all day. She knows you're here."

"That really depends on her connection to the living world," Flynt said. It felt like a betrayal to Ieyil to explain it out loud, but Flynt was supposed to be on Nightshade's side. "I think her connection to this side of the veil is stronger at night. Not because of the night itself, but the living are closer to death in their sleep. It is easier for her to feel us."

"No. She senses us. What is she waiting for?" Nightshade said.

Darkness, Flynt thought, but she had given away more than she'd really wanted to already. Yet she'd say one more thing, let Nightshade choose whether or not to listen at her own discretion. "Me."

"There are six Defenders missing out there," Nightshade said. "Prince's Defender Jium explained it to me back at base camp, in great detail. Six Defenders—three of whom are Queen's Defenders. Sizsan, Myuka, and Nekolai... I knew them all as friends once. Remember them, Flynt. They are who this mission is about."

Flynt's body tensed. Nightshade was both sharing and accusing—there must have been a reason. "Nekolai is my friend, as well. He was Cyniel's best friend and after Cyn died... Nekolai took care of me."

Nightshade folded her arms and tilted her head in a very human display of incredulity. "You allowed someone to take care of you?"

"No. But he did it anyhow." Flynt smiled, facing out at the darkening world.

"Remember him, Flynt. Whatever reason Ieyil has for her silence, you're right, it probably relates to you. In life, she was loyal to her fellow servants of Ayal—but that loyalty is twisted. You would be far from the first child of Death whom she warped with the poison of her love."

"Stop," Flynt snapped. The sudden anger was illogical and Flynt recognized that but couldn't change the flare inside her. Ieyil had no one but Flynt. She deserved someone to at least consider her side. "You don't know anything about her. Stop!"

"I know she will not hesitate to kill me or the captain. I know she will happily kill your friend Nekolai."

And they would kill Ieyil without pause. But Flynt kept that thought to herself. Again, she knew it wasn't really the same thing, but her gut refused to agree.

"Hey!" Lem shouted. Flynt and Nightshade turned back toward the sheltering outcropping of rock. Lem motioned to both of them. "Stick close where I can protect you. This part of the process may have a backlash."

Flynt shoved past Nightshade, guilt buried in anger. Nightshade was correct. And yet the same could be said in reverse. Nightshade would destroy Ieyil without compunction. So would Lem.

Lem had set up a few feet from the deepest curve of the rock. He'd laid a small stack of rocks and at the center lay the Gate-stone.

The Gate-stone now glowed a brilliant orange, and little metal extremities shoved from the center of each Aspect stone. Flynt didn't know how much time had passed; she guessed the better part of an hour, which meant Lem must have been nearly finished.

But Flynt's stomach felt tighter, and the back of her neck prickled. The Death-aspect out in the nearby ruins didn't feel as benign as it had when they'd arrived. Bubbles of the bound Aspect moved ever closer, stalking closer and closer, coming from the east and the west.

Lem stood in front of the Gate-stone not moving, but the pulse of Aspect around him made it hard to concentrate on anything else. Other than Death, she couldn't really feel the differences between Aspects, but this must have been Chaos, and that idea alone fascinated her. Flynt's mind shifted entirely to the captain. He wasn't using or manipulating the Aspect around him, simply standing and looking scared, marshaling the Aspect, his hands moving like a mother braiding her child's hair. The strands were in place but not yet twisted.

Flynt walked up and set her velvet fingers on his arm. "It's okay. There is always a risk."

"I can't avoid using Chaos," he said, focusing on the swirls of orange drifting up from the stone. "If I try to stop, it just slips out uncontrolled. At least like this, on purpose, I can try to guide the Chaos."

His words themselves were assured and assuring, but his tone was far less so. She gave his arm what she hoped was a reassuring squeeze. "I'm here with you."

"That just makes it worse," he said, lifting one hand over the stone.

Why worse? She wanted to ask, but she kept her mouth shut. Soon, she forgot as Lem twisted the strands of Aspect around him.

Flynt had only experienced him moving Chaos-aspect once and that day she had been so distracted, she hadn't really noticed what his true manipulations felt like. Though she remembered the butterflies he'd created from the body of a Defender well—as that unexpected winged creature seemed to represent the Aspect of Chaos perfectly. This time, the twisting storm that undercut the air slammed into her. For a moment, she feared her molecules would fall apart—perhaps this time, it would be she who became a flurry of butterflies. Instead, time split and moved in all directions, unfamiliar landscapes portrayed within each wind-like burst of fiery orange Aspect energy.

For a split second, the Life temple refreshed—pure-white columns decorated in red filigree unstained by the Bone Yard's citrusy winds. Small, blue flowers climbed the lower parts of the column and lined the temple walls. The frigid warmth of polar summer brushed her cheek. Then the landscape was bare, the temple gone, and a stand of green scrubs filled the area.

A flash of Aspect brought Flynt's eyes back to the captain.

She stumbled away from Lem and watched as the stone glowed and twitched on the ground. Bolts of orange shot out, and the stone shivered.

Flynt could have stared for hours, but five minutes into the process, when the stone had broken open and the frame of the gate had formed from the Aspect stones, rising into the rock behind it and arching up over their heads, another awareness set in.

Death. Close, not somewhere off in the ruins anymore—Death was approaching.

Flynt turned and saw Nightshade staring to the west at the landscape, broken only by half-crumbled walls and an archway that had outlived the tomb it had been built for. In the old ruins, outside the cage of scraggly trees, something moved. Flynt walked toward the edge of their little seed-defined area, her troop of critters following, bones making hard, dry clacks as they jerked along. The tundra outside their safe circle frothed with Death, just out of sight. Only the old Life temple remained relatively clear. Jerking, bony, and pulsing with purple Aspect energy, they came.

"Nightshade," she called. "They're coming."

Flynt's critters moved in front of her to stand just outside the circle of seeds, between Flynt and the oncoming horde. Her body ached with the discordant Aspect pouring off the massive number of approaching dead. The few critters she'd called to her during the trek would not be enough to hold for long. Not long enough by half.

Nightshade fell in beside her, took one look out into the night, and bent to touch the soil. The seeds on the ground shivered, Life-aspect twirling around them with a pale, silver-white glow.

The undead were close enough to smell, close enough that taste and smell melded into one slick, rotted sensation. Flynt spread her fingers and heard the distinct click of her finger-cuffs. She let her mind balance on the pressure between her fingers as the Death-aspect from the other side sang to her.

Chapter 12

Flynt's creatures clacked their jaws and lunged. They took down the first two oncoming critters. Then more reached them and Flynt felt her careful Aspect control stretching and breaking as the critters fought each other, bone to bone.

Nightshade's seeds sprouted, vines flowing upward, twining together in the air and reaching skyward.

The first of Flynt's critters fell.

"Lem?" Flynt called over her shoulder. They had to get out of there.

Nightshade's vines closed, blocking the horde from sight, leaving Flynt with one last glimpse of a skull. Dried, rotted flesh still clung around the eye, the few remaining teeth yellowed and rotten, but the finger bones sharp and clawing at the vines.

"Hold them off," Lem said from behind them.

Flynt braved a glance at him. He hadn't turned away from the Chaos-gate. Nightshade remained with her finger pressed to the dirt, head tilted up toward the wall. Aspect glowed from beneath the vines that formed her flesh, whitish like a fog.

Outside the vine wall, the remaining critters tied to Flynt fell with silent shrieks that tore into her soul.

Nightshade winced.

Flynt moved toward glowing vines. The Death-aspect on the other side was massive and all-consuming. She felt the vines shiver under her touch as the creatures on the other side tore into them and screamed with their massless lungs. Screams only her ears could hear.

100

They wanted in. They wanted to kill.

A skeletal arm burst through.

Farther along the wall, a vined ripped, and Flynt saw the angry faces of the risen critters outside, slamming into the weakened spot.

Nightshade stood and stumbled back a few steps from the wall. The chemical stench of preserved flesh mingled with the maggoty mold already in Flynt's lungs and throat.

Lem shot a look back at the Diethyrian. "We need more time."

"I'm working on it," Nightshade said, though the purple of her vines was fading toward gray. She held her hand out, white Aspect threaded with a golden color, flickered from her fingers and darted off to patch the vines. The two holes filled.

Four more opened.

They filled. Nightshade swayed on her feet.

Flynt crouched low, helpless. The voices of the dead cried to her—all these bodies, bones, and clinging flesh, Life-spark binding them to the spirits that had once occupied them. They all had stories and their Death-aspects told these histories and desires to her in eerie whispers.

Lives ended in the service of the Coil—taken in battle, assassinated, brought low by disease or age. None of it mattered to them. Death was a release or a curse. That didn't matter, either. Death had taken them and now they walked, driven by a will outside their own.

They told her they were coming in and that they would kill. That was all they existed for now—the command of their mistress. Kill the invaders. Stop those who came to stop Ieyil. This simple command animated them and gave them purpose. There would be no way to sway that purpose.

Flynt had to do something before they came inside.

Lem leaned toward the Chaos-gate, mouth in a hard line.

Flynt rose and reached her bone arm toward the wall of vines. Her fingers moved in the air until the desperation of the dead flickered over her bones and the skin of her shoulder.

Then she knelt and plunged her skeletal hand into the soil. If Nightshade could do this to call the seeds, Flynt could use it to aid her own call to the other things that lived in the soil. Ieyil had taken all the complete human skeletons and made her critters, but there were other Death creatures there, smaller creatures, malformed humanoids, and those bones that had aged to brittle or lost pieces to time and unkind fate.

Flynt shoved her fingers down and forced herself to endure the press of the critters outside the wall. Then past, out farther, farther until she touched more Death-aspect. The curved yellowed bones of grave after grave. She pulled hard against these old battle bones, demanding they part the soil, crawl up, up, up.

Dimly, Flynt heard Nightshade cry out.

Flynt called her creations, several conglomerations of the deformed dead. Pure animations, not true critters but spliced beings of size and force. She gave them one command of their own. Tear apart the critters at the wall.

She saw them come through her inner eye, a disorganized pile of old bones glowing purple—mismatched parts of long-forgotten soldiers—not elegant, just wrecking balls.

Nightshade gripped her arm. "Away from the wall. They are coming through."

Cool hands pulled Flynt to her feet.

Her creations struck out of sight, but with a crunching, cracking, splintering of bone. The assault on Nightshade's wall paused.

Flynt's creations tore themselves apart in their repeated strikes. Not built for life, they clung to their Deaths with a cracked and broken grip.

The beauty of their dance, of the Aspect dancing through her, was hypnotic. They could all sink under those waves and be content. Death's beauty flowed. Flynt pulled free of Nightshade.

Flynt could join them. Nightshade and Lem could join them in that swaying dance of death. All life led there. Why resist? Why not fall?

"You're slipping," Nightshade said. "Watch the abyss."

Shaking, Flynt lifted her right arm, held out her finger-cuffs, and the chain clinked. Life and Death slid back into a teetering balance.

But the creatures cried a symphony of Death. She wanted to fall with them, to sing to Death. She resisted, keeping part of her focus on the throb of her heart, the push and pull of her breath.

Nightshade's cool hand gripped Flynt's wrist, and once more, Flynt spread her fingers and let the chain tighten.

She gasped, feeling her feet on the ground and the evening air on her skin. The vine wall was torn, rotting in places and peeling away in others. She could see through it to the writhing mass of bone beyond. Nightshade hung close to her, and Flynt allowed herself to lean into the queen's spy.

Flynt's insides ached with exhaustion, but the desire to be one with Death was gone.

"They stopped," Flynt said. *I stopped them*, she thought, watching the bones fly outside the wall. It was just a mess of parts.

Nightshade shivered. "Not for long. Those monstrosities you summoned are being torn apart. Ieyil's creatures are too numerous."

That was true. Flynt had forgotten for a moment that there was a difference between the different pieces of Death outside the vines. Flynt watched as the first of Ieyil's critters dragged itself back to the wall, now missing its legs. More moved behind it.

"Lem!" Flynt called, spinning toward him.

"Not yet," he said. The unstable gate shivered in front of him. "Hold them a little longer... Just... a little..."

"I can't," Nightshade said. The hood of her robes hid her painted eyes, but her mouth looked drawn and pale. She drew a long knife from her belt and approached the wall, hacking at a skeletal arm that reached through, then slamming the pommel into the gnashing jaws of another critter.

Flynt turned too—just in time to see a section of the wall beside her tear open, the vines' thick, middle section breaking in a clean line as it gave to the weight and pressure of the undead. Crawling, leaping, and scratching, they came at Flynt, empty eye sockets staring blindly. They saw only life to snuff.

She dodged the first, ducking and rolling away from the second. She'd done this back when she'd trained to be a soldier. But she'd never been good at the physical maneuverings. And with her body drained, her speed just couldn't maintain. She kicked at a third, her foot sliding above its pelvic bones into the space below its ribs. The base of her heel caught its hip a glancing blow. The critter stumbled in its stride and then lunged, biting hard into her shoulder.

A fourth critter leaped on top of her. One bony arm shoved into her collar, just above where the other gnawed on velvet. The creature on top of her brought back its free arm, finger bones hooked into claws, and thrust toward her face.

Flynt screamed.

The world flashed a marigold orange. A gut-churning scent like melted plastic overtook the corpse smell.

The creature atop Flynt melted, bones and rotted sinews flowing away into a dusty drip. The air shrieked in agony. Other critters writhed. Flynt forced her body up and witnessed the critters falling apart, crumbling and melting into piles. And all the bits flowed out into a column.

Swirls of dust and liquid bone coalesced into a trunk, talon-like roots dug into the ground, splitting dirt and rock. Long-searching limbs grew out, reaching upward. A great tree clawed toward the sky. The forms of screaming souls were written over its bark and writhing over its windless branches.

The air stank of Aspect beneath the choking plastic stench, and then the Aspect rolled away toward the horizon.

Flynt's reaction stalled. She knew this magic without knowing it, without having seen it. This was wish-magic—the one type of Chaos that was most firmly forbidden. To twist the world to one's desires had an endless power and equally endless risk. Nothing ever came without a price.

The tree was agony. Its mere presence burned her and inside, the sparks were suspending in hellish torment.

Nightshade launched herself past Flynt toward Lem and the Chaos-gate.

Flynt turned, still dazed.

The gate swirled—completed and a solid, crackling, orange.

Nightshade slid her knife against Lem's throat. He stared at the screaming tree as if mesmerized by the souls he'd trapped there. All the remnants of Life-spark that his manipulation had pulled into the deathly gristly of unlife voiced a chorus of agony —audible to all mortal ears. The impossible entity he'd created didn't respond to him. It simply screeched in terror. Then Lem looked at Nightshade and dropped his hands. The remaining orange Aspect light faded into him.

"On your knees," Nightshade said. Each word fell and spread like acid.

Flynt's ears rang with the screams. Standing up seemed impossible.

Lem complied, not even a whisper of resistance. "I couldn't watch her die."

"Shut up," Nightshade said. "You'd be dead already if you hadn't stopped. You should be dead, and I will report this."

"Don't touch him," Flynt heard herself say. She still felt nothing but a pounding in her chest and the screams in her ears. The image of the risen critter loomed over her, teeth dripping, hunger in its bone eye sockets. She felt its boney fingers digging into her shoulder.

Lem kept his hands low and tilted his head up to allow Nightshade easy access to his throat. He was so much larger than her, but he didn't fight. "I couldn't watch her die. I've said that all along."

"And that's why you shouldn't ever be near each other," Nightshade returned. "This mission is foolish. Queen Milisade would have sent another in her place. *You* wanted this. *You* said you could handle it."

"Only Flynt can do this."

Flynt lurched to her feet and stumbled in their direction, eyes slowly focusing. Their words made sense and somewhere inside her, she stored them away, but on the surface, she simply refused to understand. She didn't have room for this in her mind or heart. The only thing that mattered was the knife at Lem's throat. "I won't let you kill him." This time, her voice was strong, fuller. Aspect crackled inside her. Could she take Nightshade down?

Did she really want to?

"You want him alive?" Nightshade asked, not turning her head to Flynt. "Go through the gate. He and I need to talk."

Flynt eyed that blade. "Not alone."

"Alone," Nightshade said. "You'll be safe enough for a minute."

She wasn't worried about herself. "Lem?" Flynt asked. He still hadn't looked at her. But he'd said he couldn't let her die... That was what he'd meant? Right? But how could he care about her living so much?

"Go," he said. "Nightshade's not wrong about any of this."

Flynt touched his arm, letting her fingers move to his shoulder. So near that knife, yet so far. She glared at Nightshade. The blade remained steady and firm.

Lem's eyes flickered over to her, and he smiled. "There are consequences to my actions, Flynt. Consequences for all actions."

Flynt swallowed and nodded. Without further hesitation, she stepped into the gate. The rose-gold energy welcomed her. Flynt walked into the arms of the portal and knew instantly what Lem had meant about the energy being different from an Order-built portal. The other portals she'd been through always felt slightly electric, like dry water washing over her. A sharp, liquid feeling. This felt dizzy and heady like a sudden drunk.

Then it faded, and she stood in a room filled with ancient torches, which burned only dimly but with a cool, purple fire that Flynt didn't recognize. Someone must have ignited them recently and they appeared to heat the space. It was the first time Flynt had felt warm air all day. The room had four doors—three of which were shut and barred. The locks were ancient but bore the queen's seal. Each had the marking for a different Aspect symbol. The fourth door was shut but not barred, the Aspect symbol for that one at the threshold.

Flynt gave only a cursory glance to the room, which contained a series of recesses in the walls designed for bodies and a large slab in the center of the room surrounded by torches.

Around the slab were dusty piles of bones, and at the edge of the room stood twenty skeletons, their bones warded against Death-aspect use. Dressed in rotted scarves and ancient armor, they had clearly been important and the blades they held in their hands were dulled by dust but not rust.

All of this would not have held her attention, given what Flynt feared was happening on the other side of the portal, but her eyes and heart focused in on the center slab and what lay there.

Bones had been laid carefully on the flat, stone top, newer by multiple generations than anything else in the chamber. Bones she knew. Cyniel's bones.

Chapter 13

Flynt approached what remained of her husband's corpse, still dressed in the remnants of his soldier's uniform and the plate of his comm hooked to his skull. Even the glint of his Scale chip at the top of his spine remained. This had been intended as a gift for Flynt.

Ieyil had brought him here for her.

How had Ieyil known she was coming to this place? And how had she gotten the bones here unless… Flynt shivered. Her hand settled on the rib bones. The other Necro had turned him into a critter. He had walked himself here. What remained of his connection to the bones told her that.

She could feel the journey in him, jerking steps over uneven stones, moving into the light from the dark. Her throat tightened. Cyniel was meant to be at rest.

Flynt reached a hand and touched the skull, sliding down along his jaw. The bones were as warm as the room was; he must have been here for a time. Cyniel's laughter moved in her blood. She leaned in and kissed his lipless face, pressing her forehead to the front of his skull. Tears forced up behind her eyes and she shoved them and the memories down.

If this was Ieyil's gift, it was miscalculated. She didn't want Cyn's bones; she wanted him, and barring that, she would have him left in peace. He'd earned his rest. But to Ieyil, perhaps there was no difference. This was the bald truth of Death-madness. In the eyes of Ayal, Death was the only truth and bones were the core of a person. Life was a breeze, no more.

The room pressed in on her and though she felt the bones, the Aspect within them behaved oddly. She couldn't quite touch it or hold it.

Flynt backed up toward the portal, eyeing the skeletons around the room. If Ieyil had been here, could she have found a way to make these skeletons into critters? They didn't feel as though their Aspect had been manipulated and Flynt felt the disconnect differently than she had with Ieyil's creatures. They didn't belong to Ieyil—they just refused to belong to Flynt. On closer inspection, she knew these to be the uniforms of Queen's Defenders—the distinctive hoods were down around their shoulders and the scarves over the armor lay in different positions or simply rotted away. Even so, that was what they were.

The sigil of Milisade's Coil was mounted in several places around the room, along with a sigil of queenhood. This tomb must have been erected under Milisade's rule, but Flynt would guess it had been created shortly after the ancient queen had risen to power. This was a queen's burial chamber. Which meant that at one point, a queen had lain on the center slab.

Cyniel didn't belong here, but Flynt couldn't fix that until she finished her quest, until she saved Nekolai. She couldn't even begin on that alone.

Where was Lem? Flynt glanced nervously toward the Chaos gate. If Nightshade had hurt him... A rush of defeat ran through Flynt. If Nightshade had hurt him, she would do nothing, but this quest would be over for her.

He'd said he couldn't watch her die. Did that mean he'd used Chaos just to save her? And if he died as a consequence of saving her, how was she supposed to just go on?

No one came through the gate.

Cyniel's skeleton stared accusatorily at her. She couldn't meet his empty eye sockets.

Flynt counted the Queen's Defender skeletons around the room. Her estimate of twenty had been off. Fifteen—bones yellow with age—a few with petrified flesh clinging to their bones.

The dust in the room had been recently stirred, leaving tracks around the room. That made sense. Nekolai's party had to have been in here to drop the Gate-stone. But where had they gone? The three doors were barricaded from this side. No one had left through them. Though all of them had tracks. The fourth door was not barricaded. She wandered closer but couldn't see any way to open the door. The only marking on it was a Life sigil on the lintel and another on the left-hand side of the doorframe.

Cyniel was still lying on the slab.

On her next look around, Flynt realized that one of the skeletons had been moved. From the marks on the floor, she could see where it used to stand. Flynt moved over to inspect that Queen's Defender and the area around it. In the flickering purple light, the pale stones of the wall all seemed a bluish gray, but there was a discoloration. On further inspection, this seemed to be a fifth door, unbarred and with a latch—yet with the skeleton in front of it, they could not have gone out that way. Yet someone seemed to have entered it recently, based on the disturbance to the dust. There was no sigil on this door but an odd marking on the floor and at the edge of the stone that made Flynt's blood ache—the door was warded heavily and apparently against Death-aspect.

Above the door, an ancient dagger hung on the wall, its scabbard decorated with Aspect stones. The dust hanging over it kept the stones and the hilt from having much luster, but Flynt suspected it was high quality.

Before Flynt could make proper sense of any of this, Lem stepped through the portal. Alive. For a moment she forgot Cyniel and smiled.

Lem instantly flew on guard, staring at the skeletons around the room. His gaze leveled on Flynt.

"They aren't being manipulated," Flynt said. "They can't be..."

Lem moved over to her, eying the long-dead Defenders.

"This is a tomb. What were Milisade's Defenders doing here?"

"A queen's tomb, I think. Queen Sisha's." The name felt odd on her tongue after her dreams of Ieyil.

"How are you doing? The wards on this chamber must feel nasty."

That was what he wanted to talk about, the Death wards and how they affected her ability to cast? Cyniel's corpse lay on the slab and Lem had just saved her from a critter with illegal Aspect. Flynt wasn't having it. Before she brought up Cyniel, she'd better finish out the drama between her companions. She laid her velvet-covered bone fingers against his chest, then slowly set her right hand against him as well. "What happened back there? Where's Nightshade?"

Lem reached up and laid one hand over her right. His eyes still hadn't fully settled. "She's coming."

"What happened?"

"We came to an agreement."

"What agreement?" Flynt asked. Cyniel's skeleton stared up, but she still felt its gaze. For once, could Lem not give her a hard time?

Nightshade stepped through the portal, still appearing gray around the edges of her vines. She paused and surveyed the room. "Interesting."

"The skeletons... I can't manipulate them," said Flynt. "It's something in those wards on their bones."

"And the wards on the room," Nightshade said. "But you should be fine outside this room. Wards like that don't extend far."

"Nothing is warded against me," Lem said. He dropped Flynt's hand and stepped away from her.

Flynt clenched her hand on empty air.

"It was common practice in the days before the Necros were eliminated to ward important tombs against Death-manipulations so that the bodies of our leaders couldn't rise and return. I'd bet Flynt would have trouble with any manipulation here."

Flynt motioned behind her at Cyniel on the slab. No one seemed to have noticed him yet. And Flynt couldn't wait. "Then explain him."

"Him?" Nightshade asked, stalking up to the slab. "That spot should display the bones this tomb was built to honor."

"It doesn't. That's my husband. Ieyil had to have walked him in here. I mean, no way Nekolai and the Defenders would have." Or could have, but she didn't want to explain how she felt the story from the bones.

Nightshade reached out to touch the bones. The pale light from the purple torches made her seem otherworldly. "How strange... The amount of power it would have taken to keep her manipulation running inside this room. Ieyil must have been dedicated to getting him here, but why?"

"Me," Flynt said.

"It's a threat," Lem said.

Flynt didn't correct him. Ieyil hadn't meant this as a threat, but explaining that would have given away too much. "What now? I can't stay here."

Lem put an arm around her shoulders and hugged her. Flynt wondered if he even realized he'd done it as his gaze was fastened on the sealed door across the room—the one with the bars removed. "I don't think we can leave. We need to get in there... and both of you need to rest."

"There are other doors."

Nightshade nodded to the other doors. "Those two lead out into the temple. One probably is the way out and one leads into the deeper rooms." Then she nodded to the third barricaded door. "That leads to further crypts. I'll bet you all three doors have Ieyil's critters behind them."

"That door?" Flynt motioned to the unbarred slab with the fancy dagger mounted above it.

Nightshade stared long and hard and then walked over to inspect the area. Cyniel listened, and Flynt wished she could lie with him. She belonged with him—here, in this dead place.

Nightshade spoke softly. "That room back there would be

where Ieyil's bones are laid."

"Why honor her with a place here?" Flynt asked.

Lem gave a mirthless laugh. "It is not an honor; it's a trap."

"But that is where we need to go." Nightshade motioned to the last door. "That is where the Defenders went. If they are alive, that is where they still are."

"We rest first," Nightshade added. "Sleep will restore our energy. It's warm and dry here; there will be no better chance. We'll be no good to them like this." Then she turned and moved to the far side of the room, placing herself between two Queen's Defender skeletons. Facing the portal, she sat.

Lem gave a nervous glance to Cyniel's bones. "Are you okay, Flynt?"

A long day of walking followed by Death-manipulations, a near-death experience, and Lem's confusing statements came crashing in on her. "You've barely said two words to me in the past six months. Why do you care all of a sudden?"

She didn't wait for an answer. Instead, she walked around the other side of the stone slab and sat with her back against the stone.

Lem didn't follow her.

Flynt closed her eyes and waited for Ieyil to come.

Chapter 14

As Flynt slept in Queen Sisha's burial chamber, surrounded by ancient bones, her husband's remains, and two people she couldn't quite trust, she expected the Necro Queen to come to her.

But a visitor slipped into her mind. Flynt had dreamed of Cyniel often since his death, but like the "dreams" of Ieyil, this was different. This was a truth brought by the clinging connection of his bones to his spirit.

Cyniel kneeled over her, his moss-green eyes twinkling in that way they had ever since childhood, a twinkle that demonstrated not mischief, as it did in most children, but a quiet devotion. It was the twinkle in a grandparent's eyes as they looked on at their grandchildren playing. He kissed her forehead.

Tears ran from Flynt's eyes down her cheeks. She wondered if she was crying in the physical world, too. She tried to sit up, but her muscles refused to comply—somewhere, her body still slept.

"You've managed to make your life into quite a chaotic mess, haven't you?" Cyniel said, but he didn't sound like he was judging.

"I've discovered so many amazing things, Cyn. I don't have to be a Breeder and... Oh, if you were here, you'd love to study all the old crap just lying around us right now."

"I always knew you'd make it out. Ayal's flame, you're too stubborn not to."

"You were supposed to be with me."

"Go. Be happy. Live."

"But you're dead."

The twinkle in his eyes spread to a teasing smile. "I fail to see how my death should stop you from living."

Then, from behind him, walked Ieyil. Her horned crown naked of obsidian, now only bare bone. Cyniel fell aside, slipping into the rippling mists behind her.

"You've come to me at last," Ieyil said, pausing with the dreamy, white mist rolling around her ankles.

"You've been in my dreams." Flynt could do nothing but lie still and turn her head as Ieyil approached.

"Yes, but with you here, so close to my bones, we can finally speak."

"I don't want to speak to you. I want you to let my friends go." Flynt strained to see past the vision and could almost see the stone walls and burial chamber. "We can leave this place."

"I cannot do that, Flynt." Ieyil stood over her, not looking down. "You've brought me everything I needed. I appreciate the efforts."

"Why are you stronger here? Your bones?"

"You know so little, my sweet sister. Yes. Spirits are tied to their bones."

"But spirits don't last forever. Shouldn't you be gone by now?"

"No, dear one. As long as memory lingers—true memory, not just stories—a soul persists. Milisade remembers me. So do her fellow queens. With that memory and even a single bone, I am tied to the living world. Has that been forgotten?" She reached up and touched her bony crown—the remains of a queen whose very name had been lost. "How like the world to forget what it cannot control. But you should be able to control spirits, sister. Have you never tried?"

Sister. An ache spread inside Flynt at the word. Why couldn't Ieyil stop saying that? "I don't have that gift."

Ieyil laughed. "No? You are seeing me now, speaking to

me. You use that gift each time you touch bone and see the life that was—that is not a skill of the ordinary Death-magus."

"What do you want from me?"

"Nothing." Ieyil leaned down until there were only inches between their faces. Her eyes held a red gleam. "I want nothing from you. How sad that question is, that you expect the world to use you. I simply love you. Has no one ever given you that?"

"Cyniel," Flynt said. Her eyes flicked to the mist.

"And I gave him back to you."

"I didn't want that."

"Keep the bones with you and you will not lose him."

The dream faded and Flynt's eyes opened. Her cheeks were indeed wet, and Lem slept beside her, not touching but close, protectively close. His back was pressed against the wall and his feet lay over the floor, stretching toward the center slab. A blanket lay half across his legs. Flynt closed the distance and laid her head against his chest, squeezing her eyes closed to try to rid herself of Ieyil's voice and the constant hum of Cyniel's familiar bones from the slab.

Across the room, Nightshade's leg stuck out from behind a slab of stone. She appeared to be resting behind the Defender Skeletons.

Lem stroked her head. Flynt tilted her face up to find him awake and looking down at her. And suddenly, she couldn't hold her thoughts back.

"She brought Cyn here as a gift, but he hurts. I was never good to Cyn. I meant to be. But I didn't love him, not the way he wanted. I was never in love with him, not romantically. He was my best friend, my partner in crime, my everything... except that. I keep wondering if all I ever did was use him, and he just let me. And now he'll never have another chance to live his life."

Lem shifted against the wall, the purple light from the torches catching a soft expression on his face. "From experience, I can say that nothing is ever as simple as that. He made his own choices."

"Choices predicated on a future that he no longer has."

"Maybe." Lem tucked his arm around Flynt, pulling her closer to him. The stones rasped against her silk robe and a puff of dust rose to clog her nostrils. Then Lem's smell surrounded her—an overlay of the day's sweat and ship oil that always permeated his clothes. "Anything I can do?"

Flynt shook her head, but the denial was a lie. "I've never really loved anyone. He was the one person I should have loved, and I failed. Can you understand that?"

"Yes. I've failed a lot of people in my time." A weak smile wavered on his lips, then faded.

Flynt looked away from him, lowering her chin and concentrating on the sound of his heartbeat in her ear. The world was crushing her. She needed something good, something to make her want to keep going. "You said you couldn't watch me die?"

"Yes. Can we leave it at that?"

"No. Please. I'm so alone right now. When I lost Cyn, I lost everything. I have been trying to rebuild my life, make it something I want to live inside, but it's hard. When we worked together before, it felt right, like coming home. I thought we'd keep that together. I didn't know what it would mean since you were clear it wouldn't be sexual, but... I deserve to know what's going on."

"My life is a series of rules, Flynt." Lem leaned away from her, pressing his head back against the stone wall and looking up. "It's the only way for me to survive. It's like I'm walking on a cliff's edge—everything that feels right pushes me closer and, if I fall, it won't just be me who dies. I have the rules to keep my balance."

Flynt curled her fingers inward and touched the cool metal of obsidian. "Like my finger-cuffs."

"Yes." He looked at her sadly—she'd never seen him without a smile for so long. The melancholy purple light only made the expression more somber. "Except if you fall, you take only you down. I have the rules to keep me steady and to fight my natural urges. My control slips when you're nearby; I want you there. But whatever feels right is wrong. I learned that the hard way."

"But... I don't understand. I've never asked you to stay away *or* to protect me."

"*I* asked me to."

"Why?"

"I can't explain more, Flynt. I can't be near you because I want you more than I should, more than I've wanted anything in a long time. Because being with you feels easy and right."

Flynt moved, shifting her hips closer to his, and sat up to look into his face. She'd spent most of her life performing the roles that others wanted of her—albeit badly and often with subterfuge. She wouldn't live a lie anymore. "What about what *I* want?"

He lifted his hand and brushed a knuckle down her cheek and along her chin. "I'm more concerned with you surviving me than with what you want. I couldn't live with myself if I destroyed you."

Flynt hadn't ever seen him take anything so seriously and resisted the urge to say anything light, anything to allow him to pull his armor back up. "I don't want to live alone." Flynt lifted her right hand to touch his face, returning his caress with her long, black nails gliding along his jawline. Ieyil called her "sister" but fought her. Lem seemed to care for her but used those feelings to push her away. Couldn't anyone just be with her? When the pads of her fingers touched him, his skin was hot. "We hardly know each other, but I... You woke something in me. I want to see where this goes."

"I *know* where it goes." Lem leaned his face slightly into her touch. "I've known since you first asked me to sponsor you. I looked at you standing on the Magi practice field and I *knew*."

"What?"

"That if we did this, if we pursued each other, I'd love you, you'd love me. That we could be something." He looked away from her toward the slab door leading to Ieyil's burial chamber. "And that we would end in disaster."

"What about your whole monogamy thing? Was that a lie?"

"No," Lem said, his smile coming back. His arm dropped, hand settling on the ground beside her thigh. "And I'm even more convinced now that you have no clue what it means. But for the moment, it doesn't matter."

"Because you don't intend to sleep with me?"

His gaze drifted over her. "I'm having trouble answering that one."

"So now you're up for a one-night thing?" Her body didn't disagree, and she felt her heart speed at the thought, at his hand lying near her thigh.

"If it happened, it would have to be," he said.

"And if that isn't enough for me?"

"You've never taken issue before."

Flynt recoiled. She wanted to cry. "This is different. That was just sex. You're... So what is monogamy to you?"

"One person exclusively. It means giving yourself wholly to one person and receiving the same in return: trust, intimacy, loyalty."

"I'm already doing that and not getting a damn thing in return."

Lem scoffed. "You had a woman in your bed a few days ago."

"So? That's just sex." Flynt's gaze moved again to Nightshade's leg, wishing she couldn't recall their conversation on this topic so clearly. But Nightshade had also said Flynt needed to be talking to Lem, not her.

Lem rubbed his temples, his head dropping against the stone wall with a thunk. "You are a walking headache. Monogamy means only sharing yourself with one person. Don't you get that?"

"But you can have friends?" Flynt laid her hand on his chest and angled her body over his. Wasn't friendship intimacy... *more* intimacy than she had with any of her one-night stands?

"Yes." Lem chuckled. He carefully kept his eyes on hers.

"So where's the line? This concept makes no sense. My heart has been yours exclusively. How does sex mean love any more than the other bits do? I can still talk to other people?"

He laughed and his hand settled on her waist. "Are you intentionally misunderstanding?"

"Nightshade said the same thing. And no! Or only a little. I don't understand the purpose or reason. I do get the rules."

Lem paused and wetted his lips. "Flynt... Shit... We can't do this."

"What about this?" Flynt leaned in and kissed him.

His lips parted, and he gripped her lower back, drawing her against him. Flynt pulled back, keeping her lips close to his, and straddled him before leaning in again, pushing him back against the slab. His hand slid down her body, grasping her hips.

Flynt moved her mouth to nibble at his earlobe. "I don't care about anything else. I want to live before I die. Save tomorrow for tomorrow."

He gripped her shoulders and pushed her back. "I can't do that, Flynt. I can't kill you or even know that keeping you close will mean your death. After this mission, you have to leave. I've already promised Nightshade. I'm sure Milisade will have you on as her Necro."

So that was the deal he'd made with Nightshade. "And what about what *I* want? You still haven't answered that."

"I'm sorry, Flynt. I've done this before, and I can't."

Flynt's chest felt heavy. Why couldn't she get through to him? If they wanted each other, that was enough. But he had decided to send her away instead. "I love you."

Was that true? She wondered when the words were out, but they felt true.

"Don't say that," Lem said. "You don't know me."

"You love me."

He laughed and his hands moved up her waist, fingertips moving under the cloth of her robe, stroking softly on the skin over her ribs. "From the start."

"Then… we have right now."

Flynt let him pull her close, let him kiss her. This time, the kiss was soft. His hands lingered in her hair and stroked at her back. She lost herself in the kiss. Lust she was used to, but this was different, not a wave but a soft velvet wrapping around her.

Then his hand fell away. It was all Flynt could do to let him draw back from her, let him look up at her with a passion he wouldn't give to her.

"I can't be what you need," he said, and he eased her off of him and stood. He turned to walk across the room toward the sealed door. Nightshade's legs were now both in view and her head bent as if in prayer.

"I'm so sick of people deciding what I need," Flynt snapped.

"Fair enough. You aren't what *I* need." He looked away from her, jaw tight.

Flynt stood and turned her back to him, facing Cyniel's bones instead—Ieyil's gift. There was someone who wanted her.

Chapter 15

Once they'd all rested, Nightshade inspected the room. Lem and Nightshade moved the stone slab while Flynt sulked by Cyniel's bones. But as the slab moved aside, Flynt drifted over. The room inside was unlit except by the little light that trickled in from the outer room. If any part of Ieyil had been conscious, she would have been trapped here in the dark.

A light flared from Nightshade's hand as she walked up beside Flynt. They'd walked about halfway into the chamber and with light, the walls seemed made of metal blocks rather than stone. Each block bore a sigil, much like the Death Wards in the outer room. Flynt tried to tug on Death-aspect and found nothing. It was as if she'd been cut free.

"No one who used Death-aspect could cast here," Flynt said. In fact, Flynt felt weaker standing there, as if strength were being leached out of her. Breathing was difficult.

"That is the point. This was meant to be Ieyil's eternal home, except it was not." Nightshade motioned to two manacles that had been pounded into the walls. The wall between them was slightly discolored in the relative shape of a body. A pile of cloth lay on the stones below the manacles.

"I have to get out of here," Flynt said, turning to flee the room. She felt a little less like she was drowning out in the main chamber, but she felt Ieyil's burial chamber behind her like a black hole trying to pull her in and drink her.

Ieyil had been here, her corpse chained in death. Flynt could almost see her bones hanging, waiting, waiting, waiting, a red glow pouring from the eye sockets. How had she gotten free? The runes guarding the room felt heavy on Flynt's shoulders and she doubted she could do so much as raise a fly. Nor were there any flies to raise—the room was swept clean.

If only Azucena were here. Her friend would have known more about all of this. But for now, Flynt didn't even have her glove with the emeralds that had been on Azucena when she died. Any answers would need to come from Flynt.

She wanted to inspect more, but Lem called out to her from the door marked with Life sigils.

"Flynt! Nightshade found a way to open the door."

Giving one last look at Ieyil's resting place, Flynt turned around and headed over to the others.

Flynt and Lem stood back as Nightshade faced the door. She trembled visibly as her fingers moved around the edge of the door. Her hand settled over the Aspect mark—a symbol from within the Life school.

"This is the key," Nightshade said, tracing the sigil on the left hand of the door.

"To opening the door?" Flynt asked. That didn't make a lot of sense. Then again, she'd never seen sigils like these.

"Watch. I will demonstrate." Nightshade held her hand steadily in front of the sigil. A pulse of Aspect flowed off of her palm into the sigil on the wall and the one of the lintel. A third appeared on the floor and this glowed brightest of all.

Lem touched Flynt's back, then dropped to wrap his fingers in hers. Flynt clung to him. What would be behind the door? The Defenders had been missing for a while and Cyniel's eye sockets seemed to stare out, proclaiming what could be. If Nekolai was dead, then she'd failed Cyn yet again.

The Life symbol on the wall glowed, and Nightshade pressed her hand into it.

Nekolai had to be safe. With Cyniel's bones behind her, she knew a new desperation. She couldn't have Cyniel watch her fail his best friend.

Then a loud click sounded, and the door swung open,

revealing a long, black stairwell. The purple light barely cut into the darkness but sluggishly, after the door opened, silvery orbs lit along the descent, casting a shadowy glow over the slick, stone walls. Nightshade didn't hesitate; she strode down the stairs and in the dark, Flynt could see the silver light clinging to her.

Flynt followed after; the stairwell was too narrow for two people, so she stayed a few steps back. Her stride was less sure than the vine-woman's. The walls hung close and slightly damp, slick with moss that erupted from cracks in the stone. Lem clumped down behind her, the shadow of his firearm stretching along the wall.

Then Nightshade reached the bottom of the stairwell. In one fluid motion, she drew out her knife from her belt and dove forward.

Flynt sprinted to the bottom of the stairs. A clump of half-rotted critters had engaged with Nightshade.

Lem fell in beside Flynt instantly. He held his gun in one hand and also had his blade out. Before Flynt could join the fray, he spared Flynt a smile. "Let's play, Necro."

Flynt didn't have time to respond before he swung his sword into the first critter that came at them, a fanged bovine, its flesh ropy and dry and stinking of preservatives. He used the butt of his gun like a hammer on its skull before driving his blade into its spine. A sword blow alone would have done nothing but slow them, but Lem used the weapon as a focus—channeling Chaos into the bones until they broke apart in a pile on the floor.

Flynt glanced over at Nightshade, afraid of her reaction to the Chaos.

Nightshade didn't pause in her own casting.

What made this Chaos manipulation okay but not the earlier one? But Flynt didn't have time to wonder. She was already moving as the question rolled through her mind. Her finger-cuffs snapped tight, and she pulled the strange cow-creature's bones as the old bindings on them broke, twisting the Death-aspect to her will. Flynt gave the first critter a command, sending her creation against another: the bones of a risen warrior and an armored canine.

When the two crumpled to rotten piles of flesh and bone, Flynt pulled the fragile essence inside them to her, binding it with Death-aspect. These bones remembered battle, and unlike the critters before, they were easy to turn to battle. She'd remember that for future reference. Animals might be easier to raise, but the bones remembered their lives and that made the bones of warriors more useful.

Lem ploughed through the critters and Flynt swept out, claiming the fallen bones and pulling them to her, bringing them back to their feet. The effort hissed inside her like a longing rather than a drain. She wanted more.

Purple puffed in front of her as she swept her hand, pulling a new critter to its feet. Hers now outnumbered the opposing side. She wanted them all. Hunger ate out of her—they were hers. The call of the abyss burned inside her, wanting to dance with her, roll inside her.

But that ecstasy would wait. Lem was out there—if she fell, he fell. Even floating on the edge as she was, her heart recalled.

She would not let him die.

By the time Nightshade reached the last of the opposing critters, Flynt had the skeleton's energy tucked inside her, tiny leashes running from her skin.

"Shit," Nightshade said.

Flynt hurried across the dark room to her. Nothing seemed to occupy it but the critters and the moss-slicked floor. But as she moved, water splashed under her feet. She saw Nightshade's glow reflected out in an underground stream, coming from a solid wall. On this wall were dried smears. Even in the dark she knew these. Blood.

"Nekolai!" Flynt called.

"Hush," Nightshade said. "There's something else here with us."

Lem splashed into the stream touching the wall. "No,

there's something back here."

Nightshade followed him, touching the wall. "Something alive."

"Nekolai!" Flynt repeated, lunging forward.

Lem caught her shoulders. "Is there Death back there?"

Flynt shook her head, not even checking. Instead, she followed the blood and at the base of the wall, found a chink. "This isn't a wall. It opens." But she saw no handle, latch, or release.

Lem came over to investigate and Flynt stood back, staring nervously at the wall. "Can you feel them, Nightshade?"

"I feel nothing, but... it's as if the wall is blocking it. I should feel something and so should you. Death and life exist everywhere in a place like this."

Lem looked to Flynt.

Flynt closed her eyes and reached out with her mind. No Death-aspect beyond the wall, either, but it wasn't like feeling an emptiness. Instead, there was nothing, as if the universe simply didn't exist behind the wall. She opened her eyes and shook her head. "Nothing. It's blocked, though. Maybe there's a sigil blocking us?"

Lem inspected the ground and, finally seeming to see what he wished to, he motioned to a set of sigils. Unlike the sigils on the door that had led down to this place, these were two symbols stacked in the same outline. Order and Water.

"It's a trap," Nightshade said. "The latch is here on this side somewhere, but not the other. Careful. Even if we open it, stepping inside may be deadly."

"To open it, we'd need Order and Water anyhow," Flynt said, staring at the symbols.

"Just one," Lem said. "Whoever built this intended for it to be opened by any official party, which means..." Lem kept looking, then gave up and looked over at Nightshade and Flynt. "I suspect there is another symbol here. Anyone with Aspect should be able to open this trick wall. But I should have enough command of Order to use this one."

"Showoff," Flynt said, not feeling the judgement in her words. She was new to the world of Aspect manipulation.

"You should be able to activate Life Aspect sigils," Nightshade said. The judgement in her voice was real. "Linked elements are meant to be studied."

Lem ignored them and held out his hand. The Aspect glow was yellower than his usual and weaker. Sweat broke on his brow, but the symbol lit up. The wall protested briefly with a puff of dust and pieces of rock wall sheering away.

Flynt stood back as a panel in the wall popped free and two doors swung open in the center of the wall. The smell of death hit her hard. Fresh decomposition lingered with the older smells of age and rot.

All three of them ran to the opening and looked inside. Several inches of murky water covered a sloped floor—only six feet wide and three times as long. Someone had wedged a metal torch into the space between the rock tiles of the wall. It still glowed with fresh power, casting a cool blue light over a water-logged room. By this light, they saw the people they'd come for.

None of them moved, not even to breathe. They seemed frozen.

One, a Prince's Defender revealed only by the vivid red embroidery on his death-soiled hood, lay face-down in the water. Judging by the smell, he'd been dead a while and with the door open, the Death-aspect hung heavily in the air. Flynt would have said he'd died almost forty-eight hours before. The other five sat in a line along the back wall. Perhaps they had once been lined up neatly, but each had moved in whatever time they'd been trapped. One woman had shoved herself back against the corner and stared at the door with her mouth agape, dried drool along her chin.

Nekolai, face hidden by blond hair, sat hunched over a smaller man. Alive, thank Ayal. Thought she didn't know for how long considering everything else around them. Even frozen, he managed to look protective. The man he leaned over was dead, though clearly for a shorter time than the other corpse

—as his Death-aspect was less frenzied at the realization of being trapped there.

None of them moved. Four of the six were still living, but the heavy presence of Death-aspect said that was not for long. The room was hungry and feeding. Flynt gasped. She could feel the leaching Death-aspect drained from them, driven by a will.

"The Time-aspect in this room is off. It has been meddled with," Lem said. "But the Aspect is bordering on Chaos... I might be able to adjust it."

"Not yet. We figure the trap out first." Nightshade hovered in the doorway, wringing her hands and looking on. "Their Life-sparks are so weak. How do we move them?"

"We don't until we stop the Death-aspect," Flynt said. She let her hands dance out on the air, reaching to touch of one of the invisible strings of Death-aspect from which the people were being drained. "They're chained to Ieyil. Anything we do could kill them. Their lives are feeding her... There will be wards protecting her Aspect drain."

"How did she get a body?" Lem asked. "She shouldn't be able to manipulate without a physical form."

"I don't think she did," said Flynt with a shudder. She took a few steps toward Nekolai, careful of the trails of Aspect. Closer, she could see his face through the locks of blond hair. His blue eyes didn't move at all. He seemed unconscious despite his eyes being wide. No, not unconscious, absent... Somehow, Ieyil had suspended their souls.

"Stop moving. Now," Lem said.

Flynt froze but continued her study of the Aspect strands around her. "She's remaking her own body and I don't recognize any of what she's doing. It wasn't in the books in the Death Compound. I need to look at this closely."

"Careful," Lem said. "The trap itself isn't hers. This is a blend of Time and Chaos, and it isn't pretty. I can probably cut a path for you, but it'll take a moment."

Flynt glanced back at him and smiled softly. "I trust you."

Nightshade scoffed. "Whether or not the trap is Ieyil's, she lured them here and if she is draining them, she is using Aspect."

"No one is arguing against that," Flynt said. "And we need to stop whatever plan it is she has concocted. I get it."

"She couldn't manipulate without a body or create a new one," Nightshade insisted. "That requires Life-aspect."

Flynt glared. "Do you understand what a Necro-equitem is? You speak in ignorance and sound so sure. Our powers are from Ayal and we do work with Death-aspect, but what makes us strong is that the fingers of that power reach over into the Life-spectrum. That's why we can drain Life-aspect. You asked what I thought. I told you."

Lem knelt in front of the dead Prince's Defender. The waters rippled out and soaked his robe. He inspected him and the invisible Aspect around him in silence, letting the women fight.

"My apologies." Nightshade ducked her head.

"How do we free them?" Lem chimed in. "Before they're all like this guy?"

"Can't you break the manipulation, as you did with the critters?" Flynt asked, still feeling out the energy. "I can find the source and…"

"No." Lem cut in and motioned Flynt forward. "It should be safe to approach."

Flynt splashed a few steps farther and heard Nightshade and Lem moving as well.

"Why won't it work?" Flynt asked.

Lem stood in front of one of the living Defenders and didn't look over at her, just down. "That won't work unless you want them dead. Chaos isn't an art of precision. If I destroy the link, I'll destroy pieces of anyone held as well."

Maybe not, Flynt thought as she turned slowly away from Nekolai. The water churned around her ankles—cool enough to burn against her skin and reeking of bodily fluids. She followed the Aspect strands to a small orb on the wall.

"We need time," Flynt said. The Defenders were so weak. "Nightshade, can you… keep them alive?"

"I can try. I can't heal them, though. All I can do is make sure they don't expire. Some are so drained, they might die after we free them from the manipulation. It might be wiser to let the weaker ones perish."

"Nekolai?" Flynt asked. He didn't seem the weakest, but she couldn't sense Life-spark except when she drained it.

"He is no more important than the others," Nightshade said with a cool haughtiness.

"He is to me," Flynt snapped. "Your inability to understand human relationships doesn't invalidate them."

Nightshade paused, as if taking in the comment, and then ignored it. "Me stabilizing their Life-spark does nothing if the two of you can't free them."

"I think we can," Flynt said. She pointed to the small orb in the wall. "The spell is rooted there. Lem should be able to dismantle the connection and I..." How did she even explain what she needed to do? She only half-understood it herself. "I need to make sure they're fully connected to their bodies when that happens. Whatever Ieyil has done seems to have pulled bits of their... Life-spark, soul, will, whatever you want to call it, from their bodies. It's why they're not responsive. If we break the connection with those floating free, they'll die."

"So how do I know when you've done so?" Lem asked, standing over the woman in the corner. He reached out to shut her mouth, wiping away the drool.

"I'll tell you," Flynt said.

"You think you can battle Ieyil's magic and chat with us at the same time?" Lem asked. He glanced back at Flynt, his smile taunting.

"Does either of you have a better plan?" Flynt snapped. "Or shall we just sit here until they die?" She turned to glare solely at Lem, her hands planted on her hips and feet spread apart in the murky water. "Or do you just like giving up on people? Maybe you'd rather fail now than take a chance of failing later?"

She'd meant to insult him, anger him, but the continued smile on his face gave no hint if she had succeeded.

"One last thing," Nightshade said, leaning close to one of the Defenders, a woman who wore a mask over her entire lower face. Then the vine woman looked up. "We should consider what to do if their loyalty has been compromised."

Flynt frowned. What? That was impossible. Defenders didn't get compromised... and Nightshade should have known that. No amount of magic could twist them.

Then Nightshade smiled.

"Was that a joke? Did you just tell a joke?" Lem asked, laughing. The sound echoed from the walls.

Flynt gave a small laugh, as much of surprise as anything. "Your timing could use work."

Nightshade shook her head, one pale-green hand hovering over the fallen Defender next to her. "The timing seems perfect to me. Shall we get started?"

Flynt nodded and watched as Nightshade kneeled in the center of the room and spread out her hands. Water lapped around her, leaving a dirty ring on her white robes. A shimmer moved from her fingers and covered the air, for a moment lighting the room evenly with her foggy Aspect light. Lem moved over to the gem and waited, arms folded.

Taking in one long, shaky breath, Flynt closed her eyes and reached out. She'd never played the ghost game before and didn't really know where to start. She focused on the feeling she'd had when Cyniel had come to her and how Ieyil had felt in this last dream. Slowly, the Defenders flickered to existence in her inner sight, the same way she saw the lives inside bones. They didn't seem aware, as frozen and still as their physical bodies.

These souls twisted in the air, terror and pain burning out from them like a scent of scorched meat. Without moving a physical limb, Flynt stood and moved to the masked woman. She took her hand and guided her Life-spark down to the warmth and heat of the body. Something invisible resisted her. Flynt pressed through it and felt a snap in the air, but the masked woman's essence remained inside her. Flynt went to the next, a man huddled alone on the wall. He was harder to move—his spirit fought her blindly, growing more agitated, not less. Even so, Flynt managed to guide him back and felt another snap, louder. It reverberated through her bones. Through her physical fingers, Flynt felt the man's corporeal body fall, slumped to the ground.

Flynt went to the woman in the corner, intentionally leaving Nekolai until last—she didn't know what she was doing and refused to experiment on him. As she guided this woman, the Aspect in the room shifted. A new spirit had joined them, and this one, Flynt knew.

"Stop this. I need them," Ieyil said.

Flynt forced the spirit back into the body, only to feel it spring free again as Ieyil's Aspect fought her.

"You have most of their Life already," Flynt said. "Let me take them home. It doesn't hurt you."

"It *does* hurt me." Ieyil's eyes looked as black as the obsidian horns thrusting up from her head. "They are mine and you wish to take them from me. They came to me, and I claimed them."

"Please," Flynt said, looking beyond Ieyil to Nekolai. "He's my friend. There have been those in your existence whom you sought to protect... He is one of mine. Please, don't take him away from me."

Ieyil turned. Her robes, composed now of Death-aspect, swirled around her and she looked at Nekolai. "I am taking his life, nothing else. He can still be yours. Did I not return your husband to you?"

"I need Nekolai alive."

"Why?" Ieyil hissed. She moved through the waters without stirring them. "I can see no reason for this other than your misguided faith to your queen and these clowns you travel with."

"They are my family!" Flynt snapped.

"No. I am. Can you be so blind? They don't even want you."

Flynt wrapped her astral arms close to her body. "Nekolai

does. Nekolai is like a brother to me—please. Give these people to me. They won't harm you. They're too weak."

"They won't harm me if they remain, either. In fact, here, they will feed me what little they have left."

"You keep what they've given you, even if the spell breaks?"

"Aye. I learned from our last battle, sister."

"Then please…" Flynt breathed deep. She'd heard stories of dealing with devils. This was a proven path. "Do it as a favor."

Ieyil stared with Death-black eyes into Flynt and Flynt waited for the retort, waited for the debt she would need to carry. "No. A favor implies repayment. If I do something for you, it is out of the warmth I hold for you in my heart. I will not lower myself to favors."

"Then please, for me."

Ieyil sighed. "For you, sister, I will not stop this. I will not aid you… but I will allow you to remove my toys from this place."

"You ask for nothing in return?"

"No. Though I would like you to recall who in all this mess is willing to sacrifice for you. I am your family, Flynt. We are all the family the other will ever have."

"But I'm here fighting you… I…"

"Families fight. That does not change that you are all of my heart that walks in the world." Then Ieyil was gone, her power retreating.

Flynt fumbled for the soul of the woman beside her, but it was gone as well. The Death-aspect from the form on the wall told her that they would not be retrieving her from Ieyil. Flynt went to Nekolai and took his hand. She brushed back the long, blond hair from his face. It was not as neatly kept now. She supposed a week trapped in a tomb could do that.

"It's okay now," she whispered, and she led him back to the warmth of his flesh. Keeping one hand on Nekolai, she stretched her being back to her body and lifted a physical hand to Lem. The words caught in her throat, and she couldn't command it.

Then she snapped back into her body. Her heart felt heavy.

She'd won. She'd received what she'd wanted without even a fight... but Ieyil was correct. Even as she floundered in the world to find a place to belong—she already had one.

What kind of person tried to fight their own family? This would be the second time Flynt set herself in the way of Ieyil's plans. Ieyil was insane, but Flynt was all the ancient Necro had, and really, Ieyil was all that Flynt had left.

There wasn't much time to stop and consider this. Of the six original Defenders, three rose slowly to their feet. Nightshade moved immediately to support the masked woman. Nekolai gasped and clutched at the dead man in front of him, pulling the corpse's face from the water. Lem watched Flynt with concern.

She didn't want his concern—he'd made it clear there was a timeline involved and as much as trusting him would have lifted much off her shoulders, she couldn't risk doing so. Instead, she stood and walked over to Nekolai, who remained seated, checking on the man beside him.

"He's dead," she said. "I'm sorry."

Nekolai looked up at her and Flynt expected to see confusion, weakness. Instead, there was only a steady coolness. "You were speaking with Ieyil. What did you say?"

"Ieyil was here?" Lem asked. He splashed loudly toward them.

Fuck. "She asked me to stop. I said I wouldn't."

"And? She didn't fight you. Why?" Nekolai asked. Fatigue crept into his voice and his pallor paled.

Flynt glared at him. He wasn't strong enough to fight. "You realize I just saved you."

"Thank you. And that doesn't matter a bit if you made some sort of deal with that witch. She wants Queen Milisade dead. I need to know what you said. Please..." Nekolai paused and forced himself to his feet. He wavered, barely able to keep his balance. "As thankful as I am, my duty to my queen comes first."

Of course. Blasted Defenders... And this was the man she'd been willing to risk her life for? Flynt slid her arm around

Nekolai, helping him balance. "She didn't stop me because I asked her not to."

"So a favor?" Lem asked. He was carrying the woman who'd been against the wall. She appeared to no longer be conscious, but she was still breathing.

"No. She was clear that it wasn't that. Ieyil said that." Flynt hesitated. This felt like a betrayal. "She said that she would do it for me because we're family, and she loves me."

Lem swore under his breath and adjusted his hold on the woman. Across the room, Nightshade was helping the remaining man and the masked woman across the room, speaking in tones too soft for Flynt to hear.

"Oh, Flynt," Nekolai said. "Ieyil is dangerous."

"I haven't forgotten that." Flynt helped him toward the exit. They were all dangerous, especially Nightshade.

Lem followed. "We need to stop her once and for all. Are you going to be able to do that?"

Flynt really didn't want to think about that. She stepped into the dry corridor. Her feet were numb, and her socks oozed water inside her boots. "Why don't we worry about that when we actually know her plot and have a way to stop it?"

"We do. In the tomb," Nekolai said in a breathless wheeze. Still, his words were clear. "We have her bones."

"We are not desecrating bones," Flynt snapped.

"First things first." Lem cut in. "We get you four back to the base camp. You're in no condition to fight. You can tell us everything there."

Flynt gritted her teeth at Nekolai's weight and trudged toward the stairs. She'd known this would come down to stopping Ieyil, but suddenly, that seemed harder to square away. Maybe Ieyil deserved another chance.

Chapter 16

On the other side of the Chaos-gate, the sun nearly blinded Flynt after the dimness of the tomb. Bones from the fight the evening before lay scattered and broken across the soil and the Chaos tree was silent, though souls still writhed within its limbs.

"What's that thing?" Nekolai asked. Leaning heavily on Flynt, he squinted up at it.

Her feet and back already hurt from Nekolai's added weight. But the remnant of the critters reminded her she didn't have to manage this alone. And that she had more people than just Nekolai to protect. "Shh. We'll talk back at the base camp."

"I doubt we can walk," Nekolai said. As if to demonstrate, he stopped and glanced back at the others. Lem carried a woman whose spark had departed sometime in the last minute or two, though Flynt doubted if anyone but her had noticed. And Nightshade helped the two other survivors. The rest of the dead remained in the tomb waiting to be reclaimed. "You should leave us here and go back inside."

Lem laid the Defender in his arms on the ground, then turned to help Nightshade, leaving Flynt to guess that he at least had noticed the woman in his arms expire. All the more reason they couldn't just let the remaining survivors fend for themselves.

"No. I'll summon help and we'll carry you back if we must. I came here to rescue you. I'll consider a new mission only when that is done." Flynt figured Nekolai would understand the idea of a stated goal. And he didn't argue.

Nightshade and Lem led the others over to the temple and leaned them against one of the planet's natural twisting trees and turned back to the gate. Then Lem reentered the tomb with Nightshade.

"They're returning for the dead?" Nekolai asked.

"They've been trapped there long enough," Flynt said as she helped Nekolai to sit on the ground. Flynt waited with the three living Defenders and one newly dead Defender as Nightshade and Lem pulled the remaining two corpses through the Chaos-gate.

Internally, Flynt thanked Lem and Nightshade for not making her explain that those bodies mattered. There were people who would mourn them, and it was easy enough for Flynt to walk them across the distance. Their loved ones deserved to get them back as soon as possible. And with Flynt's use of Aspect, they could help carry the wounded. Though she should probably wait a bit for that, feel out how the others would take it.

The only bones they wouldn't retrieve were Cyn's—and that was also good. She wouldn't be able to bring herself to animate those and wasn't up to explaining their presence to Nekolai.

The Queen's Defender shivered, taking her attention off of the bones. Flynt's robes were freezing, having sucked up the water, and Nekolai was in worse shape—soaking clothes, life drain, and the cold air of the tundra couldn't be good for him. Flynt removed her own cloak, wet only at the hem, and replaced his wet one.

Nekolai shook his head and tugged off the cloak. He nodded over to the other Defenders. "Them first."

Flynt rolled her eyes. "You take it, or I put it back on. Lem and Nightshade will take care of them."

Nekolai looked unsure, yet his lips were too gray for Flynt's taste. *It might be time for a low blow.*

"Cyniel would have wanted it," she said, firmly placing the

cloak back around his shoulders.

Nightshade emerged first, followed by Lem.

Once everyone was out, they huddled together around the corpses, staring up at the Chaos tree. Something about those limbs drove a cold terror into Flynt, and judging by the gazes of the others, she wasn't alone. They had to get away from that thing.

"Just give me a moment," Flynt said, shifting Nekolai away from her. He seemed to have passed out, clutching the cloak. Lem watched with concern but didn't intercede. No one else spoke.

Flynt could feel the dead out there in the world—bones just waiting to be claimed. A five-minute walk took her far enough to enable her to call eight critters to her. They'd be able to take the injured back to base camp—she guessed the living Defenders wouldn't agree with their dead being used to carry them. Once they passed out, of course, she could use the dead Defender's corpses to help her bone critters.

Walking back to the temple, Flynt tried to ignore the weight of eyes on her and was thankful that Nekolai hadn't reopened his eyes. She still didn't know what he'd think of her controlling critters so brazenly.

Nightshade stood and walked to the edge of the area to stand with Flynt. Lem followed the Diethyrian to the border, giving them a little space from the others.

"We take them back to base camp," Nightshade said. "What then? We need a solid plan."

"Solid plans are for solid situations," Lem said, also keeping his voice low. "This isn't that. What comes next depends on what they tell us."

Flynt wasn't entirely sure what was driving this conversation. What was there even to plan? If they were going to talk around something, they could at least let her in on it. "No matter what, we can come back here, right? To stop Ieyil?"

"I'd suggest either Lem or you remain on the base," Nightshade said.

Oh. Well, that was what she'd been talking around. She'd meant the plan with regard to *them* specifically.

"No," Lem said. His voice had resumed its usual booming quality. "That isn't happening."

His voice moved through Flynt, and she relaxed slightly.

"I'm not even certain which of you is the bigger threat," Nightshade said, glaring at Lem. Even her vines seemed to tighten over her body. But then she turned that anger on Flynt. "How long have you been chatting with Ieyil? Do you begin to understand how moronic that activity is?"

"Back off," Lem said, moving to stand with his broad shoulder between them, not quite putting himself in the way, but making it clear that was where he stood.

"Oh, don't you start!" Nightshade snapped. "You're going to get us all killed if you don't get a handle on yourself. I recommended you for this. I said you could control yourself! Everything you do hangs on my head as well as yours."

This time, it was Flynt who pushed forward. "We saved the Defenders," Flynt said. Then she grabbed Nightshade's arm and pulled her a few paces forward, away from Lem. She lowered her voice. She hoped that Lem wouldn't hear, that he would understand that some things required privacy. "Please, Nightshade, let the slip go this once. Anything you can say to him, he's already saying to himself."

Nightshade stared coldly back at Flynt. "Tell your critters to grab the Defenders. We should get going or we risk losing the light."

Flynt did as asked, and the critters started off at the front, holding the Defenders. Nightshade and Lem followed, with Flynt trailing just behind them.

The day was frigid, and Flynt missed her cloak as her breath puffed white in the air.

Nightshade spoke. "I realize how frustrated the captain is." Nightshade kept her voice low, though a quick glance said that Lem was a decent distance away studying the walking dead. "I understand you far less."

"You're referring to Ieyil?"

Nightshade said nothing, but assent was clear in every line of her body.

"They were just dreams until we reached this planet. And then... She keeps showing me the past."

"That makes sense. But you cannot listen to her. She was Death-mad even before she died. No matter what softness she shows you, she would tear the universe apart if she were freed."

Lem clapped a hand down on Flynt's shoulder, making her jump. Then he said, "It's even more frightening that she asked for nothing in return."

Flynt wondered how much he had heard.

"I agree with the captain," Nightshade said. "She's building emotional ties and playing on your guilt and sense of fair play. You owe her nothing. Remember that."

Flynt looked over at Lem and then up to the critters that carried Nekolai. She owed Ieyil more than they knew, and that debt only hung heavier because Ieyil wouldn't name it a debt. "Ieyil could have killed all of the Defenders—drained them completely. She let us take them."

"You," Lem corrected. "She let *you* take them."

Nightshade picked up her pace to move ahead of them and spoke over her shoulder. "And when she drains the entire Coil and creates an army of critters, she will retake those she freed and kill them. This is only a delay."

"She's not planning that!" Flynt cried, then she flinched. She had no idea what Ieyill was planning and she sounded like a petulant child even to herself.

"Oh? You know her plans?" Nightshade said, with a completely straight tone of voice.

"No, all I'm saying is we should learn her true intentions, not assume the worst," Flynt replied. She looked to Lem, hoping for aid, but he didn't even seem to be listening. His eyes were distant.

"Then trust me," Nightshade said, again over her shoulder. "That is what Ieyil wants."

After that, Nightshade hurried to catch up to the critters and Flynt sent the fresh dead to help carry the still-living defenders—four critters to each made for a more comfortable transport. Lem walked beside her the rest of the way, but they didn't utter a word to each other. Occasionally, Lem would look over at her with a flash of panic, then turn his eyes back to the path.

Was he having one of his moments where he knew something he wasn't sharing with her? If so, it didn't seem to be anything good. Flynt really didn't want to know.

Flynt heard the base camp before the black smudges of movement appeared. Shouts carried on the still, cold air. Apparently, the critters were causing quite a stir. Belatedly, Flynt recalled that the inhabitants of the camp had been battling Ieyil's minions for a while and had no way of knowing that these undead belonged to Flynt.

Flynt commanded them to stop.

Flynt, Nightshade, and Lem moved through the undead toward the front.

The same dead-pale Defender as before came out to meet them, followed by a troupe of Queen's Guards whom Flynt didn't recall seeing before—in fact, they looked fresh and clean. The queen must have sent fresh reinforcements from the Coil.

"Those are your creatures?" the dead-pale woman asked.

Flynt scoffed. "Clearly. And they're carrying precious cargo. Let us in."

Nightshade stiffened and her hand flew up to her heart. Flynt didn't think she'd been rude enough to warrant a reaction like that.

"Don't do that," the dead-pale woman said, only she seemed to be speaking to Nightshade, not Flynt.

Flynt searched the guards behind her for an explanation. Four new faces. Two women and two men, all humanoids and all wearing the queen's blue around their shoulders. One of the men had long, rather messy hair, but both of the women kept their hair warrior-short.

Then Lem reacted to one of the women. "Srikes. No. Why?"

And one of the guards lifted her hand to tap at her heart, then motioned back toward the fallen Defenders. "Because they are mine."

Flynt knew that voice. Yet her brain still took a while to process what her eyes saw and her ears heard. The woman was small-boned, with a weak, mousy sort of prettiness and brown hair. Only her thin, elegant neck held a vestige of the beauty Flynt usually associated with the woman. Without the blonde wig and jewels, without the frothy gowns and cosmetics, Milisade didn't retain any physical aspects of the queen. She had an enviable figure, though, in the snug officer's uniform.

Flynt quickly diverted her thoughts from that. Milisade could hear her thoughts and that should not be the first thought that the queen got from her after months away from each other.

"Milisade?" she whispered. It felt wrong to use the honorific here.

"Hush," the dead-faced woman said. "The fewer who know, the better—and the soldiers who came with you cannot find out. You must behave accordingly. In public, treat her as exactly what she appears to be."

"Why?" Flynt repeated Lem's original question. Queen Milisade being here was insane. There was no one whom Ieyil wished dead as much as her, and no single life that mattered more to the survival of the Coil.

Milisade said nothing to clear the confusion.

The dead-pale woman spoke up. "You will reconvene with our new arrival in the command tent once you are washed and fed."

The critters reached them and walked by. Milisade turned, craning to see. In that moment, it was easy to see her as just a woman. A woman in love.

"Nekolai was able to communicate a little," Flynt said, careful with his name. She needed Milisade to pick up that he was okay, but anything too forward would give away the improper connection she guessed existed between the queen and her Defender. "He'll probably be on his feet soon. Do we have a healer?"

The pale woman looked to Milisade.

The queen turned to one of the other guards and nodded. They said nothing, but Flynt would guess these were more Queen's Defenders in disguise along with their mistress. Though they couldn't actually read minds, they knew the queen well enough to predict her desires. That guard trailed after the critters into camp.

Weary and confused, Flynt followed. Milisade couldn't be here.

Her death would be a disaster that would shake the foundations of society.

And yet part of Flynt wished she could tell Ieyil.

Chapter 17

Clean and fresh as could be after a few hours' rest and a towel bath, Flynt went to the command tent with a taciturn Nightshade. Flynt had returned her glove to cover her bone arm, and she rubbed at the smooth satin with her right hand. Lem's laugh came from inside and they entered to find him seated on the desk with Milisade leaning against the wood next to him, her hand resting on his arm as she leaned in to speak.

Flynt's eyes narrowed. He'd adamantly denied he was Milisade's lover when she'd asked him and with Milisade's interest in Nekolai, Flynt had believed him. Plus… wasn't he the one going on about how Leshmen didn't know how to be faithful? Milisade was queen, but that didn't change her species.

Nightshade let the tent flap fall shut with an intentional *flwap*.

Milisade didn't remove her hand as they entered, but her posture did shift, drawing inward a little. Lem, however, pulled back as if her touch had burned him. He didn't meet Flynt's gaze.

"May the Coil's waters run pure," Nightshade said, bowing low.

"Rise," Milisade said. "No bowing, even here. If you wondered, my dear, that is a command."

Nightshade acknowledged this with a slight dip of her chin.

Flynt waited, knowing Milisade would be picking up what she needed from their minds anyhow. She didn't even know what she would say... Too much was going on to find the words.

Milisade stood fully and folded her hands in front of her. "I wish to speak about the coming mission."

"And tell us why you're here?" Flynt asked, keeping her voice low. It was only half a question; the other half was accusation. *She shouldn't be here!*

Milisade drifted to the center of the room, seeming not to have heard Flynt's outburst. Flynt hadn't realized how soft the queen's curves were, how full her hips. She was sexy. Flynt could see why men desired her... women too, though Flynt hadn't seen that happen yet.

Flynt desired her.

Milisade's mouth quirked into a smile. "But first, before I address the mission or your questions, I must speak with each of you separately." Milisade turned back to Lem. Flynt saw him smile in return to whatever look the queen had given him. "Lem, I have what I require from you—though I will need to see this soul tree you created."

Soul tree was an interesting word. Flynt would have gone with Chaos but the descriptor worked.

Nightshade seemed to relax slightly.

Milisade turned to Flynt and pulled her just outside the tent. "You have been speaking with Ieyil. I'm afraid what she's shown you is true, but not complete. I ask that you not make any judgements of her rebellion until I can show you my side."

Flynt stumbled back a step. That was a sudden admission. "You have a side?"

Milisade frowned. "Don't pretend to be stupid. It doesn't suit you. I took the throne after Ieyil's revolt, that is well known, as it is known that I faced her on the battlefield after Queen Sisha was killed and turned into one of Ieyil's critters."

Flynt's face felt hot. "Sorry. I know."

"My story will take time to impart, more than we have at this particular moment."

Flynt sighed. She wanted to push for the queen's explanation right away, but ordering a queen around wouldn't produce the results she wanted. "So? What else did you need to say?"

"That depends, child."

"On what?"

"On what you wish to ask. Pretend I don't know your mind —I try not to take things or respond to thoughts of a personal nature."

Well, then, they didn't have to discuss anything to do with anyone's sex life. Flynt didn't know that she wanted to know... and it wasn't really the queen she wanted answers from. It was up to Lem. The queen's sex life wasn't any of her damn business. Maybe Lem's wasn't either, but she felt more of a right there. But she did still have questions about Lem.

"Would you really let Nightshade kill Lem?"

"Yes. I don't wish him dead. He's a nice distraction, but I will not risk my Coil for one man's life—any man."

Flynt nodded. That was the only question she dared to voice.

"Yet his life is important to me and to the Federation of Coils' survival. Do you know why I wanted a Chaos Magister?" Milisade asked.

Flynt jumped and blushed. Did she mean that sexually? No, she couldn't. "Why?"

"Because the Coils are dying. No one talks about it—but one by one, the Coils fall, and no new ones are born."

"Our people used to create new ones."

"Not in a very long time. Tell me: How do the Gate-stones work? Come on, Flynt. I see in your heart. You've seen it."

"They have Aspects condensed into stones..." Flynt felt the answer and pushed it away. There was a Chaos-stone.

"Seven, not six. Not Order, Water, Earth, Air, Death & Life. No, there is a Chaos-stone as well. And even the Gate-stones are running short—we cannot make them with no one to work Chaos. Fear rules too many people. I believe in risk. Risk can mean a swift death, but refusing to take risks simply means a death of slow starvation."

Flynt stared into Milisade's dark eyes.

"Chaos destroys; Nightshade sees that. Lem sees that too. But creation is not possible without destruction. I wanted a Chaos-magister to create something new." Milisade leaned in closer, a spark of mischief in her eyes. "You tell him that, my sweet child. You tell him that stagnation is worse than death."

Flynt was positive this last aside had nothing to do with creating Coils anymore. "Thank you."

Milisade nodded. "Let us go in. I must speak with Nightshade."

Flynt followed Milisade inside and stared, hearing nothing over her heart as Nightshade left the tent with the queen. Flynt turned to Lem—Milisade's words burned in her, but now was not the time for that. She needed to feel the truth before she brought anything to Lem.

She marched up to him. She wouldn't pose a question about their future together, but there was still air to clear. "When you accused me of not being able to manage monogamy... what experience did you have with a Leshman to base your statement on?"

Lem laughed.

"I'm going to slap you. I swear to Ayal!"

"You know the answer, Necro. I was involved with one."

"With Milisade." Flynt sat heavily on the wooden deck.

He plopped down beside her. "Yes."

"You said you weren't."

"Well, our fling was long over by the time you asked." Lem's eyes twinkled. "You asked if I was screwing her, not if I *ever* had been involved."

Flynt glared. "When?"

"When she first found me—about ten years ago. I was clear with her from the start that sex only worked for me with monogamy. She said she understood. She didn't."

"You were in love?"

He guffawed at that. "No. Hell no. But we had fun until I realized that from her perspective, monogamy meant not fucking other people while I was physically on the Coil with her. I'd never ask someone to change for me, but I also know what I can deal with. I can't do sharing. We parted on good terms; it's easier to do that without love involved."

"So you've walked out on women you loved, too?"

He nodded. "Not a pleasant subject."

Flynt took in a deep breath. "I'm sorry. You're right, but... you should know: I really think I *could* be with just one person, if it was the right person."

"You shouldn't have to change yourself, Flynt." He sighed. "I don't want to give you rules—you should do what feels right."

"Why? You already said you aren't doing what feels right to you. In fact, just the opposite. You have rules *against* doing what feels right. Lem. It doesn't make sense."

He stared down at the bunched fabric of his robe in his hands. "I know that either I'd kill you or eventually you'd kill me."

Flynt stood and paced across the tent and then returned. As discontent as all of this made her, she wasn't going to make herself or him miserable over it. There was never any telling how long life was going to go on—Flynt was determined to enjoy what she had while she had it.

"If I'd bedded the Queen... I think I'd tell everyone." She stopped her stride a few feet away from him. "It'd be worth it just for the reactions from people like Nightshade..." And Nekolai, but that idea wasn't as pretty. Annoying Nightshade was one thing, but hurting a man who'd done nothing but help her?

"Trust me, the Nightshades of the world don't think it's as funny as you do." But his grin said that *he* did.

"That's what makes it funny."

"Yeah?" His eyes sparkled, and he leaned in conspiratorially. "Tell Nekolai that."

"Nope. I think he'd be my exception. Is that why he hates you?"

Lem laughed, any tension dropping from his shoulders. "His hatred is righteously earned based on his love affair with the law and my open opinion that laws are up for interpretation. There might have been a small smuggling affair some of my men were involved in, that I may—allegedly, you understand—have helped cover up."

Flynt was about to inquire more about this alleged infraction when Milisade and Nightshade returned to the tent. Lem's smile lasted, seeming to gain fuel from Nightshade's presence. The queen didn't glance at any of them but walked behind the desk, keeping the other three on the far side.

The art of positioning mattered. Flynt had learned that early from her mother. When you spent most of your life laid up in a bed, where your inferiors stood could matter a lot and her mom had played that dynamic like a game of chess. Milisade had a knack for the game.

"There is no time to mince words," Milisade said, pressing her fingertips against the wooden top of the desk. Flynt wondered if she was standing on tiptoe to gain height, but the queen probably didn't lower herself to tricks like that. "Before meeting with all of you, I went to see Nekolai. He has yet to wake, but the healer assures me there is little actual damage and most of what is needed is simply bolstering his Life-spark. But his mind has shown me what must be done in the old crypts—or what we must discover."

"Wonderful," Lem said, keeping his distance from the desk. He showed less talent at the positioning game.

"Tell us and we will plan a mission," Nightshade said, standing with her hands linked behind her back.

"Are you giving me orders?" Milisade asked, mouth tightening slightly.

Flynt thought Nightshade's posture made it clear she wasn't, but she watched the scene play out anyhow.

"No," Nightshade said, taking a half-step back. "I apologize."

"I will not be telling you what I believe must be done because I am going with you." Milisade leaned forward on her fingertips.

"No!" Flynt and Lem said together.

"They mean, my queen," Nightshade said, cutting in, "that this is dangerous, and our enemy wishes you harm."

"Nevertheless, I will be accompanying you. I hope Nekolai will be on his feet in the morning to aid us, but if not, the four of us will travel alone."

Nightshade said, "You need an escort, at the very least."

"An escort will not aid me against Ieyil." Milisade moved away from the desk, rounding it again to move to the front, still commanding the room.

"Nekolai would never agree to this," Flynt said, and she hoped that Milisade might care more about his opinion than theirs. "Why suggest he come if this is your plan?"

"Oh, smart girl," Milisade purred, smiling in a way far too wicked for a queen. "Because Nekolai would understand, even if you do not. Though you, sweet child, may also understand by the end. But I don't ask for any such comprehension. I am telling you that I am going to the crypt with you. We must find Ieyil's bones and destroy them—along with any anchors she has."

"Hold on," Lem said. "How is having you along going to help anything? You'll just make it harder."

Can he say that to her? Flynt wondered before seeing by Milisade's relaxed reaction that apparently, he could.

"Like Flynt, though in a different fashion, I can speak with Ieyil." Milisade spoke softly and walked through the line the three of them had unconsciously made toward the tent's exit. "But more importantly, even if I am no help, I must be there for her destruction. And I will not be turned away."

"This is madness!" Lem said, sounding excited rather than scared.

"The choice is made. Be ready to head out in the morning." Milisade lifted a hand and pulled back the door flap. She waved Lem and Nightshade through but gave a slight shake of her head to Flynt. "Captain Lem, Magister Nightshade, you may both leave now. Flynt and I have a further engagement."

Lem leaned in to Flynt's ear before leaving. "You intending

to have something to brag about to Nightshade?"

Flynt choked down a laugh and elbowed him in the arm. "Go. She can hear you just thinking it... I don't think whispering helps!"

He grinned. "Nightshade didn't hear."

In fact, Nightshade had already walked out the door. Lem followed and the tent flap fell closed. This was the first time Flynt had ever been truly alone with the queen—no guards and no Defenders anywhere near them. Even more intimate was the lack of gown and wig. Whether she wanted it or not, this exchange would be a link that forever held her to the queen.

Flynt only hoped that she could honor that link.

Chapter 18

With the others gone, Milisade sat in one of the padded wooden chairs that lined the sides of the command tent. A bowl of incense, unlit, lay on a short table beside her. Milisade patted the chair on the other side of the incense table. Flynt crossed the room slowly. The area smelled of cloves and some sort of bitter flower, but this civilized scene didn't entirely drown the lemony trees and camp smoke from outside.

Flynt was glad she'd bathed on returning to camp or her own smell would have been another competing force to drown it out. And that was no way to have a moment with a queen. Flynt sat.

Milisade fished in the deep leg pocket of her uniform and pulled out her hand in a closed fist, holding something hidden from Flynt. "There is something that I must show you, but first..." Milisade waited until Flynt met her eyes. "You have let Ieyil speak into your soul. Will you allow me to commune so with your mind?"

"What?" Flynt gripped the arm of her chair and leaned toward the queen eagerly. Milisade couldn't mean mind speech. That was impossible!

"Not impossible, just rather unheard of. Considering how few queens there are, you shouldn't make assumptions about what I can do."

Flynt swallowed and tucked one leg up under her on the chair. "Okay. I'm dying to know what's going on. Do whatever you need."

"Back when my queen powers had activated, but before I had a Coil to lead, I used to share dreams with another Necro-equitem." Milisade opened her hand to reveal a set of jade finger-cuffs—identical to the obsidian ones Flynt had. Milisade slipped her fingers into the jade loops and twisted her hand to gaze at them. "It has been so very long since I've put these on."

"They look..." Flynt fingered the chain that bound her own finger-cuffs.

"Just like yours? Yes. Because they were created as a matching set." Milisade lifted her hand and partially spread her fingers. "Now let yours guide you. The obsidian remembers the path. Stone never forgets." Milisade let the chain between her fingers snap tight. Then she rotated her palm so her hand hovered over the bowl of incense.

Flynt lifted her own hand and felt the obsidian chain snap tight. The cuffs sang in a new way and Flynt let them pull her, bringing her hand up against Milisade's palm. Ieyil's black stone clicked against the queen's jade.

Then the world blurred, fading to a dream state.

The brown command tent became a green garden and the wooden chairs turned into a wool blanket spread out beside a Coil-pool and its rainbow waters.

Flynt sat on the ground between two women who lazed back on the blanket. She recognized them both instantly, though they wore their hair and clothes in outdated fashions. Milisade looked halfway between her soldier self and the queen she'd become, wearing a flowing, silver gown with long, tight sleeves and a sleek, blonde wig pulled into a high-tail. Across from her sat Ieyil, looking less skeletal than Flynt had ever seen her and with a rosy lip-stain.

Milisade held out a rosewood box tied shut with a green, silk ribbon in her palm.

"A gift?" Ieyil asked, shaking her head and causing a riot of black curls to bounce beside her thin face. "There's nothing I need, Millie. You don't need to buy my love."

"Open it, will you?" Milisade laughed and shoved the box at Ieyil.

Flynt watched. Though she was in the moment, it moved around her like a dream. She knew she wasn't actually in the timestream.

Ieyil sighed, but she sounded content and her long, slender fingers tugged at the silk ribbon until it fell away. She folded it neatly beside her on the blanket and then opened the box. Inside were the two sets of finger-cuffs, lying on a bed of rainbow-colored beads.

Milisade bounced on her knees, as giddy as a child. "I read about the finger-cuffs—to help your balance. And I read about this technique to let us talk into each other's minds."

Ieyil looked up, tears making her eyes swim. "Oh, Millie... I..."

Milisade took the other woman's hand, stroking her knuckles with her thumb. "I'll never forget you. We are forever. I'll be a queen, but I was yours first."

Ieyil threw her arms around Milisade, and Flynt lowered her eyes, awkwardly stranded amid a personal moment.

Had the two women been lovers? It was evident that they had loved each other, at the least.

Then the scene faded, air rippling with shifting colors. The garden disappeared from view and then came rows of windows and moss-colored carpet and marble walls. Milisade trailed after Queen Sisha down a hallway, looking out over the bright lights of the Coil. Voyagecraft zoomed by in the sky, and the floating compounds bobbed like gems in the air. Both women were in full queen array, though Flynt guessed that Milisade was still training under Sisha at that point in time. Flynt moved like a silent spy beside them, drawn on without her will to witness.

Sisha's face was exactly as Flynt recalled—aged and somehow dry, as if she could turn to dust and yet her eyes were the embers that burned away at her.

"You can't ask this of her!" Milisade shouted. "She's

slipping. Please. Not Ieyil. Don't do this."

"And who else can?" Sisha snapped. "I know you care for the Necro. I understand your emotional bond, but I'm sorry. This is what being a queen is. People die. They burn out. Necros go insane. The Coil comes first. Anyone is disposable to that end."

"Not her."

"There is no one else. I need a queen dead. This isn't just some throwaway job. I require my best tools for the work."

Flynt winced at hearing Ieyil referred to as "a tool." People weren't tools.

The scene faded again. And this time, Flynt was struck first by the stench of death. Rot filled everything with a thick, deadly-sweet odor.

Milisade stood at the edge of what Flynt took to be a battlefield. Her blonde wig was in disarray, smeared with blood, and the arm of her dress was shredded along with the skin beneath. Milisade huddled mostly hidden behind a column, shivering.

But out past the queen, the world became a hellscape.

Flynt had never seen so much death. Fresh corpses and rotting critters lurched together, missing limbs or eyes, or with holes blown through their torsos. In the distance, people screamed. Warriors ran across the blood-drenched courtyard.

The screams echoed.

The scene before her hardly resembled the Coil's palace district, but that was where they stood. Flynt knew it by the floating compounds in the sky and the shape of the courtyard that led up to the palace. She wanted to search for familiar markings. However, Flynt couldn't choose what to watch. This was Milisade's memory and Milisade stared at Sisha.

The once-queen's eyes had been ripped from her head and mold made patterns over her skin, yet she stood at the center of a group of living people—Queen's Defenders. Even after death, some must have remained true to her.

Someone grabbed Milisade's arm, and she spun to face a man with blood-streaked green skin—not critter green, but smooth and even, as if this were a species trait. His orange eyes seemed to glow especially bright over the dark bags that rimmed them. "Ieyil is by the Coil's heart. The waters cannot take much more—you must go now. Stop her."

Milisade looked at her hands, where he'd pressed a thick blade. Glowing runes ran up the hilt. Flynt could swear she'd seen that same blade in the tomb "I can't stab Ieyil."

"Then we all die," the man said.

"She will link to the Coil... Maybe it can heal her," Milisade sounded close to tears.

Part of Flynt wanted to reach out to her. Another part just hung back, wishing she could escape the smell and the screams that hung like macabre party decorations on the air.

"If you believe she can be healed, even by the Coil," the green man said, "then I was a fool to think you were queen material. It cannot heal her, Milisade. She is too far gone to Ayal. She will corrupt the Coil. Killing her is the kindest act you can do for her."

Milisade folded her hand around the hilt of the dagger.

Flynt's connection broke, and she nearly fell from the chair. Her hand flew out, knocking the bowl of incense from the table to spill over the floor. Flynt righted herself but sat as far back in her chair as she could. She could still smell rot on the air and she gagged, tasting bile at the back of her throat.

Milisade sat impassively and waited, her jade finger-cuffs now resting on the arm of her chair.

Flynt cleared her throat, trying to get rid of the stench. "Ieyil was your lover."

"We were not so simply defined," Milisade said softly. "That would have been easier to forget, I suspect. I've had many lovers."

"Then what?"

"She was like a sister to me—she worked in my home when we were children. I paid to have her privately trained in Death-aspect so she could choose if she wanted her gift or not. She was like a second mother to my children. She was my sister, my best friend, and *on occasion*, my lover, but foremost, she was my heart." Milisade stopped, opened her mouth to speak, then stopped again and waited.

Flynt looked at the spilled incense. Tiny red flecks glowed within it, slowly flickering out.

"Queen Sisha," Milisade said at last, "used her Magisters as tools—used them for a purpose. But Ieyil didn't see that right away. She wanted to serve the Coil and give of herself for the greater good; she lost herself completely and it is my greatest regret that in the end, she believed she lost me." Milisade made a low, choked sound.

The last of the red embers disappeared on the ground, leaving only ash. Flynt looked up.

Milisade wiped at her eyes. "If I'm going to order Ieyil's plan to be stopped... which I know I must... I cannot do so as Sisha did, using those around me to do the dirty work. Ieyil's death was personal, and so is her reaching beyond the grave. If I die, so be it. She deserves this much from me."

Flynt reached over to clasp the queen's hand in hers. "You killed her?"

"Stabbed her in the back... in every way that phrase can be meant."

"But the whole story of her, the way it's told, makes her out to be some demon. Isn't that your story?"

"It's not mine. I let the Coil's people tell their version of what happened in those months, and I stood behind it. They needed to rebuild, and they needed a queen to support them."

"There was never any sign that you and she weren't always enemies."

"Really? You used to portal into my rooms. In my chambers, you must have seen her portrait there. Many have remarked on it."

Flynt thought back, but the only portrait had been one hanging in the queen's antechamber, which Flynt had glimpsed while in the midst of battle. She'd hardly noted it. But being reminded, she could picture the painted depiction of Ieyil hanging on the wall, not in her full obsidian array as the portrait in the Death compound had her, but in simple robes and a smile. "No one ever questions the portrait?"

"They do, but a perk of being queen is I only answer what and when I wish. I am old now, too old for such passions to come easily. I love differently than I did in my first years—without the high passions. One would think that after nearly one thousand years, memories would fade, but it isn't so."

Flynt touched Azucena's emeralds. The loss was not the same—she'd only known Azucena a few weeks, but in a way, Azucena's death had been Flynt's fault. Flynt's guilt and regret had not faded yet, but it hadn't been anything like one thousand years. "You never tried to forget her?"

"The weight of her memory is mine to carry, and it helps remind me of the woman I intend to be. I am Sisha's heir, but the moment I see Sisha in myself, I will know I am not fit to be queen. I love my Coil, but the weight of all cannot erase or replace the plight of the few."

"And you never loved again?"

At that, Milisade's mouth curved in a smile so brief, it was almost lost. "You guessed already how my heart errs of late. My dearest Defender holds more of me than I can ever admit. Nekolai is not a man I would have cared for in my wild youth. He's..." She stopped, visibly thinking.

Dull, Flynt thought. She blushed because Milisade would hear the thought as loud as if she'd shouted. And because it was not a fair thought.

"At your age," Milisade said, with a sad little smile, "I would have seen just that, but no. He is deep and pure. And he will never know how I feel; he cannot. Yet I fear that Ieyil does. It surprises me that she let him go. The others perhaps, but not him. Surely, that means something."

"He's a good man," Flynt said, avoiding the Ieyil issue entirely. "I guess I just never saw him sexually."

Milisade laughed. "I doubt he sees himself that way. He is not Leshman, and I have known other humans like him in that way. Sex doesn't drive him; his desires are more cerebral and where they are physical, they are simple. You are young yet, but passion need not always mean sex. I love him as he is."

"But..." Romantic love without sex didn't make any blasted sense.

"Sometimes, child, you must weigh your natural urges against those of the people you love. If anyone asks you to deny yourself, they are not worth such an act... but sometimes, to choose such a denial is, in and of itself, a declaration of love."

"You're not talking about Nekolai anymore," Flynt said.

"Clever girl." Milisade stood and tucked her finger-cuffs into her pocket. Then, as if she had just thought of something, she half-turned with a finger raised. Flynt was certain the queen had known all along what she intended to say next. "Oh, and we must bring Cyniel's bones out of that temple. The entire tomb will need to be sealed and his bones deserve to return to the soil."

Flynt flinched thinking of Cyniel's bones sinking into the frigid soil here, lost to her forever.

"And Flynt?" Milisade asked, commanding her attention. "Remember why you're on this mission. Proving yourself here means you can emerge publicly as a Necro-equitem. It means you can live openly as you choose." Then Milisade turned her head away.

Sensing she was dismissed, Flynt fled the tent. Running around here, Flynt had almost forgotten the feeling of constantly hiding her powers and lying about herself. With Nekolai safe, she could have walked away if not for that the hope of being able to do exactly what Milisade promised..

At the edge of camp, Nightshade stood watching the tundra, the pale Defender standing by her. Lem sat by the fire with a bunch of soldiers. Flynt didn't belong in either place. She certainly didn't belong with Defenders in any capacity, and she'd tried for years to fit in with soldiers. And for all of those years, she'd failed.

I don't belong here with them, she thought. Even the Diethyrian and the Chaos-magister fit in better than she did. In order to belong, she had to follow Milisade's wishes. She had to stop Ieyil.

Flynt switched on her comm device. She'd been too distracted by the queen's arrival to do it before, but now she needed the distraction. Maybe some good news from the society she was working so hard to be part of.

A message waited for her. Nothing from her father or any of the various acquaintances she'd left behind; any true friend she'd ever made was either with her on this adventure or dead. But the message was from the mercenary guild that had agreed to track down Azucena's arm.

Flynt flicked her eyes to open it.

Then she gulped. A note of termination. They were ending the contract, stating that the desired object was not to be found.

"Ayal!" she swore and closed the message. What now? It wasn't the first group she'd hired, but she couldn't give up. She's sworn to Azucena. Flynt had failed to save her friend's life. At the very least, she could honor the other woman's last request.

But how? Flynt wasn't even on the Coil.

The easiest way would be to finally prove herself as a Necro-equitem so she could go home. Maybe if she was physically there, the people who she hired would take her more seriously.

Shortly thereafter, Milisade left the command tent and walked quietly to the tent where the newly returned Defenders were resting. She certainly didn't belong in that tent, either, but curiosity was a potent driving force. Flynt heard the rumble of voices and a laugh. She moved around the tent to draw nearer the voices.

Even so, she couldn't make out many words, not enough to put the conversation together until the words grew heated.

"If you go, I go," Nekolai said.

"Don't be foolhardy. This is my choice."

"Command me and I stay," he said, but something in his tone threatened that he would not soon forgive her. "But my place is at your side."

"Recover first…" The rest of the queen's statement was too quiet to completely make out.

"If you go, I go," Nekolai repeated. Then his voice, too, fell to a softer tenor.

Flynt turned and walked away. Likely, the queen already knew she was there, but if not, Flynt had heard enough.

Nekolai knew his place.

Chapter 19

Mud coated the entire party by the time they reached the Chaos gate that they'd planted. Flynt was thankful for the warmer day and the amusement of watching the others deal with the ensuing mud. The muck looked especially odd on Queen Milisade; the drizzle had plastered her short, dark hair to her skull, and she looked a bit like a half-drowned child.

Nekolai hadn't complained at all during the walk, but Flynt kept her eye on him. The queen really should have ordered him to stay behind, but it wasn't Flynt's place to comment.

The warm twinkle of the Chaos-gate and the mind-curdling terror pouring off of the tree made it seem like a very different place from the one they'd come to only a few days before. Even the nearby crypts looked different, slouched as if being slowly beaten in by the inaudible shrieks.

The Life temple seemed to have curled inward, aging as it did.

Nekolai and Nightshade hung at the back, nervously watching the queen while Lem walked at Milisade's side and Flynt drifted like a planet in orbit around them all. But when they stepped into the ring of twisted vines that sheltered the gate, leftover from Nightshade's wall, Flynt shuffled up beside Lem and pressed a hand to his bicep, trying to impart comfort with the touch.

Milisade gazed up at the tree of souls with a solemn expression before moving up to set her hand on the sickly orange bark. The shrieks intensified.

"Flynt?" Milisade called softly.

Water dripped into Flynt's eyes from her hair, which hung in heavy tangles around her face. She walked up to the queen.

"Can you free the sparks trapped here?"

"I wouldn't know how. It's not Death-aspect that binds them, even though they're tied to Death-aspect themselves. I..." She glanced over at Lem. He was close enough to hear. Whatever she chose to say, he'd know it. But lying served no one, not even him. "This shouldn't be possible. It feels wrong right down to my bones."

Lem didn't appear to give any reaction. He just stood there, looking as wet and muddy as the rest of them, and stared up at the tree.

"That's how wish manipulation functions: uncontrollable and unpredictable," Queen Milisade said, letting her finger run along the trunk. A ghost face lunged at her finger, mouth wide. She didn't even flinch away, though Flynt did on her behalf. "Nightshade believes that our captain stepped over the line. What do you say?"

Flynt glanced over her other shoulder back at Nightshade and Nekolai, who stood under the meager shelter of the outer ring of trees. Of all of them, Nightshade seemed to thrive the most in the rain, seeming not wet, cold, and tired, but energized with the green of her vines giving off warm hues and the purple like a ripe berry. Nightshade meant no harm, but perhaps like the berry she took her name from, her seeming innocence and beauty could be deadly.

"Power exists for a reason," Flynt said, careful not to look at Lem. Though he could hear, this speech really was for the queen. "Why would we have it, if not to use? There has to be a way to release the sparks, given time. And beyond all that, which is all theoretical, Captain Lem saved me."

Milisade dropped her hand from the bark and turned to the Chaos-gate. Flynt stood a moment longer, staring at the souls. Whatever had occurred had been done to protect Flynt.

There was a decent amount of pressure in that. She had to make it right, somehow.

And if Lem died for it, his death would rest on her shoulders.

The queen gave her no time to get lost in these thoughts.

"Nekolai," Milisade said, motioning him forward. "You'll need to guide us through the tomb."

Nekolai still looked too pale, and the walk hadn't helped improve his condition, but he stood straighter and stronger when Milisade's gaze fell on him. They both looked a little less bedraggled with the glow that came from their exchanged smiles.

How could he not see her love? Surely, no one was that oblivious, not with the amount of attention he paid to her every whim.

Given that level of commitment from him, Flynt also wondered how much he knew about Milisade and Ieyil but didn't dare ask.

"Let us get in out of the elements," Nekolai suggested. He brushed a lock of sopping, blond hair from his forehead. "The burial chamber is warded against Ieyil's magic—we are safer there."

Milisade nodded. "Captain Lem, you go first. Nekolai, you will follow."

They entered as she said, and Milisade followed, leaving Flynt and Nightshade to use the Chaos-gate last.

The burial chamber was exactly as they'd left it. Right down to Cyniel's bones, lying neatly on the stone slab in the center. Flynt took a moment to inspect the weapons on the wall, mostly to confirm that the dagger hanging above Ieyil's intended resting place was indeed the one that Milisade had stabbed her with. With the image of that gem encrusted hilt burned into her brain from the memory transfer, the blade was undeniably the same.

A shiver ran through Flynt and she wrapped her arms around herself.

Nekolai had moved over to the barred doors with his back to the stone slab and its skeletal contents. Flynt wondered if he knew that Cyniel's bones were resting there. Perhaps she'd been wrong and Ieyil hadn't placed them there. Perhaps Flynt had been wrong about the song of the bones; maybe no Death-aspect had been used. Though even given that, Flynt couldn't imagine Nekolai gathering the bones; she couldn't imagine him laying them out so neatly.

The question was bound to come up, as Milisade wanted to move the bones. Flynt decided that was better done sooner than later.

"Should we gather the bones now?" Flynt asked no one in particular. It was more a statement of intent than a true question. "Who knows what will happen once we leave this room."

Milisade moved up to the slab and looked down. "Yes. You can't move them with Aspect in this room?"

"No," Flynt said. If Death-aspect had moved him here, Ayal only knew how Ieyil had managed to get him to the slab.

Lem and Nightshade both moved closer. The whole group gathered around the bones.

"There wasn't a corpse here before," Nekolai said. He moved across from Milisade and reverently touched the uniform. "It's the current uniform. He doesn't belong here."

Lem took Flynt's hand. After a moment of shocked surprise, she squeezed his fingers, glad of the support.

"Those bones were placed there for me," Flynt said, her tone measured.

Recognition crossed Nekolai's face almost immediately. He couldn't feel the story from the remains, but a closer inspection of the uniform would have told him much, and the fact that the body would matter to Flynt must have given him no doubts. "Cyniel?"

Flynt nodded. "We won't leave him here."

"I will gather the bones," Nekolai said softly. Yet his hands pulled in closer to his chest.

"You don't need to." Lem cut in. "Nightshade and I can handle it."

"No," Nekolai said. "This is a matter of honor. To you, he is just bones. Whatever spirit still clings deserves more. Go. We will discuss the rest further when this is done."

"We don't have a lot of time," Nightshade remarked. "Ieyil knows we are here."

"This is time we will take," Milisade said firmly. "Go inspect her burial chamber if you wish to be useful. What was or was not left behind may tell us something about how Ieyil was freed from the room in the first place."

Nightshade nodded and turned to go.

"Lem," Milisade said, "aid her. This is a private moment."

Lem and Nightshade both left and Milisade pulled out a thin, silver shroud from her pack. She handed it to Nekolai. The material was barely thicker than a spider's weave, but it didn't tear as Nekolai unfolded it. The queen stood back before doing a circuit of the room, touching all of the wards and whispering to herself. As she did this, Flynt and Nekolai moved the bones, gathering them to wrap in a piece of thin fabric that Milisade had provided. Flynt folded his uniform carefully to place with the skull.

When the bones were fully bound, Nekolai left them next to the gate. Sending them through unaccompanied would mean that Ieyil could easily manipulate them. Nekolai and Flynt stood, waiting, head bowed, and words trapped within their heads.

They had already buried him once. It seemed unfair to Flynt to repeat the process. She'd said her goodbyes and Cyniel should have been free by now.

Lem came back into the chamber ahead of Nightshade. His eyes were broodingly dark, but he still held a hint of a smile around his mouth. "Where is Ieyil? Nekolai, you said before that you knew."

Nekolai straightened, looking every bit the Queen's Defender and shedding any softness that had come with handling Cyniel's bones. "Not exactly. I apologize if I misrepresented myself. I have an *idea* where she is."

"We must find her remains," Milisade said. She pointed to the chamber. "Ieyil's bones should be in there. We bound her carefully and warded the chamber against her powers, even more strongly than this room... and she made it through both. There is no way she could have overcome it alone. If we can get her bones back in that room, it should stop her current plots."

"Someone let her out," Nekolai said with a small nod. "We found evidence of an intruder when we first arrived, and the manacles were broken."

"Picked, not broken," Lem corrected, leaning casually against the gray stone wall. "It wasn't a bungled job. Someone came here with the intent of letting her out."

"And it was done several years ago. Before her last attack, I'd say," Nightshade added. "I'd suggest Hiirshal, but he wouldn't have had the skills. He might have orchestrated it, but he had help."

Flynt winced. They'd already stopped Hiirshal once. Why must his influence linger? Maybe Ieyil would be resting peacefully if not for him.

"Hiirshal's involvement seems more than likely," Nekolai said. "From the evidence we observed, multiple people with multiple skill sets would have been needed. To enter this crypt through the main doors, someone of a royal bloodline would be needed and there were traces of Life-manipulation in the burial room as well as traces of Earth-manipulation on the outer doorway. But *who* is not the concern for now. The concern is *where*."

Flynt crept closer to Lem. If only he'd wrap those powerful arms around her, maybe she could settle the frenzied rush of nerves inside her.

"Agreed. Once Ieyil is defeated, I can set a full investigation to find the culprits," Milisade said. "But I suspect it was led by Hiirshal, royal blood or not. There are enough fallen royals out there that it would not be too hard to hire one. And Hiirshal made a trip here around two years ago—it would coincide with the timeframe I did not meet with him and couldn't access his mind. He is causing us trouble even after death."

"He had more in common with Ieyil than he knew," Lem joked.

Flynt nudged him with her shoulder but couldn't help a smile.

Neither Nekolai's face nor tone reflected their levity. "Someone with knowledge moved her. Our Death-magus would explain better, but he was the first to die in that trap. That's why we were down there; he sensed her bones below us, not from this chamber, obviously. But we were exploring when..."

"Where are the bones?" Flynt asked, hoping to distract from the memories.

Nekolai pointed down. "He said there, but when we took those stairs, it was a trap. So all I know is the remains are on a lower level. It must be one of the other passages." Nekolai motioned to the doors. "Only I never saw a way to a lower level out there. We'd be exploring it all again."

The hallways beyond would be outside the anti-Necro warding and that alone made Flynt wish to rush there.

"Then we explore," Milisade said, striding toward a door.

"No!" Nekolai shouted. "Those halls are crawling with her creatures. We endanger no one until we have a proper plan."

"I don't know. Creatures sound fun," Lem said. He took Flynt's hand in his again. "All this talking is dull. Flynt? Ready to play?"

Flynt grinned up at him. "This little game of yours... how do I win?"

"Points for style."

Nekolai made a disgusted sound and shook his head in disapproval.

"Flynt," Nightshade snapped, "don't encourage this."

"Milisade is here," Lem said, calm and good natured, though Flynt felt tension in his fingers. "You don't need to play guard dog."

Nightshade smiled. "*Someone* must hold your leash."

Milisade frowned and clapped her hands together. "Nightshade, boost them and send them out to clear the way—we'll walk one hall at a time." Then she softened her posture. Flynt assumed it was an intentional shift. "I realize many of you are uncomfortable with my presence, and I will endeavor not to overburden you and stay out of danger. But this exploration will be done."

"Send me with them," Nekolai said. "Two will not be enough. You haven't seen those hallways, my queen. There are hundreds of those things."

Milisade's mouth tightened.

"You're still weak," Nightshade said, eyeing Nekolai.

Flynt winced—there was no single worse thing she could have said to Nekolai in that moment.

"No, he's right," Lem said. "Milisade will need a guard here with her—Nightshade will have to do. Flynt can't manipulate in this room and my skills lend better to boosting others—but we'll need Nekolai as a rear guard if he's at all correct about the critter numbers."

Nekolai stood frozen, still unsure. He looked to the queen.

Milisade clasped her hands in front of her. That didn't appear to be intentional to Flynt. It looked like a genuine nervous gesture from the heart.

"And a lot of the wards here require a specific type of Aspect manipulation," Nekolai said. "We'll have more mobility with at least one representative of each of the linked Aspect focuses. I can't use Water or Earth in any meaningful way, but I'm close enough to send a spark to open a door. I assume that Flynt and Lem both have the same capability for their linked Aspect pair."

Lem grinned. "I have been using Order magic for years... nasty stuff, but possible. And I've seen Flynt nudge the edge into Life manipulations."

"There's no one I'd trust more than you," Flynt said. She squeezed Lem's hand again, wanting to hug him. Nekolai needed a chance to defend his queen. With Cyniel's disturbed bones so near, it was imperative that he feel useful.

Milisade gave a slight nod.

"Then it's settled, I suppose," Nightshade said.

"Which door?" Lem asked, turning to the barred doors along the stone wall. "Flip a coin?"

"There are three doors," Flynt said. "You have a three-sided coin?"

"Start from the left and move right," Milisade said.

"Basic layout? What's out there?" Lem asked, looking at Nekolai.

"A short hallway with no doors leads out to a wider hallway with these windows—only they don't look out on this world. It's old Aspect."

Old Aspect? Flynt wondered.

"Chaos," Milisade said. "Back when people still played with Chaos on occasion."

Nekolai gave a stilted nod. "There are a few doors on the opposite walls—then two smaller hallways we barely explored, and the main passage back out to world."

"So not likely we'll find anything but a good warmup out that door." Lem dropped Flynt's hand. She wondered if he had only just realized he'd been holding it. As the others talked specifics, Flynt walked over to the weapons display and pulled down the knife.

The metal was heavier than it ought to have been; it weighed in her arms as if she held something four times the size. She touched one finger to the edge and jerked back. Red bloomed up on her fingertip. She hadn't expected the sharpness, not after it had gone so long unused. A scabbard was tied to it with a piece of red-metal twine and Aspect stones decorated the surface.

Milisade must not have been kidding—Aspect stones would never be used so casually now. They were precious, especially the Death- and Chaos-stones... but here they were used as decoration.

Footsteps followed her and Lem spoke, his tone deep in a

way that rumbled inside her. "Feeling the need to cut and slash a bit?"

"Who would use these stones like decorations?" Flynt asked. She held the blade and scabbard out on her palms. Though perhaps they weren't just decoration given the blade's previous use.

Lem leaned closer and ran a thumb over them. "My honest guess? Someone who saw the future. Bring it with you."

Flynt sheathed the blade and hooked it into her boot. There was no way her flimsy robes would support the weight. Oddly, she felt more prepared with its weight there. Aspect hummed against her ankle. Then she turned to find Milisade watching them. The queen quickly turned away, but not before Flynt caught a dark, angry expression on her face.

Chapter 20

Lem ended up being right about the first hallway in the crypt being little more than a practice round. The three of them encountered no hidden stairways down to where Ieyil's body lay. Out of the crypt where the wards suppressed her power, Flynt could feel the location just as the Death-magus with Nekolai had. Ieyil's bones hummed louder than anybody Flynt had ever known. It was hard not to listen.

Room upon room of bones dressed in jewels and walls lined with statues, frescoes and time-faded paintings filling the hallways. Flynt avoided gazing too long into the windows into other worlds, afraid of what might look back. They found many treasures, but they weren't there to rob the tomb. Nor did they have time. "Hundreds of critters" had been accurate.

Lem moved at the front, smashing through the skeletons while Flynt gathered the bones into her own creations. Nekolai had to defend the rear several times when Flynt failed to take control of all the bones or a new group made their way over.

Lem was fighting with a disadvantage—using only his time-based spells and his sword. If he was uncomfortable using anything obviously Chaos in front of Nekolai, she wouldn't question him, but she knew from experience that he tired faster this way. It also slowed them down, which she found unbearable. Smashing critters apart with a sword was far less effective than pulling them apart with Chaos.

By the time they returned to the queen's burial chamber, Flynt already felt the beginnings of exhaustion nipping at her innards. Her arms and legs dragged, and a headache was forming behind her eyes. She had dismissed the critters she'd claimed, sending them all out into the tundra to roam. Not having to actively control them helped conserve energy, but it also meant she had no army to aid her.

"How many halls are there?" Flynt asked. Even to herself she sounded weary.

Milisade eyed both her and the men, then turned to Nightshade. "They will need your strength out there. We wish them to survive."

Nightshade stared bravely at Milisade. "I need my strength to protect you."

Milisade gave a small smile that, to Flynt, implied the queen already knew she'd won. "But disobeying me now could mean Ieyil's success and messy deaths for all of us."

Nightshade spun to Flynt. "You remember how to hold a boost?"

Flynt nodded.

The Diethyrian reached out and laid a hand on Flynt's chest. "Breathe in deeply. It will help you absorb more."

With no more warning, a foggy glow grew around Nightshade and lunged forward, driving its pale Aspect fingers into Flynt. As it had on the *Seer's Sword*, the boost filled her and for a moment, she imagined herself as an overripe fruit, splitting at the seams. She pulled air into her body and the pressure eased. Her eyes fogged over with clouds.

By the time Flynt had marshalled the power inside her, Nightshade had moved on to Lem. Flynt watched as his brown eyes suddenly glowed a foggy white, shots of green shimmering within. Other than this, he showed no outward sign of the boost.

Nightshade moved on to Nekolai, but he shook his head and stepped back.

"I'll be fine," he said. "You must be strong enough to defend her." His eyes flicked to the queen.

Milisade made a choked sound of annoyance and her mouth opened as if to argue. Then she stopped and simply turned away from them.

Why doesn't she just command him to accept it? Flynt held the question inside. Love made people behave in strange ways and with the queen's mind reading ability, she might well have information that the rest of them didn't.

Nightshade's boost had Flynt feeling renewed, and when they ventured into the second hall, she felt much more capable. Except that it made Ieyil's call that much louder. Not only could Flynt feel where the bones were, there was an insane urge to drop everything and run to them.

The second hallway started off with no promising advances, which made resisting the call harder. The blade that had killed Ieyil weighed down Flynt's boot, its cool metal no longer seeming relieving, but like a needle injecting poison into her skin.

The blade had killed Ieyil once and Flynt had stopped Ieyil's attempt to regain a hold on the world. Why continue to fight her?

They moved slowly down a short hallway. There were no critters in sight and an eerie stillness around them. The tomb waited, biding its time.

"Wait," Nekolai called, staring at a panel at the side of the room.

Flynt had taken it for a stone carving in the wall, but as she looked, she saw the deep grooves on either side. The carving was of twelve kneeling figures in Death-magi robes and at the front of the carving, deeper lines formed the thing that they knelt to—Ieyil's horned crown.

"Who carved that?" Lem asked, a sheen of sweat slicking his forehead. "From what I know of Queen Sisha, no way her vassals commissioned this."

"Ieyil held a lot of power back then," Nekolai said. "I wonder how much of this tomb is unofficially in her honor. More importantly, the dust on the ground is disturbed."

A hidden door had been opened. Flynt nudged Nekolai out of the way and felt around the edge, looking for any call to her

Aspect. If this was a door meant for Ieyil's people, for those who worshiped her, then Flynt could open it.

The scuffs in the dust were bold. Now that they had been pointed out, she could follow them clearly, but the disturbance didn't bring any sigils into sight.

"We should go get the others before opening this," Nekolai said. "Whether or not Ieyil's body is back there, *something* is."

"No," Flynt said. Her fingers twitched in the dust. Waiting wasn't an option. Answers were here—she felt it. *Maybe I can save Ieyil and the queen. Maybe if I find the right answers, everyone can win this time,* she thought. "We need to check it out first."

"This feels wrong," Lem said. "This whole space resonates badly. Nekolai, maybe you should go back... go get help. The halls are clear. No reason Milisade can't come here."

Flynt found the Call of Death-aspect and held her fingers out to wipe the dust away from the sigil. She didn't even need to do anything, not even manipulate the Aspect. A panel on the floor lit up with green light that spread over the crack around the carving and then the carving itself fell into the floor.

There was no time to discuss who went where. The door opened on gears driven by a throbbing, purple light. A smell swept out, old and bitter like Aspect gone rotten and consumed by maggots.

Behind the door were a dozen undead, not critters. Flynt sensed the difference in their Aspect immediately. These were much more complex than critters, each mummified in appearance with hungry, red eyes and Death-magister robes hanging loosely over their shriveled limbs. These creatures had been changed prior to dying—the purpose in their bones was at least partly their own.

One at the front lifted its shriveled finger and gave an equally shriveled wail. Its red eyes seemed to see Flynt—see into her.

Bone critters erupted from the dirt at the undead Magister's feet, crawling from the packed dirt.

Nekolai murmured a prayer, his gun out in one hand, a

blade in the other.

Lem slammed into the critters erupting from the floor and Flynt tried to grab them and harness their power, but the old bones simply disintegrated. Nekolai fired into the skulls of several, and they fell. But it wasn't enough, not fast enough. Critters rose faster than they fell.

The floor was made of bone. Layer upon layer of death.

A third and then a fourth wave erupted from the earth. Their numbers grew faster than Lem and Nekolai could deplete them.

"We're being overrun," Flynt said.

There was nothing more she could do. She couldn't overcome the wills holding the critters... And then a realization hit her. The will came from the creatures at the back. And in order to manipulate Aspect, a being needed Life-spark—not much, maybe, as they clearly weren't alive. But she might be able to kill them and cut off the waves.

"Lem!" Flynt shouted.

He stumbled back away from the oncoming critters.

"Get me back to the originals."

Without a pause, he fell back to her, grabbed her waist, and swung her in front of him.

Bones in unnatural forms surged for her—human skulls on canine bodies, lizard bodies matched with large, mammalian arms. But each was hungry, a hunger that shuddered in her with each reflection. But behind them, the undead masters watched, hate in their red embers of eyes.

Behind her, Lem shouted. "Nekolai, fire there!"

First one critter then another disappeared where Lem pointed.

Flynt felt Lem's energy fold around her, as smooth and sweet as honey. Time slowed. She ran forward, then leaped up onto a critter who had fallen and launched herself through. Death-aspect grew in her, filling her limbs and her mouth, spilling from her eyes to color the world in purple.

Hunger lapped at her skin, igniting an answering

gnawing inside her.

Lem moved behind her, smashing things, and little bone fragments hit her. Flynt hit the first of the creatures and let the Death-aspect at her fingers drive into the creature. She found the Life-spark inside it. And she tried to drink in.

She pulled the Aspect through her fingers. The Life-spark was warped and dry. Wrong.

Something cold and sour filled her, and her flesh ached. Her blood revolted, trying to pull back. Flynt struggled against that instinct to stop. She had to kill it; she drank deeper of the sour-wine Life-spark. The creature fell, but Flynt could barely stand. There was so little life to drink… and it was tainted with death. How much could she drink without dying?

There were eleven more.

Behind them, the carved stone door slammed back up into place, smashing several critters in its ascent. Flynt half-turned back to catch sight of Nekolai on the opposite side. A critter had him by the shoulders.

Ayal, everything hurt.

Then Nekolai was gone—locked on the outside of the room.

Flynt swayed, vision graying.

"Flynt!" Lem called. She saw him as if through a haze, striking through the critters, then his sword slamming into the chest of one of the ancient Death-magi.

Flynt moved toward him. She lifted shaking fingers and tried to gather Death to her.

A creature grabbed her and pulled her to the floor. Flynt hardly saw it, even as the mummified fingers slipped into her mouth. She bit down but couldn't pierce the skin.

Then the creature was gone, flying back. Lem ripped Flynt to her feet.

"There!" he called, pulling her away from the creatures. With her vision still black and spotty, she saw a slender, stone stairwell at the back of the room leading down.

Down was where they had wanted to go. And the thought

hurt almost as much as the poison running through her. Lem lifted her up onto his shoulder and ran toward the stairs.

"Nekolai!" Flynt protested. They couldn't leave him.

Lem ignored her, thundering down the first few steps into darkness. As they moved, the darkness seemed to deepen, easing the pain of Flynt's eyes. Once they were fully submerged in the murky black, Lem turned to look back. He jerked her forward.

Then she was falling. Not far, but farther than his height. She landed on stones, and he crashed beside her. Something even heavier fell moments after, stone hitting stone.

Flynt groaned.

Lem let out a string of curses.

Managing to pull herself into a sitting position, then around, she crawled toward where the stair had been. Only now, there was nothing but black, no sign of the world above, and when she reached out, she found a wall. Forcing her aching limbs to obey, she stood and felt out with her hands.

"The stairs are gone," she choked out. "There's a wall."

"Well... the creatures can't get at us," Lem said. His arm slipped around her. "You need to sit down. Whatever that thing did to you, I don't think you're okay."

He didn't really need to tell her; consciousness was already fleeing until all that remained of her waking mind was a terrified voice, screaming that they were trapped.

Trapped in the dark with Ieyil.

Chapter 21

Flynt's blood burned inside her. Demons crawled out of her flesh; the pain rocked through her. Dripping liquid metal, the gates to the afterlife opened and Ayal wept tears of acid. Then slowly, slowly, it faded away. She felt Lem seated at her side but saw nothing. The dark reigned complete. Flynt wanted to ask how much time had passed, but if she opened her mouth, it would be to scream or cry. Nekolai's face kept running through her mind, how he'd looked as the wall had slammed into place and the way contaminated Life-spark had tasted in her mouth.

Waiting in the dark, drowning in the pain, Flynt drifted inside her mind.

When Ieyil appeared, she floated in a soft, gray light. Flynt wasn't certain if she'd fallen asleep or even died, or if the ghost herself was standing in the tight room. Which one didn't matter.

The Necro Queen wore her horned crown, but her hair fell in loose curls down her back as it had in Milisade's memory. Her face seemed unsure where to settle except for the brilliant red of her eyes.

Ieyil hissed. "You should have died above; things would be so much easier then."

"We're trapped in here, aren't we?" Flynt didn't hear her own voice but knew she had spoken and that Ieyil had heard her.

"I have been trapped here for a thousand years—so I've been told." Ieyil leaned close. "You'll grow accustomed."

"Can you show me the way out?"

"You came here to thwart me, to destroy my dream for all of our kind. Now you ask me yet again to help you? No, I must insist this time. You'll die and then you'll be free. You will simply be one of Ayal's servants—like me."

"Please. Save us." Flynt looked to the side in the black, eyes wide as if they could pierce through the lightless murk. Lem's breathing rustled in her ears. "Save him. I will stop everyone from this mission... keep them from hurting you. Please."

Ieyil's face changed, eyes sinking until there was little difference between her countenance and a screaming skull. "No! Why should I care for him? Why? None of his kind ever took care of me."

"I am not ready to die."

"Your problems are nothing." Ieyil's anger seethed on the air, a sheen of red over the black. "Death happens. You will die. All die and it won't matter."

"I can't let him die. I'll do anything."

"I don't need your help. And he... he stinks of Chaos. He'll be better dead. I'll like you better dead."

Flynt bit back another plea. There was no point.

"I can help..." Ieyil said after a moment, drifting closer. But she was still just a skeleton in robes. "I can kill you now. Waiting is the worst part. If I take you now, you'll never have to endure your man there sinking a blade into your flesh, as the knife you carry was once buried in mine."

Agony bloomed between her shoulder blades—Life-aspect curdled inside her and Death-aspect slithered forward. She endured the sensations of the knife sinking through her muscles, scraping over bone.

Flynt screamed and Ieyil was gone. The pain left with her.

Only blackness remained, dark and high around Flynt. Her panicked scream echoed in the emptiness.

"That was loud..." Lem said sleepily from her right.

"Lem?" She choked out his name. The pain in her blood was gone, but the terror pressing in with the dark was almost as bad—worse in some ways. She couldn't see the room around her, but the energy in the walls gave her an awareness of the space. The Death-aspect floated through the thick stone wall that had fallen to block the stairs they'd used to descend into this place. And she felt Ieyil through the far wall, hidden and blocked but there, waiting. The weight of the knife in Flynt's boot pressed against her ankle.

"Are you doing better?" Lem asked.

"The wall fell. Where are we?"

"I have no idea. There's no exit," he said. "Five foot by seven foot… size of a big bed. No breaks in the wall. I searched for sigils but couldn't find any—that has seemed to be the method of opening the secret doors so far."

"No levers or switches or anything?"

"None I can find. You're welcome to check for yourself."

"We're trapped," Flynt said. She struggled to her feet, arms extended, and walked the length of the room. It only took a few steps. His estimate of the room's size had been accurate, and the ceiling above couldn't have been more than seven feet high. She searched with her fingertips for any breaks in the stone but found none—it was almost as if there had never been an opening. The air was hot and sticky. Would they run out of oxygen? "Ayal help us."

"There has to be a way out built in." Lem's voice came from the same place, low by the wall. "We'll figure it out. Now that you're back on your feet."

"Why does there have to be a way out? This is a trap. The one we found Nekolai in didn't have a way out."

"It did, just not one they could use. But there has to be an option here because I'm not dying here. You're not dying here." Lem sounded calm, but without seeing him, Flynt couldn't be certain.

Flynt spent a fruitless time exploring the walls entirely. Unlike Lem, she located a Death sigil near the far wall. The glow of her Death-aspect ignited the sigil. Nothing happened.

Perhaps there were others, but Flynt's body ached. She needed to rest.

She sank back down to the floor beside Lem, close enough to feel his heat and the brush of his pants on her leg. He was the only thing there to make her feel at all safe, especially since through the fallen wall Death-aspect shuffled around. The undead things were still there. "This is a tomb. And those things up there…"

"I've never even heard of creatures like those. What did they do to you?"

"I don't know exactly. They weren't entirely dead; it was like the Life-spark remained in them. I thought I could kill them by draining the spark, and it worked, but the Life-spark wasn't right. It was like drinking death, like poison." Flynt reached up her right hand, settling it on her throat, which tightened at the recollection.

"Did we leave Nekolai with them?" Lem asked.

"He was on the other side of the wall, but…" Flynt swallowed words. There had been critters attacking him, and Nekolai had still been weak. "No one's coming for us."

"They'll come," Lem said.

Flynt bit back her words. How would they come? How would they even know where to come unless Nekolai got away? She'd been the one to open the door into the main chamber and she was the only person who could manipulate Death. Even if they returned, how would they ever know how to activate the wall? Nightshade's powers didn't appear to lean at all to the center of the Life-Death-aspect pair. They could use a Death gem —she recalled Nightshade mentioning that about the Life door in the crypt—but they'd have to know where to look.

These fears and exhaustion warred for dominance over her mind. The damage the attack had done to her body seemed to wipe away any ability to do anything except lie there in the dark.

Whether or not Flynt had been asleep before, this time, she drifted off. Her dreams were as black and cold as the tomb around her. She woke to the sound of Lem pacing the short length of the room. Every so often, she heard the clash of metal or a thump, presumably as Lem tried to use pressure and force to shift the wall.

"How long have we been here?" she asked.

"Long enough that we should have heard something. Can you hear the creatures up there anymore? I can't."

"No," Flynt said, then she lifted her bone hand to tug at the Aspect. And she couldn't feel the creatures, either.

"Six hours, eight? Who knows? Maybe only four."

"And how long have you been beating up the walls?"

"Oh, at least half that time. Strong buggers."

And how much air was there? It already felt heavy in her lungs. They needed to get out. Waiting wasn't an option and Lem controlled his wishes in his own way. "Could you...?" Flynt leaned out to touch his leg as she moved by—rather than continuing, Lem sat on the edge across from her. Their boots bumped into each other.

"Can I what?"

"You could use Chaos to get us out? Just wish it and we can deal with the consequences."

Lem sighed. "I've been thinking about nothing else, Flynt, but I won't do it."

"Why? You must. We're going to die."

"I'm sorry, but no matter how I twist it in my head, the risk is too great. Nightshade's up there—Milisade, Nekolai... all those Defenders and soldiers. It's too big a wish. I can't risk all of them for us."

"But..." Flynt stopped herself. She didn't want to die despite the ease Ieyil spoke of death; being on the other side of the veil had changed the Necro Queen. Life was more than a waiting room for death. Life was the whole point. "You're right. I know you're right, but I'm scared. I'm not ready to die."

"Me, either," Lem said.

"Please? Maybe nothing will go wrong. It could save us, and no one could get hurt."

"Or it could rip the entire planet apart and everyone on it could die. I won't risk it. Before I acted in the moment, now

I have no such excuse. No matter what I want, using Chaos for this is wrong, and I cannot."

"Maybe—"

"Stop. Please. Saying I can't save you is difficult enough, but I *can't*. Ask something else. Pretend we aren't Magisters, just people. How can I help?"

By not dying, Flynt thought, but those were words for her, not to be shared. "Sit next to me? Hold me?"

Lem shuffled over to her, sitting with his shoulder against hers and a hand on her knee. "Do Leshmen play hide and seek?"

"Random," Flynt responded. "But yes, of course, but we called it 'Dark Corners.'"

"That fits. Pretend that's what this is. We're hiding in the dark, waiting for our friends to find us."

"That seems painfully close to the truth." Flynt leaned toward him, resting her head on his shoulder. "In 'Dark Corners,' we always told secrets in the dark."

"Oh? Tell me a secret, then."

"A few years back, I went to see a doctor—the off-the-books kind who works on 1s. I booked a sterilization..." Flynt swallowed. She'd never said those words aloud. Not even to Cyniel. Her father would have disowned her even for thinking of it and even though she knew Lem wasn't Leshmen and wouldn't think as they did, fear still made her heart pound at voicing her unthinkable desire to desecrate her body. "I didn't do it, but I still wonder what life would have been like if I had."

"Those doctors are butchers." His voice came out lightly, without judgement.

"I know. That's why I chickened out. When I still thought I was going, though, I felt this new freedom. Cyniel came back from one of his missions and I figured, why not? I was already planning to have myself altered." She paused, kicking the toe of her boot against the stone. "I tell everyone that we never slept together, but we did that once. He admitted he thought about having children with me sometimes. It's how I know that he would have followed me if I'd decided to become a Mother. I didn't conceive, but it was the idea that I might be with child that stopped me from completing the procedure in the end. Your turn: What did you mean before when you said you'd been through this issue before with Chaos and love?"

There was a long pause. "That's not a fun secret."

"You think mine was?" Flynt's eyes struggled against the dark but made nothing out. "That's the point. To share the things that weigh us down... to do so in the dark where we don't have to see the eyes of those we confide in. Tell me."

"You're certain..." He sounded oddly unsure. He must have wanted to share, which made the truth hovering over them seem even more frightening.

"I don't want *fun*. I want to know what it is that scares you, that weighs down your spark." If they died, it was better to have such things out in the open.

"Back before I was a captain, I made a living on a variety of vessels. I knew what I was and knew better than to use Chaos-aspect—so I didn't. I didn't know yet how the need to use Chaos would build inside me."

Flynt set her hand over Lem's where it rested on his knee, and he turned his palm up to twine his fingers in hers. His flesh felt clammy.

"One day we were on Uvus unloading a Coil shipment on the docks. Mags and I were happily married at the time. She was pregnant with our daughter. Mags, the baby, and my son, they were all in the universe that really mattered to me. I'd told her I was on planet that afternoon, but that we wouldn't be staying the night on planet."

He fell silent. The next part must have been the true weight. This was all just history. She had only one reassurance to give him. "But they lived. I've met them... whatever happened."

Lem pulled his hand away. "Do you want to hear or tell me?"

"That's a bit uncalled for."

"I know. I'm sorry."

"Go on."

"I got pissed at a fellow worker—I don't recall why. But I was angry. So I wished him away. It was barely more than a thought. I didn't wish to hurt him; I liked the guy. But I wanted him gone. I never *chose* to use Aspect. Need and desire took over."

"And he went away?"

"Him and half the section of dock just disappeared. I found out later that they reappeared five miles away and fell on a farmhouse—nineteen total dead. Two of those were children."

Flynt opened her mouth to speak but didn't have words. So she said the only ones that even slightly fit. "I'm sorry."

"Not done." Lem reached out to her, and Flynt took his hand back.

She nodded into the dark, hoping he felt what he couldn't see.

Lem continued. "I didn't know where the disappeared bits of dock had gone yet. I *did* know that over this new nothing space I'd just created—this emptiness... Just past it was a walkway. Mags and the kids had come down to the docks to have lunch with me. If I'd been standing ten feet farther forward when I'd wished—they'd have been among the dead."

"Ayal," Flynt swore. "But they weren't."

"That didn't matter. It doesn't matter. I knew that the next time, and the next, and the next... all to infinity, they could be the ones I hurt. I decided I couldn't be near them, not when I was so dangerous. I left Mags, joined up with a warship... I love them too much to put them in danger."

"Mags was okay with this?"

"She hated me for a long time. I'm not sure she was wrong to feel that way. She used to say that I tried to kill her, and then I had the gall to leave her."

Flynt squeezed his hand. "She's not wrong."

"She's not. And it didn't help that after a while, I didn't even want to come back to her. I was a different person. Those kids are still my world, but Mags... She's a remnant of an older life that I've outgrown, and that isn't her fault. I visit as often as feels safe, but they can never be my home. The best thing I've ever done in my life is not kill them. I'd like to not kill you as well, but here we are."

Flynt snuggled up closer to him, trying to reassure him with her body.

He spoke again, soft as a breath this time. "By not risking the others, am I as good as killing you?"

"Maybe, but that's okay." Flynt had the words this time. They came in a flood. "If I die because of your actions, that's part of the deal. It's part of the lives we've chosen. If we get out of here and you happen to slip and a twist of your manipulation kills me, know that I won't blame you. I've already forgiven you. Death comes with the territory. You're killing me right here and now, and I don't blame you."

Lem turned, his fingers moving to seek out her face. Flynt felt him shift in the dark and turned toward him. He cupped her cheek, his fingers stroking down to run over her lips. Flynt sank into the movement, waiting for him to come closer, to kiss her.

Chapter 22

Flynt crawled to the far side of the room. Her lungs ached, and she felt out of breath, though she'd been doing nothing but sitting. She needed to relieve her bladder and there wasn't much choice when it came to where to do so in a room this size. Crouched in the corner, she used a container from her field kit made for cooking—it had the benefit of a lid.

Finished, she touched the solid wall beside her. Somewhere behind that wall was the way out—she could feel the pulse of Ieyil's Death behind it. But she'd never reach Ieyil. After everything, this was the end. After struggling to escape becoming a Mother and being condemned by the customs of her people to birth children until her body gave out, she'd finally found a new way. Then after entering the Death-aspect order and accepting that the Aspect would likely drain her, after watching Azucena die by the hands of a wicked man in an attempt to frame Flynt... After all of it, she was going to suffocate in this little tomb.

She'd never even been able to live her new life freely, never walked the streets of the Coil as a Necroequitem. This quest was supposed to give her the right to live as herself. She'd finally found true friends. She'd never get a chance to enjoy any of it.

Lem and she hadn't exchanged a word since they'd kissed. Flynt couldn't guarantee why that was for Lem, but she wanted to preserve the air. They had made their confessions. It seemed idiotic to be holding out hope that someone would rescue them. But to just give up struck her as worse.

The silence from the creatures in the room above concerned her, but that was a distant worry. They couldn't affect her now, not running about or silent.

The only thing that mattered now was breathing and the stone wall between her and the air. Well, two things, because Lem breathing mattered too.

And neither one of them was going to get the air they required for much longer.

Flynt's bone fingers ran over the wall, checking for chinks.

Dying became progressively less frightening as she stared into the unquenchable black.

She sat back down and dropped her face to her knees.

Whoever would have thought it would be her inability to open a door that killed her? Lem wanted her to think about their problem as people, not Magisters... but even ordinary people could open a door.

Except the doors here in the tomb, she realized. These all had the same elite mechanism for opening. The thought pierced the cloud of haze over her brain. Every door they'd opened had required some form of Aspect to activate. This one could require Death or Chaos.

She'd found the Death sigil, but what if that wasn't the only one? What if they'd somehow missed more? If she and Lem searched together, maybe they could use the light from the Chaos and Death sigils to locate any others.

"Lem," she croaked. She should have thought of it sooner and could only blame her exhaustion and panic from the battle. "Help me look. There may be more of those Aspect panels here... Maybe one for Chaos."

The rustle of cloth and the more forceful sound of breathing let her know that he was moving. She reached out to touch the strands of Aspect in the room. She'd been able to feel the one outside the Magisters' room on the carving. Both her hands slid over the stone, searching from floor to ceiling.

"Here," Lem said.

Flynt turned to see an orange glow near the floor. She

fumbled to the space where she'd found the Death sigil and activated that as well. She held her breath, waiting for the wall to move. Nothing changed.

"Keep looking," Lem said, sitting down. She could see the outline of him in the light. "Sometimes these have multiple activations."

Flynt kept looking, but she worried—what if it wasn't a Death-aspect panel?

Her bone fingertips picked up on a trace at last and she set her palm down on the floor. A low green glow lit the room a little more. Life.

Flynt's eyes flew up to the wall.

"Nothing," Lem said.

But there could be more. For the second time that day, she recalled the Aspect crystals. Then, the realization hit, and she recalled the scabbard tucked in her boot.

Flynt lifted her hand, and the light went out. She fished the knife out of her boot and pried a stone from the old leather. She couldn't tell in the dark what stone it was. Carefully, she slid her hand with the stone in her palm facing down over the floor against the wall. She was almost over to Lem and nothing had stirred.

She reached him. In the light from his Chaos, she could see the color of the stone. Earth.

She pried Air free from the scabbard and quickly found its home. A pale blue light came to join the others. Still, the wall didn't move. Flynt went through all the stones until five lights glowed—missing only Earth and Death.

"If it needs six, it'll need the seventh... but I looked," Flynt said.

"Try again."

Flynt crawled again with the stone in her hand from the wall over to Lem. Nothing.

"Other side of me," he said. "Here." His free hand came up to claim the stone, and he turned to run the stone along the floor behind him. Sure enough, a warm, brown light bloomed up.

Flynt went back to her spot, and with a shaking hand, placed her palm down.

Purple light lit her fingers. With all the Aspects lit at once, she could see the fear on Lem's face. She wished that she couldn't.

The wall behind them rumbled, lifting to show the stairs. Then, as if it were a star performer waiting for the warmup act to finish, the wall next to them lifted. Air poured in—and light.

Flynt turned to stare down a long hallway. She couldn't see where it went. The idea of walking deeper terrified her. Then she spun back to the stairs.

"The Undead Magisters," she said. No oncoming Death-aspect flowed to her, but that wasn't proof. "Are they coming?"

Lem stood, his hand going to his sword.

A shadow moved on the stairs.

Chapter 23

Flynt gripped tightly on to Lem's arm as they stared behind them, toward the revealed stairwell. The shadow moved slowly, sliding down one step. Without feeling the Death-aspect of the creatures up above, Flynt didn't know what they were doing. Could they come down the stairs? Would they?

Heart hammering, Flynt wanted to sink to her knees and pray to Ayal. But if any creature in the world belonged more fully to Ayal than Flynt, it would be those monsters. Why would the Ayal protect Flynt? Her knees grew watery, but she would not let herself fall.

She turned and took one step out in front of Lem.

The shadow slid down another step and Flynt saw the tip of boot move into view and another shadow hovered beside the first.

Flynt searched the boot and the leg as it moved—no neon-green rags or shriveled flesh. No. The boots were new and black, and the legs covered in an officer's uniform.

"Hello?" Flynt asked.

Lem gripped her waist.

Milisade, delicate as a flower, descended the steps, one hand clasped over her heart, the other trailing on the wall. Behind her, Nekolai and Nightshade followed. Flynt scanned the area behind them, but nothing followed.

"How?" Flynt asked. "What?" The questions weren't exactly well-formed, but they came out with the pure confusion she felt. There had been monsters in that room. Monsters that she couldn't see how these three could possibly have defeated.

"Where are those things?" Lem said.

"Disabled," Nightshade said.

Nekolai walked past the others, examining the chamber and the Aspect stones laid out on the floor.

"I took the ward sigil from Ieyil's chamber," Milisade said, crossing the room toward them. Her brown eyes shifted over both of them, but what she saw, Flynt had no clue. "When Nekolai described what was in the chamber above, I recognized the description from old stories."

"What were they?" Flynt asked.

"Liches," Milisade said. "They can only be destroyed by cutting off their access to Death-aspect. My guess after seeing them is that those were some of the Death-magisters bound to Ieyil during her life."

"So you think that she raised them?"

Milisade glanced behind them at Nekolai, then returned her attention to them. "That is impossible to say. It is entirely possible that when she brought herself back, her connection to them allowed them to resurrect themselves. I use the term 'resurrect' loosely."

"She will realize they aren't functional anymore," Nightshade remarked. "If they're bound to her, then she knew the minute they went down. We do not have time to have this discussion."

"We don't have time to skip it," Lem said. "We run down that hallway as we are, the mega-lich lady kills us."

"We must kill her first," Milisade said sadly. "Permanently. Her bones are here. We destroy them."

"No," Flynt snapped. Destroying Ieyil entirely was just too cruel. "We just need to stop her."

"If she is inhabiting her old bones, it is no longer a matter of stopping a plot." Milisade sounded weary.

Nekolai touched Milisade's hand. Just a brief brush. "At this point, stopping her plot means destroying her. She has connected them."

Flynt swallowed against a welling sadness inside. She feared they were correct, but she didn't know if she could actually do what they were asking. Was this what it took to earn her true place in Coil society?

She tried to focus on their words, but she kept seeing Ieyil as she had been in life. The Coils had destroyed her, Death-madness had fed on her, and now the only way to stop her from tearing the veil between life and death was to desecrate her remains. But Ieyil wasn't the only person in danger and Flynt focused on Nekolai. Seeing him alive and well helped steady her.

Milisade said, "Nekolai, are we safe here?"

"I see no sign that this door will shut." Nekolai inspected the door on the far wall, his back to the stairs that led up to the liches' chamber. "The other had marks... I apologize that I didn't recognize them in time, but we were being attacked."

"No one is blaming you," Flynt said, though she realized she'd inched onto the stairs. "I was afraid... I saw the door going back up and I thought the creatures might have..."

"I survived. I saw you go down," Nekolai said. "You looked ill. Dying. I'm glad we were able to find you alive."

"If the door is safe, let's go," Nightshade said. "Let us complete our mission. The faster we can leave here, the better. I don't like it here."

"No one likes it here," Lem said. "Plan? Do we have one?"

"None yet. We were still planning how we could get the stairwell open and free you," Nekolai admitted. "And those creatures stink. The one you touched was practically a puddle. What did you do?"

"I tried to drain the Life?" Was that the right word? "There was a Life-spark in there, sort of. I knew I could kill lich if I drank its Aspect, but the manipulation hurt."

Milisade nodded. "I'm surprised you're on your feet."

Flynt turned, taking a step off the stairs back into the small chamber, eyes peering into the darkness at the other end of the hall. Something was moving down there. "None of us will be on our feet if we don't get out. Ieyil is regrouping, and you can assume she knows your goals have changed."

"*Our* goals?" Nekolai said. It wasn't really a question, more of an accusation.

Flynt breathed deeply. When it came to it, could she really help them kill Ieyil? She would do so, impossible or not. The day before, she might have answered differently, but something had changed between her and Lem. Something that made her believe she had a compatriot in this world. "Our goals."

Milisade took a few steps closer toward the tunnel that led deeper, closer to Ieyil. "But Lem is correct and so is Nightshade. It is time to have a plan. Unfortunately, this time, I don't know what it should be. Running madly to meet Ieyil isn't wise, but if it's the only plan we have…"

"It is. We must venture down the hall, find her," Nightshade said.

"It isn't," Flynt said, trying to focus her thoughts. The liches were dead bodies, like any others. Now that they were disabled, she could control them… Only she didn't know how quickly they would take control of themselves without the rune.

The rune. Why hadn't Ieyil come to them? This room wasn't warded. "We need to find out why Ieyil hasn't reached us. The very fact that we have the choice of timing implies she's still contained in some way."

"So I'm correct," Nightshade said, not sounding as smug as Flynt would have in her position. "We go down the hall."

Before anyone could answer, Lem stepped scooped up the Aspect stones and handed them over to Flynt. "Opening the door will have used some of the energy stored in them, but not all."

After speaking, he stepped into the dark and walked forward. Nightshade and Nekolai followed, leaving Flynt and Milisade at the back.

"With all the life she's drained," Flynt asked slowly, wedging the first of the Aspect-stones back into the dagger's hilt. Then she started in on the remaining stones. "Ieyil will be like those things, those liches, won't she?"

"Somewhat," Milisade said. "She's likely been their source,

as we said, so like them, but much more. Why? What are you considering?"

Couldn't she see it in Flynt's mind? But then, Flynt didn't know, either. She was feeling out some nebulous thought. At the heart of it was the fear that none of them would be able to stop Ieyil. "I can't hurt her, not if I couldn't handle them."

"It's true that Death-aspect cannot hurt her directly. Life? Perhaps Nightshade will be able to damage the Death inside her, weaken her somehow." Milisade smiled softly at Nightshade when she glanced back at her name. "Lem and Nekolai also have powers that might touch her."

"There is no plan," Nekolai said. "That is what the queen is avoiding saying. We are going in with a prayer."

"Such opinions are not helpful," Milisade said with a glare into the dark. Nekolai wasn't looking back to see it. "What I do know is that we must destroy her bones once we have brought her down. Then seal this entrance to the tomb off."

"We could wait," Flynt said, already knowing why they couldn't. The more time Ieyil had, the less chance they had of succeeding. This was her playground.

"That is a desperate suggestion," Nightshade said. "I didn't believe you were in a hurry to die. Ieyil will come after us soon and by then she will be stronger."

Lem set a hand on Flynt's lower back and smiled at her. "Ready to play?"

"As much as I'll ever be," Flynt whispered back.

The five of them started off down the hall but didn't get far.

A flare of Aspect slammed into Flynt, tugging hungrily at the Death-aspect around her.

Then she saw the mark on the wall. It was a dull purple that pulled at the Death-aspect. A ward. Like the one into the burial chamber, only stronger.

Lem had passed it and Nightshade stepped over the line.

Flynt stopped; her hand hovered in the air. These were runes similar to the one above, but on closer inspection, different. It was a line, four marks on the wall delineating a chunk of tunnel. A chunk that no Death-aspect would survive through.

A wall built to contain Ieyil.

But Ieyil was back there. So this must have been like the wall of her cage—rather than its effects carrying on over space, it was simply an impenetrable line. Meaning Ieyil was free inside but could not leave. Why would Hiirshal have put her bones into such a cage? Perhaps when this had begun, he had hoped to master the Necro Queen. That didn't matter now. Things were as they were.

"Stop!" Flynt yelled. "Come back now!"

Nekolai stopped and turned back. Nightshade paused, but Lem took another step, staring out in front of him.

Did he see the Necro Queen? Could she be that close?

"It's a trap!" Flynt shouted. No one was listening.

"Return to me, now," Milisade commanded.

Lem pivoted back and Nekolai and Nightshade both hurried to Milisade's side.

Under other circumstances, it might have annoyed Flynt that the others responded so much quicker to the queen, but for the moment, all that mattered was that they didn't move past the barrier. With everyone back with her, Flynt explained.

"Those marks are keeping her contained. As soon as we go in, we have to be ready to face her."

"Can you get in?" Lem asked.

"I would have trouble controlling Aspect near this spot, but I am not composed of Death-aspect. It will have no serious effects on anything living, including me."

"We walk in together," Nightshade said. "*We* are not getting stronger."

The rest of the statement—"she is"—hung unspoken.

"No," Flynt said, rustling through the information. Milisade wanted to destroy the bones once they stopped Ieyil. But Flynt had other constructs who had been stopped. Flynt hadn't been able to take the liches over before, but... "Go back.

Nekolai, Nightshade, Lem... go get three of the liches from that room. Break them in pieces, above the hips, and at the neck. Separate the three focuses of life energy: head, heart, groin. They won't be able to reassemble themselves."

"So...

"I can reassemble them once I pass the ward," Flynt said. "There is a lot of strength in those bodies. We'll need it. And there won't be anything for me to play with in there except these. It's not a plan, but it gives us tools that she doesn't know we have."

Lem grinned. "And you get to play with corpses."

Flynt sighed. She didn't want to return to the room Lem and she had been trapped in. As Nekolai and Lem started off, followed by Nightshade, Flynt stood at Milisade's side. She ought to help, yet something voiceless inside told her to remain. "We should help them carry the bodies."

"No. You are following instinct and that told you to be here alone with me. Why?"

"The thing about instinct is it doesn't explain itself."

"Then think."

Well, the warriors were stronger. The trapped room terrified her, but she didn't really want Lem and Nekolai being in there, either. The thing was, everything right now was about destroying Ieyil, and Flynt didn't want to. She saw the need, but her soul resisted the idea.

"How did you do it before?" Flynt asked. "How did you kill Ieyil when you wanted not to?"

"She meant more to me than any single person in the universe. But I knew that she didn't mean more than the universe. I also knew she'd never be at peace as she was. She'd been driven to a place where she was in freefall internally. As much as it hurt me, and her, killing her was the only way to free her." Milisade gave a small laugh. "Or so I thought."

"She wanted me dead... When I was locked in there, I saw her. She said I was better off dead." Flynt stared hard at the wards. "Maybe she understands what you did."

Milisade shook her head. "I wish I had another chance to do it correctly, to save her before she fell so far. I wish. I wish I'd known before this she had come back. If I could have gotten to her while she was still weak, maybe I could have reached her."

"Are you strong enough to do this?"

"No, but I will do it anyhow. Are *you* strong enough, child? Sometimes I think you're strong and other times, I feel the weaknesses in your soul."

Flynt pulled the knife from her boot and started to pry at the sigil on the wall. If Milisade could remove them, then so could she.

"Ieyil will feel it the minute you break that seal." Milisade touched her arm. "Stop. You can assemble your creations on the other side. We cannot remove this barrier... If we fail, it is all that stands between the universe and Ieyil's vision of the future."

Flynt touched the emeralds in her glove. Azucena's emeralds. Ieyil's actions had led to her death, but Ieyil was the only other person Flynt knew of who had worked to see a better universe for the followers of Ayal. Would Azucena have understood Flynt's need to belong or condemned her for betraying her own kind? Flynt had already failed her friend once —she might never find her friend's lost arm bones. She couldn't even say what Azucena would have wanted, and she couldn't return to the Coil and ask her ghost. This was something Flynt had to decide alone.

The two women stood in silence until the others returned with the dismantled liches. Flynt still held the blade. It had killed Ieyil once. Hopefully, its powers had not been spent quite yet.

Flynt stepped past the ward, the sensation of it leeching off her energy stinging as if it were nibbling at her flesh. Then she was past it. The others followed.

The hallway, lit only with the Life-aspect around Nightshade and traces of Air-aspect from Nekolai, was long and curved. It sloped downward until Flynt was uncertain that it wasn't simply some endless spiral down. The featureless walls occasionally sported a crack of a black smudge to differentiate them, but otherwise, they might have been walking in circles.

Maintaining the three cobbled-together lich bodies was difficult. Their power constantly shoved against her mind as if their wills were pushing for domination. Flynt refused to give in and they shuffled along behind her.

"You're certain she's down here?" Nekolai asked after a while of walking.

"Yes," Milisade said for Flynt. "I realize she hasn't appeared yet, but that may simply be because she feels stronger where she is. And we did not build this tunnel when the crypt was erected. I'm not aware of every Aspect, but something this massive I would have known."

"Why build it? Anyone who did so had a purpose." Nightshade said.

"Earth magic created it," Milisade said, though how she knew was unclear—she shouldn't have been able to feel Aspects she didn't control. "All of these walls were formed by the hand of a Magister, a remnant of her remains. This deep, Ieyil's power would not be so obvious from the surface. Someone meant to build her a prison... What they intended for after is unclear still."

"Why not ward the room she was in... Why the hall?"

"Because whoever did this wanted her to work Aspect. They probably meant her to grow strong."

Flynt wondered if that person had been Hiirshal. If so, he'd already paid the price for his folly. If there were more out there, people he'd been working with, she really hoped that would end up as someone else's problem.

"Quiet," Lem commanded from the front. He didn't need to say any more than that. They all saw the huge, metal doors, rivets of jewels reflecting back Nightshade's light.

Ieyil was in there.

The weight of Milisade's ancient dagger doubled against Flynt's arm—it was the weight of dread rather than any true conversion of matter. A blade like this carried death. Crafted to kill, it longed to fulfill its function, and its one function, the hope

200

in the heart of its creator was simple: Stop Ieyil permanently.

Chapter 24

The door opened to an earthen chamber. With only one light shining from near the door, the sides and back fell into complete blackness, leading the room to look infinite. But with the amount of Death-aspect and her bone sight, Flynt knew otherwise. She could "see" the perimeter clearly from the hundreds of corpses gathered in the darkness.

She'd never controlled so many, never knew it was possible.

"You came to have me kill you?" Ieyil's voice rang out.

Flynt thought the sound was in her head until the others reacted. Lem, Nekolai, and Nightshade fell into battle posture and Milisade froze like a statue, not even blinking. The liches seemed to quiver.

"Come in. You've traveled far. Now is no time to give up." Ieyil's voice differed from the dream version, rougher with a grating rasp. "You wish to destroy me again, Millie? It will not be so easy to sneak up behind me."

"If I thought there was another way to save my Coil," Milisade said, her voice somehow younger, "I would take it. Even if it meant staying here with you in the dark. But even my death would not satiate you."

A shape moved at the back of the room, and Flynt gathered as much Death-aspect as she could in her hands. Ieyil stepped out into the light, not a skeleton or a corpse, but Ieyil as she had looked in Milisade's vision of the war. A skeleton dressed in flesh, with a free tumble of black hair and a gown made from bone.

Finger bones curved over her hair, holding it back from her face. Ribs encased her chest and thousands of tiny animal bones make a skirt around her legs, parting and clicking as she walked.

"As always, you are correct," Ieyil said, white, cracked lips parting to reveal the black void of her mouth. "I will pull your precious Coil through the veil with me. We will all live in this perfect nothingness of Death. I will be queen."

Flynt commanded her creatures to surround Milisade. Eventually, all the dead that hovered at the edge of the room would move. Milisade was the only person who had to survive this.

So why was the queen bating her old love?

"No," Ieyil said, looking directly at Flynt. "She does not need to survive. The queen is irrelevant."

Flynt gasped for a moment before speaking. Ieyil had pulled that thought from Flynt's mind, which seemed to prove Flynt's suspicions.

"You can read minds."

"And for that, because I was her equal, your dear queen murdered me... and now she brings you, my only remaining sister, to slay me again."

Flynt moved forward until she stood in the center of the light. "You were the one who said that Death is not to be feared."

Ieyil lifted one thin arm. "Yet you fear it. Step aside, and I can let you live. We can build a new world together."

There was no chance to respond. Energy smashed into Ieyil's hip, jerking her to the side. Flynt didn't know which of her companions had broken the standstill, but Ieyil didn't delay her response. The creatures around the room burst forward, a sea of yellowed bone, fabric scraps, and smashing jaws. Many held weapons—rusted axes, swords, even wooden clubs and poles.

A burst of air swept forward, at its core a twist of orange Chaos. Several skeletons fell. Flynt sent her Aspect to gather them to her, but they were already back in Ieyil's claws, reassembling and standing.

The army surged forward.

"Get to Ieyil," Milisade commanded.

Flynt felt Nightshade's hand brush her back, boosting her until the room spun with the reach of her power. White filled her, the glow blending together with the Death-aspect inside her and the well that held the power filled until it brimmed over in her blood, nearly spilling from her skin.

"Up and over, Necro." Lem knelt down, lowering his hands. On instinct, Flynt stepped onto his hands.

He thrust her up as the horde reached them. His energy burned around her. She leaped onto the head of one skeleton and Lem's Chaos burned through it, disintegrating bone. Flynt launched herself forward, clearing a path. Her feet found the creatures on instinct, leaning toward the strongest Death-aspect. She pulled two of her creations behind her, circling Nightshade and Lem, who followed.

Nekolai stood in front of Milisade, a whirling wall of air already forming in front of him, sheering off bits of bone and dirt where it touched the floor.

Milisade needed more than one to guard her, but they couldn't spare it. Unless Ieyil fell, they would just have an endless horde after them. Flynt prayed that Nekolai could protect her long enough. She'd never seen him use Aspect for anything but small things before. Still, his shield felt strong to her, the pulse of Aspect steady and powerful.

She ran, her boot hitting down on one of the creature's shoulders. The Chaos around her had weakened, and it turned, biting hard into her ankle. Flynt brought her other foot into its face and felt the crunch of bone.

Then Chaos melted the bone and Flynt fell. She landed on her knees and one of her liches broke through the final line of defense. The bite on her ankle bled, but she seemed able to stand on it. Lem grabbed her arm, pulling her up and through.

Nightshade darted directly at Ieyil, white encasing her body. A vine rose from the dirt behind the Necro Queen and struck through her chest.

Ieyil laughed as the vine rotted and turned to dust. Her

red, glowing eyes hung on Flynt. "Is this it? This is all you have with you, sister?"

Lem struck Ieyil's side with his sword, a gun in his other hand. The blade hummed with Chaos. The rib bones over her chest melted, but the Aspect-covered weapon passed through her flesh, leaving no mark.

"You bring the weapons of man." Ieyil turned as she spoke and slammed a bony foot into Lem's chest.

He fired at her.

The impact rocked the Necro Queen back even as he toppled down, clutching his chest.

Nightshade hit Ieyil again.

Flynt froze, simply watching. They would fail. She saw that. Past the horde, Nekolai had an air shield surrounding him and Milisade. He swung out with his sword at as many creatures as he could. They shattered in bursts of air, dozens already at his feet, skulls shattering and bits flying to join the fortress of air he'd built around his queen. He looked stronger than she'd ever seen him. But the critters kept coming.

Her frontmost lich had been overrun, lying pinned beneath critters.

Lem hadn't risen yet.

All Flynt would have to do is just let Ieyil win. She could let this decide itself, step aside and let death walk unabated. But Azucena's emeralds were buried in satin at her wrist—the Death-aspect there spoke differently—spoke of life lost too soon, of pain.

Ieyil hadn't managed to find a life within the Coil, but Flynt still could.

She wouldn't step aside. Flynt raised the knife—it had killed Ieyil once. Maybe it could again. That was its only purpose.

Flynt sent her liches to hold the crowd back and then ran up past Lem. She lifted the knife. Ieyil's eyes met Flynt's as she tossed Nightshade back. Flynt hesitated.

She was fighting the one person who accepted her—the one person who had never pushed her away.

Her arm dropped.

Ieyil smiled, purple gathered at her hands, and she turned to Lem, stepping on bony feet. Flynt knew that power. Death. She would kill him, and not just him, all of them.

As Ieyil reached out, Flynt slammed the blade of the knife into the Necro Queen's neck, driving down.

A scream filled her mind and then the room. Ieyil reached back and ripped the knife out. She threw it to the ground. "I would build a world for you, and this is my payment."

"Not for me," Flynt said, trying her best to hide her trembling. The dagger should have worked. "I believe in your dream as it was... but you've warped it. I won't let you kill them."

"Then I'll kill all of you," Ieyil said.

Lem rose behind her. His chest was burned with necrotic flesh in the shape of her foot. This time, the burst of Chaos was bigger; it encased her.

Nightshade's energy still surged inside Flynt, making her feel powerful, but there was nowhere to place that power.

A rush of deep purple melted the orange energy, and Ieyil stepped out, facing Lem. "You, I don't like. You die first."

"Let's see how that works for you," he said. Orange gathered again. With Nightshade's boost, he was nearly invincible. But *nearly* wasn't good enough. He would go down.

Flynt pulled one of the liches to her, meaning to send it at Ieyil, to defend Lem. Then she knew. They'd been animated with some sort of Life-spark before. Likely, the Life in Ieyil was the same energy that had animated them—after all, Flynt had used a bit of hers to bring these three. Which meant, somewhere in Ieyil, was a true Life-spark.

If only Flynt could isolate that spark. It was what her mind had fought for earlier. Drinking that Life-spark nearly killed her —but maybe there was a way to avoid the poison.

She could if...

Flynt grabbed Nightshade and whispered as low as she could, "Boost Ieyil. Now."

Nightshade froze for just a moment.

Please, Flynt thought. *Trust me.*

Chapter 25

Then Nightshade lunged toward Ieyil, hand extended. Aspect flared.

Flynt ducked low and rolled over the ground to pick up the knife. It had been meant to kill a living Ieyil. So that was what she'd give it.

Ieyil laughed, purple now encasing her body. Lem hit her with something, but it rolled off, hitting the ground at her feet where the dirt turned momentarily to lava, then hardened into a pure-black rock. The black coated Ieyil's feet like boots.

Yet the Necro Queen turned away from Lem. Flynt knew how she must have been feeling: invincible. Good. Let her. Flynt could feel the Death-aspect in Ieyil. It burned like a heaving mass of molten metal in her mind. And from this, she knew exactly where the Life-spark was—the one place she couldn't feel—a cavity in that liquid burning.

Ieyil's hands flicked out and a purple mist slammed into both Lem and Nightshade. "Your puny efforts won't save you," Ieyil said.

Flynt lifted the knife, light in her hand now, as if it knew what she intended. And she struck down, throwing her body weight into the blow, directly between the shoulder blades. Feeling through all the Death, she aimed for the cavity. She shoved her own Death-aspect through the blade, hitting that Life-spark.

The twining and interlocking Death-aspect in the air exploded. Flynt flew back, trying to pull in all the Aspect and turn it to her command. For a moment, all she saw were the twists of souls in the air. Cyniel looked down at her from the writhing Aspect and smiled. Then her vision cleared.

Ieyil's bones had crumpled to the dirt and all her critters lay, no more than yellowed bone on the earthen floor. Flynt's heart pinched at the sight, but she didn't have time to mourn. Lem was hurt.

Flynt pressed up on her arms. Nekolai and Milisade stood together at the opposite end of the room. Aside from the ashen look of terror and grief on her face, Milisade appeared completely unharmed. Nekolai held a bleeding arm and several claw marks and teeth marks bled from his chest and legs—but he was standing.

Lem was not.

Nightshade stood on shaky legs, protected by her Life-aspect.

Flynt shoved to her feet and took the few steps to Lem. He wasn't moving.

"Move aside," Nightshade said softly.

Flynt turned with a snarl, but Nightshade only regarded her softly.

"He isn't dead. I can boost Life-spark. If you want him to remain not dead, let me by."

Moving aside was the hardest thing she'd ever done, but she did it. Her ankle, where a creature had bitten her, resisted her attempts at movement, but her heart resisted harder.

Nightshade knelt at Lem's side, her hands glowing softly.

Flynt knelt and watched, not wanting to breathe. If he died, she'd as good as killed him. She'd let Ieyil attack. And she'd used him like bait. She could have acted faster.

Milisade knelt beside her, setting one hand over hers. Flynt accepted the comfort, but her eyes remained on Lem. Ieyil's bruising marks stood out on his skin.

Lem gave a gasp of breath and curled inward with a groan. Flynt took in a shaking breath and smiled down at him.

Milisade squeezed Flynt's hand. But when she spoke, it was

in a calm voice to Nightshade. "We must destroy the bones. Will he be able to do it?"

The Diethyrian lifted her hands and leaned back. As before when she'd done too much, she looked gray and colorless. "Yes. Give him a few minutes."

Nekolai stood over the body. "What happened?"

"Ask Flynt," Nightshade said. "I don't understand."

Flynt shook her head. Instead of answering, she moved over to Lem. "I'm sorry. I was slow."

He turned to her, and she knew he was okay as soon as she saw his smile. "You should work on that."

"Why didn't you manipulate to protect yourself?"

"Chaos makes an awful shield... I wasn't about to redirect anything. I'll die someday—today is as good a day as any."

"Don't you dare," Flynt said. She leaned over him and kissed him gently.

To Flynt's surprise, it really did only take a few minutes for Lem to be on his feet again.

"This works best if the bones are animated," Lem said. "Can you do it, Flynt?"

She nodded. Flynt crouched beside the bones, lifting them with a wisp of Death-aspect. Her hand hovered up by Ieyil's. There was still a trace of the Necro in them and that trace was angry but also sad. So achingly sad and betrayed that it hurt to touch them, even with her mind. But she deserved to feel that. Flynt reached up to hold the bones of Ieyil's hand. Perhaps somewhere, Ieyil would feel this small comfort.

She freed Nekolai for me. Before Ieyil had been driven insane, she had been truly driven to improve the life of Death-magi. There was good in her that no one but Flynt and Milisade would remember. So Flynt held her bony hand.

A glow gathered around Lem, slower this time. Flynt remembered the bones around Ieyil's chest, which had melted and fallen to dust. All of her was to go that direction.

"Please," came the soft voice in Flynt's mind, an echo of the power Ieyil had held but still her. Perhaps a vision of the Ieyil she'd once been before her power had found her. "Please, not this."

Lem reached out and placed his hand on Ieyil's chest. The bone started to dissolve, the effect flaring outward. First the ribs, then the hip bones, then the shoulders, along the arms and legs, up the neck to the base of the skull.

Soon all of her would be gone.

And that wasn't fair. It wasn't right. *She was my sister*, Flynt thought.

With a twitch of power, Flynt released a few finger bones from her Death-aspect, letting the bones fall into her lap. With a careful movement, Flynt tucked the bones into her boot. The top of the skull disappeared and all of Ieyil, except for those finger bones, lay in a pile of dust.

Lem turned his back.

Flynt stood to find Milisade staring at her. Flynt winced— of course the queen had seen. She knew.

The queen moved to stand over the dust pile and looked down, then over at Flynt, and then she moved purposefully back to Nekolai. "There was a time when she was the best person I knew. This is a sad ending... I find I cannot celebrate, though I welcome that you will."

"Damn right," Lem said.

"Eventually," Nightshade said, still looking drained and half-dead. "First, we get out of this tomb and call for an Earth-magister to seal it, and an Alchemist to create more sigils for it. We must ensure she does not rise again. Whatever she once was, we know what she became."

Flynt watched Milisade, expecting her to say something.

Instead, the queen walked toward the door. "Then let us go."

Flynt followed, terrified, confused, and relieved. This chapter was over, and it was a chapter that Flynt was excited to close, but she was unsure what came next or what Milisade would demand.

Chapter 26

Back in the safety of the circle of trees just outside the Chaos-gate, they set up camp. They chose a stone courtyard in the center of several old crypts—a place far enough from the soul tree that the cries were only a dull roar in Flynt's blood. Milisade and Lem went to inspect the tree, leaving Nightshade to rest against one of the tombs and Nekolai and Flynt to set up a fire.

She was exhausted and Ieyil's finger bones poked into her ankle—luckily, not the ankle damaged in the fight, but she didn't dare move the things lest someone see.

Once the fire was built, Nekolai sat down on a stone step and Flynt sat across from him, stretching out her legs. Cyniel's bones were strapped to Nekolai's back, and he took that moment to carefully remove them and set them next to him on the step as if this were a third person resting in the firelight.

"Thank you, Flynt," Nekolai said. "For my life twice over and for Queen Milisade's. She told you why she needed to be here, but... I was scared she would be taken from us."

He said "us," but she wondered how much he meant "me." "Hopefully, it's over this time." And she meant it, despite the bones. She wanted the fight to be over—perhaps Ieyil's remaining bones could rest peacefully with Flynt.

"Sitting here with you feels wrong," Nekolai said. He turned his blue eyes on the wrapped bones. "He was always with us and to be with you without him... I suppose it will always feel a bit wrong—like a lost limb."

"Always," she agreed.

"Shall we rebury him while they figure out what to do with the tree? His bones deserve the honor."

Flynt stared into the fire, thinking of the cool dirt of this world—thinking also of the bones in her boot. Back on the Coil, her room in the Death compound was walled in bone and they spoke to her. She'd saved Ieyil's bones. She couldn't just let Cyniel slip away from her. "No. Now that I know my powers, I will keep him with me. Bones do not replace him, but his spirit clings."

"He deserves more respect than to be made into a table or a wall decoration."

"There is no more respect than to be cared for. I don't believe you can possibly know. Returning to the soil is lovely, but... Cyniel would have chosen to remain with me if he were given the choice."

Nekolai touched the thin cloth, dragging his fingers over it. "I cannot argue with that. He would have done anything for you. Seeing you now—seeing you fight and struggle, I begin to see why."

"Oh?" Flynt smiled and leaned forward on her knees. "You didn't before?"

Nekolai grinned back. "I did not. And I will apologize the moment you tell me that you thought any better of me."

"Then we both admit that Cyniel had better taste than we knew."

Nekolai lifted the bones. Carefully, he stood and brought them over to Flynt. "I am proud to call you 'friend'—and I know that Cyniel's spirit can rest peacefully. Call on me if you need me. At any time."

"For Cyn's sake."

"No. Because you have earned the loyalty yourself." Nekolai touched a hand to his chest and bowed his head. She'd seen him give this sign of respect many times, but never to her. "Now, excuse me. I am exhausted."

Flynt watched him walk away, hardly daring to breathe. Nekolai meant such promises and statements. He did not speak lightly.

With him safe and Ieyil gone, all that was left was seeing if Milisade could deliver on her promise to ease Flynt as a Necro-equitem into society. Well, that, and telling Azucena she'd failed yet again to honor her request.

Reminding her of yet another thing that wasn't finished, Lem headed back into camp looking worse for wear. He came up to her and Flynt went to hold him, but he held out a hand.

"Milisade wants to see you and I need to go to sleep. This feels like the worst hangover ever."

Flynt reached down to the bones, feeling the residue of Cyniel like a caress over her fingers. Lem pushing her away wasn't new, but it still stung. What did she have to do to get through to him?

As he went to lie down near Nekolai, Flynt walked away from the courtyard toward Queen Milisade by the soul tree.

The queen stood at the edge of the circle of trees around the gate. Flynt drew up beside the queen and waited. Queen Milisade simply stared up at the tree, saying nothing.

"You saw me take them and still haven't mentioned it," Flynt said. "Are you planning to take them from me?"

"Had I not seen, I would have known from your mind," Milisade said, still looking at the souls twisting on the trunk of the tree.

So no answer to the question. Flynt decided to move past that for a moment. "Why not stop me?"

Milisade twisted at the collar of her uniform. "Hope. As long as her bones exist, her spirit remains tied to this plain. I can hope, deep inside, that somehow, she'll find happiness. And while you have them—and I know you do—the bones will be observed. But this is not why I wanted you here."

"Oh?" Flynt didn't point out that Milisade hadn't called her out for taking those little bits of Ieyil, but she thought it. Loudly.

"Captain Lem tells me you will be returning to the Coil with me rather than remaining on the *Seer's Sword*."

Flynt gasped. "No? He said that? He told you that just

now?"

"Oh." Milisade pressed a finger to her temple. "I'll leave it to the two of you to discuss that—later. Taking the tree down comes first."

Flynt tried to focus on the screaming tree. "You know how to destroy it?"

"No. But cutting it down helps us achieve our goals with you. The people will want a demonstration of power. Simple enough."

"But it's not my power."

"They do not know that, and we must explain it somehow."

"Cutting it down will free the souls?"

"Most likely not. We don't know, but it will allow us to bring the wood back to the Coil to be studied. We'll find a way. There is time yet. Nekolai and Lem will bring it down in the morning."

Why did the queen need her for this?

"You are very impatient. I need you to call enough critters to carry the wood back to the base camp. Will that be an issue with the wood being what it is?"

"No. There are souls in there, but it isn't Death-aspect holding them, so it won't disrupt my manipulations." That was really it? Should she call her critters now?

"Well, that and the bones in your boot. Keep them safe, and know I will destroy them if you die before me. You should do the same if I die—we are the only insurance that they don't somehow do more damage. Agreed?"

"Why would you even let me keep them?"

The eerie Aspect light from the Chaos-gate and tree lit a timid smile on Milisade's face. "You've saved my life twice now; you have my friendship and loyalty. I am trusting you—it is not an honor I offer to many."

***

Flynt slept alone and woke the same way. Despite a newfound kinship Flynt hadn't expected, Lem still kept a barrier up between them. It was getting really old. He and Nekolai were already over at the tree and Milisade sat on a blanket, watching them. The sun was barely up—people really shouldn't have been about so early. Especially Lem, whom she'd never seen up early on the ship.

They looked close to finishing felling the tree, and Flynt figured an intrusion wouldn't be overly annoying. She was about to go over to him by the soul tree and bring the subject of her leaving the *Seer's Sword* up when Nightshade called out to her.

"May I have a word?" Nightshade asked.

Flynt nodded, moving over to stand with her under the branches of the trees. It was odd to think that the soul tree would be coming down. "I guess we all have time. What's on your mind?"

"Back with Ieyil, I doubted you."

"I know it must have sounded insane. If I'd had time to explain, I would have."

"That isn't my point. More, I realize that I, too, have left you to make assumptions with a frightening prospect lain out before you. I asked for your trust, but unlike you, I never made the truth clear."

"You mean about Lem and… killing him?"

"Yes. I have let you understand only that, but that is hardly the entirety. Emotions and personal connections are difficult for me to understand, but that doesn't mean that I don't develop them."

"You believe you owe me?"

"This isn't only about you. What I left you to see on your own, and shouldn't have, is that by all rights, I should have killed Lem when he created that tree. I had no way of knowing he'd get himself under control. If I'd followed my orders, he'd be dead. Queen Milisade chose me for my loyalty, but also my ability to see things dispassionately. Besides the Defenders and Milisade, the two of you are the only family that I have. I'm glad he saved you and glad he lives."

"Family?" What did she mean by that word?

"I believe that is the closest word to my feelings, yes. Perhaps 'team'? Those words always confuse me but know that I am not harboring ill-intent."

"We're a family?"

"Would you say differently?"

Flynt gave her a swift hug, which Nightshade did not reciprocate. "I would like nothing more. Thank you."

"Now… Milisade wishes for you to join her." Nightshade pointed over Flynt's shoulder toward the others.

This was the second time that Milisade had summoned her away from a conversation, but she was the queen and Flynt supposed it was her right. When she turned, the two men had taken a break. Nekolai had wandered out of sight and Lem stood facing the tree they were in the process of chopping.

"You wanted me?" Flynt said. *Again*, she thought.

"Yes, again. I had this thought, perhaps something you could research back on the Coil."

Flynt tried not to glare at the queen. Their last conversation still stung. Why was Lem trying to fob her off on another ship? Part of Flynt stubbornly insisted that she had no intention of going to the Coil unless it was aboard the *Seer's Sword*. Yet Milisade had made a promise that had yet to be delivered and the only way to be accepted again into the fabric of Coil society was to go there.

"As long as bones exist, a spirit is tied to this plain, but what I did not think of until I was sleeping last night was something that Ieyil studied. Theoretically, resurrection, true resurrection, is possible from bones—I don't believe this would work unless there was a full set of bones, but we must discover this."

Flynt scrunched her brow and waited for her mind to catch up to this new topic. Because if Ieyil could be brought back from the few bones Flynt had preserved, the bones needed to disappear.

"Except resurrection isn't possible at all," Flynt said.

Lem glanced over at them from the wood, sweat coating

his brow.

"No, it's not to my knowledge," Milisade said, lowering her gaze to Flynt's boot—though the bones were tucked in her pocket now. "Or I've never seen it successfully done. Ieyil tried it once—she had a spell and talked for months about all the things she meant to do with it."

"So, a Necro can perform a resurrection?" Flynt asked.

Lem was now glaring over at them.

"Ieyil swore that it was possible, but it took all the Aspects in conjunction. No one believed her and when she tried the manipulation, it failed." The queen's back was to Lem. However, his glower deepened. She dropped her voice lower, leaning away from him slightly. "However, now that I've seen how close she came on herself, I wonder if it isn't possible after all."

"Stop!" Lem barked as he strode over to them. He grabbed Flynt and pulled her back. "Don't feed Flynt that crap."

Milisade sighed. She couldn't exactly explain what the conversation was really about without mentioning the bones that Flynt had taken. "It's only speculation."

"And Flynt's holding the bones of her husband!" Lem said. "Resurrection doesn't work."

Flynt recoiled from his vehemence before the implications hit her. "A person could think that you're jealous."

Lem dropped her arm.

Milisade dipped her head. "I have stepped in the center of something. I will withdraw." Then she spoke directly to Lem. "Weigh your words—you may regret your choices."

Chapter 27

After Milisade moved away, Flynt spun on Lem. "What was that about?! First, I hear from her that you're fobbing me off again and then you start... What was that?! What do you care if I try to resurrect my husband?"

"Wasn't that clear?"

"No. No. And no! Especially since you're apparently still sending me to the Coil."

"Then I'll explain." He folded his arms and his smile remained conspicuously absent. "Resurrection isn't possible. Looking for something that doesn't exist is wasting your life and it'll just break your heart."

"And how is that your concern? All you want is to have me gone."

"You're impossible to talk to," Lem said.

Flynt grabbed his arm. Death-aspect swirled inside her, demanding release. If only he could see how beautiful it was, how... *pure* the other side of the veil could be. He feared so much, but they were such silly fears. The Aspect swirling in her told her to show him, to let him view Death with unclouded eyes.

"Let go, Necro," he said, pulling back from her. "You don't understand anything that's happening right now."

"No. *You* don't." The Death-aspect wouldn't stay inside any longer. It leaked from her fingers. She reached out to touch his chest where Ieyil had struck him. He'd felt Death there. How could he not see its beauty? His Life-spark hovered inside, waiting to satiate her. She wanted him. She wanted him to understand. It all seemed so simple.

The taste of Death in her mouth longed for company. Flynt reached inside him, encircling that precious spark. She tasted it on her lips, on her tongue.

He was honey-sweet, and the hunger rushed over her— she could drain him and be full. She could keep him with her always and soar together.

Lem didn't fight, though she saw the hollowing in his face as she pulled his Life through her fingers. He didn't fight her. The abyss lurked, opening wide, welcoming her.

Obsidian finger-cuffs pressed into his flesh, and it was that blackness and the imagined snap of the chain that brought her struggling back.

Flynt dropped her hand; the laughter from Ieyil's bones was clear in her mind. "Ayal... I..." That was Death-madness. That was what her fate would be someday. That was the end that she could not escape.

Lem gripped her shoulder, steadying himself, but also, perhaps unintentionally, offering some comfort. Even now, he was not afraid to touch her. Why? She could have killed him.

"I didn't mean to," Flynt stuttered breathlessly. "It just... In my head, it wasn't even like I was hurting you. I don't know."

"All those who deal in Aspect pay a price," Lem said, his voice shaky but amused. "This is my point, has been all along. We are dangerous for each other. Either Death-madness will take you and you will drain me—yes, I know, without ever meaning any harm—or I will slip and one of my manipulations will open a pit of lava beneath you or..."

"I've already forgiven you for that."

"True. And how did you say it? You forgave me ahead of time? I will always forgive you, Flynt. But that doesn't change what we are."

"You're sending me to the Coil."

"No. We are all going to the Coil. I thought it best if you went with Milisade—you need to bring Cyniel's bones back and the soul wood. I can't travel with the wood. Milisade plans to blame you for it. Only Death-magi will know the difference and they won't speak if you tell them not to."

"'Blame' me, but…"

"You are coming out to the world. I'm not. So all the miracles get to be yours."

"And then I'll join you on the *Seer's Sword*?"

"That, I don't know. I need to think, and I need to do it without you around. I can reconcile myself to us killing each other… though it isn't what I'd prefer."

"I'd *prefer* not to go Death-mad. I'd prefer many things that aren't possible. But no matter what, we will die—our gifts will do that even without each other. I'd rather be with you when that day comes."

"Your death isn't my ultimate worry. What I can't abide is that I will end up destroying others to save you. It's the tree that I fear… What if it had been the Defenders, Nekolai, Milisade, Nightshade that I trapped in there? And it *could* have been."

"Ayal! I think you're just afraid to admit you're wrong."

"Well, that's an interesting theory."

"Back when we were trapped, you could have saved me. You didn't. If you need to, you will let me die. You've proven that."

Lem glanced over at the stacks of wood and then back at her. Some of the stress had left his features.

"Any more excuses?" Flynt asked.

With one hand, Lem reached over to grab her waist and pull her closer. "I prefer action."

She kissed him.

When their lips parted, he held her tightly, staring down into her face. "We'd have to sort some issues out."

"I do my best to be exclusive and you… forgive me if I slip. Beyond that, let's wing it. Surprises are more fun."

"I don't want to ask you to—"

"As Milisade pointed out to me, I'm pretty sure with full knowledge of what she was saying, you aren't *asking* me to change. That's why I'm willing. You're whom I want; the rest…"

221

She shrugged. "We'll work it out."

He grinned. "Done."

"Except..." Flynt stretched up to kiss him again. Having tasted his Life, she found an odd reflection of it on his skin. Like an electric honey. "I retract all promises of exclusivity if you don't actually take me to bed."

Lem grinned, his hand moving lower on her back. He glanced back toward camp. "We should probably wait until we don't have an audience."

"Plenty of private nooks around the tombs if you're going to be a prude about it." Flynt brushed her lips over his, lingering there. But a kiss wasn't enough. It wasn't where she wanted this to end and for the first time, she really didn't think he'd object.

After a breathless moment, Lem deepened the kiss, moving her toward the marginal shelter of a stand of trees. As they moved, their hands explored. Each movement of his hands swept through Flynt, blinding and beautiful. Nothing in the world seemed to exist except the captain.

"Like this?" he whispered.

"It's a start." Flynt let her hands slide over his massive arms down to his hands. She moved them up to cover her breasts.

"You this bossy with all your toys?"

"You're not a toy; it's different. This is different."

"Good."

And then their mouths were busy with other things.

The air was bitterly cold on her bare flesh, but his body was warm.

Maybe waiting for sex had had a few positive points if this was how it felt when finally achieved.

Chapter 28

On the walk back to base camp, Lem held Flynt's hand. Not for long. Maybe five minutes, but long enough to prove to her that he wasn't regretting what they'd done and that he wasn't looking to hide their connection. It was also enough to imply he wasn't fond of public displays.

Odd. She hadn't known that. Retroactively it might explain some of the times he pulled away from her. As much as she knew about him, it occurred to her that she knew next to nothing about what a relationship with him would be like. She loved him, but he wasn't family. He wasn't home.

She glanced at where one of her creations carried Cyniel's bones. There was her family.

What if things didn't last with Lem, or she needed support he couldn't give? Her heart was too involved to turn back. Did falling in love always feel like teetering on the edge of an abyss? No wonder it was called "falling," not "settling" or "flying."

Flynt needed someone there to catch her. Again, her eyes flicked to Cyniel. Nekolai would want to rebury him, but Flynt had the final say and without question, she knew she'd be bringing him with her. Even if Milisade's rumors of resurrection led to nothing, Flynt felt better with him nearby.

Lem started whistling and Nightshade's mouth tightened in disapproval. Nekolai strode ahead of them, no emotion visible in his perfectly erect posture. Walking in the middle, Milisade glanced back toward Lem and Flynt and flashed a small smile.

This was going to be a very long walk. And surely now that

they were hauling hunks of Chaos-torn wood, they could risk calling for a pickup. But Flynt wasn't about to press.

She flicked her finger to her ear to turn on her comm. They weren't in a battle situation anymore, so there was no need to have it off.

A message waited from the mercenaries she'd hired to find Azucena's arm bones.

Flynt's heart leaped. It had to be good news. Everything was going so well. She had Cyniel's bones, rumors of resurrection, and Lem had finally come to his senses. She'd even be able to come out as Necro back on the Coil.

Everything was going so well. The unexpected message had to be good—maybe they'd found something despite the message about closing the investigation.

Flynt used a flick of her eyes to open the retinal interface and then projected the screen out like a visor in front of her eyes. She opened the message, her heart pounding.

A bill.

They'd sent a bill!

"Ayal find them," she cursed.

Lem's hand touched her lower back, fingers settling as if they belonged. "Something wrong?"

"Just... Ugh... The company I hired to find Azucena's arm bones gave up. This is the second firm to tell me that it can't be done and now they're charging me for their failure."

Lem chuckled.

Flynt glared at him. She'd forgotten how annoying he could be. "You realize you're an asshole?"

"Yes. I also realize that you're hiring this out to mercenaries when you're friends with the queen. Did you know things work better if you use your brain?"

"Careful. Monogamy means you rely on me for sex."

He flashed an irritating grin. "I also know you're a Breeder and if you withhold, I can outlast you."

"I'm going to walk away now," Flynt said.

"Before you slap me? What fun is that?"

Flynt's annoyance fled. Something about his smile had a way of worming into her. "It was you who suggested that I talk to the queen."

"You do what I say now?" He winked at her. "I need to test that."

Before either she attacked or jumped on him, Flynt picked up her pace and headed to where the queen walked. "Queen Milisade?"

"Yes, dear? Are you done aggressively flirting?" Milisade's face remained completely neutral, but her tone sounded amused.

"For the moment. I have a favor to ask."

"Then ask it."

"I need to acquire some bones—a friend's bones. She sold her arm before joining the Death school and now she's..." *Dead.* But Flynt left the word unstated. Milisade would know anyhow.

"Indeed. I recall mentions of her. You realize that those bones may be long gone—ground to make tea?"

Flynt flinched. She had always known that was the fate of the bones but thinking about it wasn't pleasant. "Not a lot them, but I've hit a dead end searching and... could you help?"

"You *are* maturing." Milisade tilted her head. If she'd been wearing her blonde queen wig, it would have fallen charmingly in her face. Her short, brown hair barely moved. "Yes. I'll see it done when we return to the Coil."

"That easily?"

"I'll speak with the Coil."

Flynt wasn't sure what exactly that meant. "I know the Coil and the queen communicate, but how does that work? How does the Coil know anything?"

"The Coil is a living being—anything created from all the Aspects of Creation is. People tend to think of Coils as machines because it's easier, but the Coil has a mind just like you do."

"Gates are created with all seven aspects."

Milisade chuckled. "Smart child. They are alive, too—they aren't sentient... More like bees. They have a purpose, and they instinctively serve that purpose. Yet they are alive."

"But the Coil can't talk to anyone but you?"

"Correct."

"How would it know where to find the bones?"

"There is always a trail. The Coil knows every breath taken, every door opened, every transaction. The difficulty is knowing which actions relate to any given event or goal. This should be simple for it to analyze."

"Why give me this lesson now?"

"In part because you asked now. The rest... Once you come out officially as my Necro, the queens of all the other Coils will be looking for a way to take you down. You and I cannot afford secrets if we are both to survive this."

Both? "You're in danger."

"Always. But it's a danger that I've chosen." Milisade glanced fully into Flynt's face and something of the queen's age showed in her eyes. "I have no more precious assets than you and Captain Lem. I have waited longer than you know to find you. The risk is worthwhile."

"And if they kill me?"

"They will want to, unless I can demonstrate that we are better off with you alive. I intend to do so."

"How?"

"I have a plan." The queen lifted her hand and motioned Flynt away. "Can you see what's bothering Nekolai?"

Flynt glanced over; he did seem even more stiff than normal. Of course, the queen would know about what was bothering him already. And if Milisade thought Flynt should be the one to talk to him, that was probably the case. Flynt hurried forward toward her friend, though she promised herself she'd question the queen more at some point. Half of her knew she was lying.

Nekolai slowed slightly to let her catch him and before she could speak, he did. "I needed to speak with you privately."

Good. This would be easier than she'd thought. "Yeah?"

"During the battle with Ieyil..." he started, but he trailed off. His hand twisted on the knife hilt at his belt.

Flynt bit her lip. If he asked about Ieyil's fingerbones, she was in deep trouble.

"I used Aspect in unexpected ways," he said at last. "I keep replaying it, trying to make sense of the battle, and I can't."

A sigh escaped Flynt's lips. "You did what was needed to protect the queen."

Nekolai leveled a piercing glare at her. "Aspect doesn't work that way. I should not have been able to create a shield powerful enough to protect us or to hold the shield and attack the creatures that got too close. Failure is the only logical result for a Magi playing with Magister-level manipulations." He looked pale and frightened.

Flynt spoke slowly, trying to control her natural edge. "Maybe you were miscategorized."

"No."

It was rare for a Magi's skill to grow or shrink, but not unheard of. Why was he freaking out so much?

"I heard my Aspect speak," he said.

That never happened. In fact, from her studies, Flynt was pretty sure it only happened to Masters or Haeres... and there hadn't been an Haeres since Ieyil. "So you wanted to what, confess?"

"No. I need a favor from you. Don't tell Milisade anything you noted me doing in battle. She can ignore what she hears from minds, but not mouths. By traditions, I should be released from service and returned to school to retrain."

"And you don't want to leave the queen."

He nodded. "All I ask is time. I will do the correct thing."

"Why tell me, just to ask me not to tell?"

"Because you or your captain would have figured it out on your own."

"And Nightshade?" No way would she keep her mouth shut.

"She didn't know I was a Magi to begin with."

Flynt giggled. "I'm not you. I have no issue with secrets."

Nekolai's shoulders slumped. "I owe you a good turn. But about Cyniel..."

"I'm not leaving Cyn's bones here. I want him with me. The first time I buried him, I didn't know what I was or what I could do. This time... I can hear his voice." *Maybe someday I can bring him back*, she thought, but she kept that to herself.

"Having his bones is not the same as having him," Nekolai said, his face hard. Something warred under the surface. "Let him go, Flynt. Move on with your life."

"Sometimes I imagine he's with me, advising me. He wasn't supposed to die. It isn't fair that he's gone."

"Fair is for children."

"No. He died. He'll never see what I became or what you did. He'll never learn all the amazing things I'm learning about the past. Imagine if he'd gotten a hold of these?" She held up her finger-cuffs. "And learned Ieyil's history? He loved that stuff."

Nekolai gave a stiff nod. "So you'll tell his bones."

"Please, don't fight me on this. I don't want to have to argue with you."

"I believe this is a mistake, but I won't fight you. This is your right as his widow, Flynt. And for the record, I miss him every day, every hour." With that, Nekolai resumed his pace and Flynt allowed herself to be left behind.

And now to face the Coil.

Chapter 29

Bone song surrounded Flynt. It echoed in her frame and rippled in her blood. As she rolled over in the soft, woven blankets, Flynt decided that this was a prime way to wake up. She'd missed the Coil and the Death Compound in her time on the Seer's Sword.

There was no natural light in her Coil suite—most Death-magisters didn't want to see outward, she suspected, or have to witness the desecration of their own flesh as they shriveled up. But the windows on the south-facing walls were all the guidance she needed as she stretched, then turned on an overhanging chandelier made of deer bone and electric wiring. The yellowed light brought all of her bedchamber into focus.

Most Coil suites didn't have fully walled-off rooms—preferring open air spaces. This was the first place on the Coil Flynt had seen with shut-off chambers for sleeping, cooking, and bathing, leaving only the eating and living areas connected in the central area. And there was no one to share it with. After the tightness of the *Seer's Sword*, Flynt appreciated the privacy, and the rooms seemed spacious enough.

She missed Nightshade as a roommate, but her new roommate was pleasant as well. Dead people were very quiet.

Flynt snuggled for a moment into the warm blankets. She'd have to thank Lem for talking her into returning here, even if he had yet to join her. Her true nature couldn't be hidden any longer and if she was going to be the sole face for Necro-equitems, she'd better learn more about them.

Ieyil was gone, but Flynt wasn't ready to let the woman's dream die. The Coils could be a more welcoming place for those who worked in Death-aspect. Flynt could make that happen, but only by proving herself and her desire to work with the Coil.

Time to go be a Necro-equitem and perform for the crowd. She rolled over in bed and dropped her feet to the floor.

Before standing, Flynt turned to the soft chair in the corner to say her good mornings. Cyniel sat there, leaned against the wall with his arms propped up on the chair arms. Clothed in a fresh uniform, hood up over his skull, he seemed to be waiting. It took only a tiny amount of Death-aspect to keep his bones joined and it was worth it to feel his bone-song twist with the others. He hadn't spoken to her since the Bone Yard, but she could be patient.

"Good morning," she said. She grabbed her glove from beside the bed and slipped it on. Now that she wasn't required to use the satin to hide herself, she found she liked it—enjoyed the feel of Azucena's emeralds over her wrist and liked the feel of velvet over bone when she touched human skin.

Flynt considered getting dressed but opted for a simple robe of black silk, the seams threaded with tiny bones, and fastened it closed with an acid-green belt.

Milisade meant to introduce her officially to the public that evening, and she'd have to prepare, but first, a decent morning drink. There was no fresh guarana stocked on the *Seer's Sword* and she'd missed her spiced guaranas.

Flynt opened the bed-chamber door and entered the living area.

"I was starting to believe that you'd never wake up."

Flynt spun to the kitchen and the speaker. "Lem! You made it."

He sat at the yellowed table on one of the many equally yellowed chairs. "Was there somewhere else to be today? This is a lot of bone. The chairs aren't comfortable. Given that you aren't likely to go blind soon, why not get some normal furniture?"

"Just to annoy you," Flynt said, then she dashed over to

him and leaned in to kiss his lips. He tasted of oranges and honey. She wondered if that honey taste would ever leave or if, having tasted the Life-spark inside him, she'd always sense it this way.

"You ready to parade yourself in front of millions?" he asked.

"I wish you were walking out there with me."

"No. I have to stay in the shadows—that's fine by me. You take the spotlight, and you're welcome to it." He stood and grabbed her waist, pulling her closer to him.

Flynt turned her face to the door. There was an energy lock on it, and no one but she was supposed to be able to get in without her permission. "Did you break my door?"

"Define 'break.' A little basic Chaos and I convinced the locks that I was the key. It works perfectly for me."

"So I need to replace them."

"Definitely. I mean, it is possible they will melt the next person to touch them." He grinned. "But considering how dead these halls are, that didn't seem like much of a risk."

"Shh. I need to get ready soon, so... we should use the time we have. Breakfast or bed?"

His eyes raked over her body. "That's not a serious question, is it?"

"I don't know. You seem remarkably capable of not sleeping with me. It's a flaw, but I forgive you."

Lem laughed and in one motion, scooped her up and carried her to the bedroom. He dropped her on the bed. Flynt reached and tugged him down to her. The bed was better suited to two people than her bed on the ship had ever been—big enough to roll around on. They kissed. Despite her words, there wasn't any big rush, except the steady hunger of her body—which spoke quite loudly.

Gaining the upper position, Flynt straddled him and shoved his hands down to the mattress. Then she sat up and removed her black robe.

"Flynt?" Lem said, his eyes caught not on her, but on

something behind her.

"You're supposed to look at me."

"That's difficult with your husband on the chair behind you."

Flynt sighed. Trust her to find a man with so many rules about sex! "It's just his bones."

"I... It's disrespectful." He sat up and kissed her before pulling back. "Maybe breakfast would be a better option."

"Oh, shush! Cyniel wouldn't have minded even alive. And I swear to Ayal, I can make you forget all about him." Then, seeing the discomfort on his face, Flynt moved back and gave him a kiss on the nose. "Or we could just use the living room... The couches aren't comprised of skeletons."

∞ ∞ ∞

Leaving Lem on her couch, Flynt went into the bedroom and pulled on a robe. Then she headed out into the hallway. Time to visit Azucena. She'd been putting it off since she'd come back because she didn't exactly have great news to give her friend.

Flynt walked the nearly empty halls of the Death School. Someday, she would be able to help the Death-magi so that the Aspect didn't drain them. That was her duty as a Necro-equitem, to help support the others. But for now, each glimpse of their drained faces only made her feel guilty.

Ieyil had tried to save them. Sure, her way had been insane, but at least it had been something. Flynt hadn't even managed to save the one Death-magi she'd sworn to protect... and now she was off to inform Azucena yet again that there was nothing she could do.

Yet.

The queen had promised to help. Maybe she would.

Flynt reached the locked door that separated her from Bone River. Even through the obstruction, Flynt felt Ayal's pure energy. There was too much Death in that river to feel anything else when near it. Even as a Necro-equitem, the river had melted the flesh and sinew off of Flynt's arm when she'd touched it.

The door opened, shoved by Flynt's will or that of the unseen Ayal.

Inside was all blackness, the only difference being that the energy of the river bisecting the room and filling the empty void of space on the far side of the chamber was darker. The bones that floated on the river of energy seemed to glow.

This time, Flynt didn't approach. She stood in the doorway and called to Azucena. After a time, a shivering apparition appeared at the river's edge. Death had erased Azucena's red skin, but not the subtle stripes that decorated her flesh, nor had it given her back her hand.

"You don't have it," Azucena said softly.

"I'm still looking. The queen has offered to help."

Azucena's dead eyes sparkled with a childish joy. "The queen knows I exist? She's helping me?"

Flynt nodded. Though she doubted that was how Milisade saw it. If the queen's attention made Azucena so happy, let the ghost be the sole recipient of that attention.

"You look better," Azucena said, not moving from the edge of the river. She couldn't. Her soul was tied to her bones and Flynt knew better than to reach in and try to reclaim them. "Happier than when I saw you last. That's good."

"Are you okay?" Flynt asked. "Is it awful here?"

"Not my favorite place ever, but I trust you'll find my hand eventually. Once I'm complete, maybe it'll be better."

Flynt smiled. "Want me to stay awhile? We can catch up?"

Azucena laughed. "I have nothing to share, but I sense you do. Come, then. Tell me."

∞∞∞

Flynt's reflection stared at her from the mirror, looking every inch a devotee of Ayal. Lem stood behind her, his reflection painting a softer picture of him than she usually saw. She didn't think she'd ever seen him look so lovestruck and doubted he would look that way if she turned to face him.

Then again, she was impressed by her new outfit herself. Given that she was no longer forced to present as a Death-magister, but something new, she'd been given the chance to design a "uniform." Aside from being cut from the same fabric of the other Death-magi and that fabric dyed the same acid green and black, it had almost nothing more in common. Twists of the queen's blue had been added to the chest piece of silk and human ribs—it seemed logical to follow Ieyil's choices, to honor her as the only other Necro Flynt had ever known. However, given the placement and the shine of bright cloth, Flynt liked how the outfit retained the terror-inducing element while adding a kick of sex appeal.

The top and skirt were joined in the back by a spinal column spaced with gold and gems and more pearly white bones dangled from the belt at her hips, making a long fringe down to her knees, which parted when she walked, revealing that the fabric beneath came only to mid-thigh.

She'd even saved a place for Azucena's bones, once she'd located them. Then the two could travel together as she'd once daydreamed.

But Flynt's favorite touch was the headpiece, designed like two bone hands reaching from her brow back to the nape of her neck. It pushed her hair in to thin streams over her shoulders and held the strands from her eyes. Among these skeletal fingers, she'd hidden Ieyil's bones. Like Cyniel, the Necro Queen had yet to speak to Flynt—honestly, Flynt didn't know if she could or ever would, but she liked having her ancient predecessor close.

Ieyil had lost her mind too soon to finish what she'd started, but now she could watch as Flynt worked to make her vision real. Sort of. Flynt wanted the Death-magi to be free of the high weight of their curse and welcomed in society, but she wouldn't displace anyone to do so.

Flynt would simply prove the worth of Death-aspect. After one thousand years without much of the Aspect to utilize around the Coil, it should be easy to display her worth. But she couldn't afford to fully show off, either. Some of her talents must be kept secret.

"All the things I have to do," Flynt said, reaching up a hand to touch the glowing rib bones, slicing just above her waist. "What if I fail? There's so much weight to being the only one of something and now everyone will know. They'll see if I fail."

"You'll do great," Lem remarked, leaning in to kiss her neck. "Just keep in mind that everyone is watching you."

Flynt glared at his reflection. "If you want to psych me out, it won't work. I'm scared about the future, not today. I like people watching me. I'm amazing. They *should* watch."

"I'm coming to realize you have a thing for people watching." Lem chuckled to himself. "But that wasn't how I meant it this time around. I was being serious. There won't be that many people physically there—a few thousand."

"'Not many'?" Flynt didn't think she'd ever been in a room with so many people.

"Given the millions, possibly billions, who will see? Everything will be recorded and broadcast. Watch your reactions. Even if no one physically there can see your facial twitches, all the people at home will."

Flynt turned away from the mirror and gave him a playful shove. "Now you're making me nervous."

"Good. They'll like you better if you're a bit nervous. They would be nervous in your shoes... It'll make you seem more like them."

Flynt let out a puff of air. "Glove or no glove?"

"No glove." He touched her shoulder gently, just above the bone. "This is your moment to show the Coil what a Necro-equitem is."

Flynt flexed her bone fingers, tightening them into a fist. But what if the people of the Coil hated her? Flynt recalled all too well all those who had recoiled from her arm or her powers.

"What if they don't accept me?"

"Better to know now… And, Flynt, you will still have the people who matter on your side—you'll have me and Nightshade, Nekolai and that creepy skeleton in your room. You'll have Milisade. The rest is fluff. You belong with us."

"You do know what to say. Why not start there?"

"That wouldn't be any fun."

"Walk with me?" Flynt asked.

"I'll see you out of the building at least."

Flynt sighed; the time had come. She turned from the mirror and swept from the room with Lem at her side. The bones hanging like fringe from her belt clattered against each other and the stiff cage of the ribs over her chest, even cushioned by cloth, kept her back straight.

They passed through the halls of the Death compound and took a portal down to the palace. Lem followed her without a word, but his closeness helped. She wasn't alone.

A set of Defenders met them outside the palace and led them to a private hallway. Flynt searched their faces and stiff bodies for evidence that Nekolai was among them, but he wasn't there. Lem parted ways from her, escaping through a doorway with a single Queen's Defender.

With him gone, Flynt struggled to hold to her blind confidence. The Defenders, intimidating in their hoods, faces hidden and only gray and blue to recommend them, led her to a huge door of frosted glass. Through the surface, she saw only light and blotches of dark.

"What now?" Flynt asked.

"We wait until it is time and walk out there. You will lead."

Flynt nodded. She'd seen a few events in her lifetime and knew the general outline of what such an unveiling meant. It happened every time some new important person was named. She'd be flaunted through a courtyard packed with the upper echelon of society and led to the queen. Then Milisade would announce her status and name her official assignment.

She reached up and touched Ieyil's finger bones in her

headpiece. Only Milisade knew they were there. Flynt briefly wondered who would end up keeping the promise to destroy the bones. With her hopes set on it being the queen, Flynt stroked the bone.

Receiving only silence, Flynt dropped her hand.

Flynt waited, watching the shadows outside the frosted door shift. At last, responding to some stimulus that she didn't see, two of the Queen's Defenders stepped forward and opened the door.

If she was to show the best that Death-aspect could produce, she needed to do this flawlessly. Flynt's throat tightened. Perfect or not, one thing she'd never do was show her fear. Squaring her shoulders, Flynt strode out onto a pale-stone pathway, the Coil sky arcing above her.

On either side of her path was a drop that, from her perspective, looked endless. It couldn't have been more than one hundred stories. These gaps were each three yards wide and past them, on both sides, waited a crowd. Generals, princes, top-tier scientists, and Magisters of all orders lined up to watch her proceed.

Flynt endured their gazes as she walked toward the far dais where Milisade and a small group of people waited under a sunshade. A glass tower rose behind them. Milisade was back to her old self, all blonde curls, silk, jewels, and brocade. Flynt tried to focus on her glittering form.

As Flynt walked, those at the edge of the courtyard lifted fists to their chests and bowed their heads. Flynt kept her eyes on Milisade—she couldn't face any disgust. In her peripheral vision, everyone was sincere. She wanted to keep it that way. Rejection hurt and she couldn't show that, not right then.

Toward the end of the walkway stood the Queen's Defenders—this, she'd expected—but also a sea of black and acid green. Death-magi and Magisters stooped over canes or floated in chairs and Death-potens still training waited behind them.

Hundreds of her people.

As one, they bowed their heads to her.

Flynt stopped and returned the motion. Her nerves were gone, and a fierce pride took its place. Let others judge. These few were hers and they were the only ones she'd be accountable to, other than the queen. This was the family that Ieyil had meant to protect. Flynt had no intention of forgetting that.

After a few moments with her head bowed, long enough to be sure that no one missed it, she turned and walked up to Queen Milisade. The queen stood partially in the shadow of the overhanging sunshade and in that shadow with her stood Lem and his officers and Magisters. She knew them all from the *Seer's Sword*, though none of the officers had really spoken with her. Nightshade appeared crisper than ever in a blindingly white robe. Her hood was up, hiding most of her face, and her hands hid inside her full sleeves. Nekolai stood with them—or perhaps just in Milisade's shadow.

Flynt didn't have more time to ponder the makeup of people on the dais. Milisade bowed her head.

"May the Coil's waters run forever pure for you, child."

Flynt touched her heart and bowed her head. The second part of the mantra was rarely voiced, but in ceremony, it was appropriate. "May the Coil's heart remain stable and true."

"Flicity, as the first servant of the Coil, I see you—we have not had a Necro-equitem to lead the followers of Ayal in some time. But you have proven your ability and loyalty."

Flynt kept her face still and swallowed her words. Anything she wanted to say wouldn't have been appropriate. Still, she had to wonder exactly to whom she'd shown loyalty.

Behind the queen, Lem broke into a smile.

The queen continued to speak. Flynt concentrated on how she held her own body and her face with such easy poise.

One by one, Lem and his upper-ranked people stepped forward. Milisade introduced them briefly as Flynt's new team. Flynt's heart responded. That was an official assignment. She was staying with Lem.

They inclined their heads to her, and Flynt returned the motion, feeling rather numb.

"Turn now, Necro-equitem Flicity," Milisade said. "Face your people."

Flynt did as bidden, turning back to the courtyard and raising her hands, and letting the fabric fall back over her bone arm.

This time the reveal was not met with disgust but with gasps of awe.

The people knelt or bowed at the waist. Flynt waited for them to rise. But these were not truly her people and Flynt waited to turn to the ones whom she would claim. First, she turned to the Death-magi. "My brothers and sisters, we will begin a new age. Trust in me. I will not fail you."

They gazed back at her, wordless but intense, they were hers just as she was thiers.

Then she turned to Milisade and bowed her head. In private later, they could talk, but not here. Milisade gave a slight nod. Flynt then moved to Lem and his leaders. They bowed again, and she returned the gesture, feeling silly for this repetitive motion. She felt ridiculous right up until she caught the smirk on Lem's face.

She shifted to catch Nekolai's painful earnestness and Nightshade's curious twinkle as she looked not at Flynt, but at the crowd.

Everyone there, under the sunshade, saw Flynt. None turned away.

No one else mattered in that moment.

These were her people, and she was home.

Join Jesse's Mailing List

Want more?

That's not problem! There is plenty more insanity to be had.

Sign up for Jesse's mailing list at Jessesprague.com (or reader's group as she likes to call it) for updates on her latest projects and extra perks like character interviews, early release information, insights into her process, and best yet FREE exclusive short stories!

Did you miss reading the first book? Check out Bone River

The Best Gift...

Is a review.

Enjoyed the book? As an independant female author, reviews are my lifeline. They are how readers find new books and decide what is right for them. Without your help, other readers may never find me!

So go on Amazon and/or Goodreads and say what you like, what you didn't like, or anything else you feel. Even just leaving a star rating can help!

Books By this Author

Aspect Wars

Bone River

5Th City Chronicles

Beneath 5th City
Project Eo
Red Angel

The Drambish Contaminate Series

Spider's Kiss
Spider's Gambit
Spider's Choice

Anthologies

Love in the Wreckage
Monster's Movies & Mayhem
Once Upon Now

Printed in Great Britain
by Amazon

21125869R00142